ESCAPING LIMBO

a novel

MIKE F. ELLIOTT

BEAVER'S
POND
PRESS

This is a work of fiction. Names, characters, places, and incidents are either the products of the author's imagination or are used in a fictitious manner, and any resemblance to actual persons, living or dead, businesses, events, or locales is purely coincidental.

Scripture quotations are taken from the *St. Joseph New American Bible* © 1970 by the Catholic Book Publishing Corp. All rights reserved.

Edited by Kerry Stapley

ISBN 13: 978-1-64343-615-9
Library of Congress Catalog Number: 2023923933
Printed in the United States of America
First Printing: 2024
28 27 26 25 24   5 4 3 2 1

Author photo by GinaRaePhotography.com.
Cover and interior design by JamesMonroeDesign.com.

Beaver's Pond Press, Inc.
939 Seventh Street West
Saint Paul, MN 55102
(952) 829-8818
www.BeaversPondPress.com

BEAVER'S
POND
PRESS

Contact Mike F. Elliott at MikeFElliott.com for speaking engagements, book club discussions, freelance writing projects, and interviews.

*To my grandmothers, Regina Elliott and Eleanor Kammerer.
Your life's journeys taught me work ethics, perseverance,
and unconditional love.*

PRELUDE

My windbreaker reeked of campfire smoke from my secret canoe trip with Izzy. Dad was still out of town for a bowling tournament, as our family's candy factory sponsored the team, but Mom was here. She made darn sure Izzy and I went to church as soon as we got back from our weekend excursion.

After Mass, we dropped Izzy off at his house and stopped at Joe's General Store for a malt. Mom started "Catholic coaching" me about being a responsible fourteen-year-old young man. She wanted to get the talk in before I joined the Catholic big leagues as a freshman at Trinity High School the following week.

But everything that transpired on my trip with Izzy had been exhausting and, if I'm honest, exhilarating. It changed me. This whole year had. And now, talks like the one from Mom and the priests and nuns the past year, they just don't make as much sense as they used to. So, when we got home, I thanked Mom and came directly to bed. I couldn't sleep, though, so I took my journal out of my safe, flipped on the reading lamp at my desk, and started writing it all down, lest I forget . . .

1

St. Paul, Minnesota

END OF AUGUST 1968

Behold, I will do something new, Now it will spring forth; Will you not be aware of it? I will even make a roadway in the wilderness, Rivers in the desert.

—ISAIAH 43:19

This past year, through all the tragedies Izzy, my little sister Mandy, my parents, and I survived, I've discovered a few things about myself. The summer is ending, but for me, it's a new beginning.

For the first time, I'm questioning whether I need all the piety and fear of God that's been pushed on me by my folks and the nuns and priests at Holy Family School. Appearing virtuous seems hypocritical if you're not living that one big commandment to actually be kind and just. Always being obedient and never questioning authority seems like a recipe to smother me. Izzy, as off the rails as he is, taught me that.

Would God really deny my salvation just for asking questions that make some under his heavenly wing uncomfortable? If I tried to be moral and just and do the right thing, would I really be punished just because I started eating a hamburger every Friday during Lent?

At my new school, I'm going to reinvent myself, start fresh. I might skip Mass and go toilet-paper a classmate's yard instead. Maybe I'll take part in a food fight and then further tick off the brothers and priests by doing a book report on *The Catcher in the Rye*, the novel banned at all Catholic school libraries in the archdiocese of St. Paul. Maybe I'll organize the school's first underground newspaper, and if I get expelled, I'll go attend public school with Izzy. And finally, since Susan left, I might try to fall in love with a new girl. I probably won't kiss an atheist, but I might give a Lutheran woman a chance.

One thing is certain: I will do what I do best, observe and write.

Because I believe that God is something more than all the fear the nuns and priests put into me at Holy Family. Maybe he's even more than all of Rich Grandma Rose's ceramic saints and Poor Grandma Patricia's handmade rosaries; he's got to be more than my mother's blind, unquestioning beliefs.

I have a new quest: to live my own spiritual journey. Because when I do, like my stillborn sister Cynthia, I too might escape Limbo.

2

The St. Croix River

END OF AUGUST 1968

From the throne came flashes of lightning, rumblings and peals of
thunder. In front of the throne, seven lamps were blazing.
These are the seven Spirits of God.

—REVELATIONS 4:5

All night, the northern lights exploded. Our eyes were glued to the skies. Fierce white streaks were dancing, performing jumping jacks in shades Crayola never knew: shimmering blues, eye-popping greens, and chartreuse, like rainbows on fire.

I inhaled the mist from the churning waters below Jack's Cliff and was soothed by the scent of cedars after a night of intense emotions. The dawn pushed the aurora borealis aside, and the wind quickened, muffling the sassy waterfalls. Izzy was sobbing, so I bear-hugged him. That's unusual for me. I'm most comfortable punching his shoulder and calling him a moron.

Earlier on that rock, when Izzy disappeared for way too long, my head spun like one of my 33-rpm albums running on 78-speed. The intensity of the past year, and then, what occurred on the trip—it had me questioning my intentions. I hoped I'd

3

helped Izzy and done more good than harm.

At that moment, I had never felt so close to another, except perhaps with Susan when she visited our candy factory wearing that red sweater, plaid skirt, and white tights. Or that time two weeks before the canoe trip when she convinced me to climb into that giant billboard's beer bottle on top of the brewery so we could explore each other.

That was the first time in my fourteen-year-old life that I made up my own prayer: *Thank you, God. Thank you, Jesus, and thank you, Saint Rose.*

When I let go, Izzy pointed to an eagle circling above the falls. The majestic bird was targeting its breakfast. We watched it descend like a speeding dart, grab a northern pike with its talons, and ascend toward the heavens, perching behind us on the tallest pine on Jack's Cliff, where it tore into its family's breakfast.

Izzy had calmed himself. He mumbled something.

"What?" I asked.

He cleared his throat.

"I guess I also had to fly through some shit to grow."

I handed him the wet stub of my Cuban cigar. Accidentally inhaling, he gagged and started coughing. I slapped him on the back.

"Me too," I said.

In that moment, I started grasping Grandma Rose's wisdom that life was more about the journey than the destination. Perhaps my blind faith, unending prayers, and sheer determination will never cure all my, or my family's, troubles, nor save good people from disappearing or dying. I like to think I really did help Izzy, but now, maybe neither me nor God have much to do with it. Now, it's up to Izzy to save Izzy.

3

Mom and Dad

1966

You shall love your neighbor as yourself.
—MATTHEW 22:39

Unlike Rich Grandma Rose, my mom felt life was only about the destination. She was a big believer in *The Baltimore Catechism* and a card-carrying member of the Holy Rosary Society.

Last year, before I entered seventh grade, she put her hand on my shoulder and said, "Francis, you are to kneel at Mass this Sunday and take the Legion of Decency pledge."

So, I took the oath. I always did what I was told by my folks and the priests and nuns at Holy Family Church and School.

"I, Francis, condemn immoral motion pictures that glorify impurity, violence, crime, and criminals. It is my obligation to form a right conscience about movies that endanger my moral life. In the name of the Father, Son, and Holy Ghost. Amen."

I said my final goodbye to Larry, Curly, Moe, and the hammers they banged on each other's heads with.

Our Paulson family hallway boasted a framed mahogany portrait of Pope Paul the VI. Next to it, a smaller frame—same

5

fancy wood, but with a real-life photograph of Mom's best friend's brother and St. Paul's young bishop, George Donald.

Mom was certain about Satan, sin, and the plenary indulgences that would make Purgatory disappear for our dead relatives if we followed the holy card instructions on All Souls Day. According to her, there were only two destinations: Heaven or Hell. Maybe three if she counted a pit stop in Purgatory. She made sure every visitor saw the bishop's photo.

"You know I was there for both ordinations," she boasted.

After Vatican II, Bishop George Donald left the priesthood and married a former nun because he disagreed with the Pope on birth control. Mother took down his picture and quit inviting his sister over for bridge club.

My father was a go-along, get-along Catholic and followed the big commandments. He never murdered, worshipped fake gods, or stole another man's goods or woman, but he worked the small sins to his advantage, like fudging a little on his tax returns, gambling, looking at his *Playboy*, and swearing at the bowling alley.

Dad worked hard at our candy factory six days per week and late into the night during the holidays, but he was always there for Mandy and me and anyone with a need. He sometimes butchered scripture verses, inventing his own, like the time we were driving and had to stop for some city workers taking a break.

"Now look, Francis. No work ethic whatsoever. Two guys coming from the toilet, two guys going, and only one filling these awful potholes."

I said, "Maybe it's break time, Dad?"

My father chuckled.

"Break time? When you run a business like we do, there's no time for breaks. The Bible even says idle hands make the devil dance and jump-rope with joy."

But my father, Antonio Paulson, always lived by that one big commandment about doing unto others. I loved him for that and wished Izzy's old man was half the man my dad was.

4

Francis and Isadore
Duck and Cover

SEPTEMBER 1964

You will be hearing of wars and rumors of wars.
See that you are not frightened, for those things must take place,
but that is not yet the end.

—MATTHEW 24:6

I met Izzy on the first day of fifth grade. Sister Ann Margarite put her hand on my shoulder. "He's new, Francis," she said. "Go make him feel welcome."

I was Sister's chosen welcome wagon for the new kid, but before I could make my move, Izzy approached me.

We were on the playground. He pointed to my new brown-framed eyeglasses and shouted, "Hey, Four Eyes!" Then he spit out his wad of gum. "I'm Izzy. And if you call me Isadore, I'll sucker punch you!"

He thrust out his right hand so I could shake it. The tip of his middle finger was all crooked and swollen. I took his eager hand and gave it a gentle shake, careful not to touch the wounded fingertip.

"That old bag of a nun said she will only call me by my Christian name. Said mine is Saint Isadore. Told me he was a farmer and liked animals. Dumb nun. I don't even own a goldfish."

Izzy opened his other fist and handed me a large steel marble the size of a golf ball.

"Here, you take it. It's a gift. My favorite. I'll win it back later. Unless you are better than me at marbles."

I accepted his trophy. It was heavy, smooth, and still warm from his hand. I had never owned a steely that large and so perfectly polished.

"Sweet! Welcome to Holy Family, Izzy. I'm Francis. I don't own an animal either, but the real Saint Francis even loved rats and snakes."

I searched my right pants pocket wanting to offer my own welcome gift. I always had a few pieces of wrapped candy on me from our candy store.

"Here, take these," I said, handing him three extreme sour balls. "Just don't suck on them in class or you'll get detention."

Izzy smiled, carefully unwrapped each one, and then jammed all three into his mouth at once, not sucking, but crushing, grinding them with his teeth. The tart made most of my friends' mouths pucker like a carp fish, but the sour did not faze Izzy. After swallowing, he started rattling and gave me the lowdown on his transfer to Holy Family.

"My old man pulled me from public school yesterday. He said the priests and nuns at this holy-roller pithole will straighten me out so I don't end up in Totem Town with all the other juvenile delinquents in St. Paul."

Sister's pet student, Susan Flannagan, was on the swing near the baseball backstop fence listening to Izzy's booming voice, gathering information about our gift exchange to get us in trouble.

I pointed toward the swing, motioning Izzy to lower his voice. Steel marbles had been banned since some eighth-grade boys shot one through the cafeteria window last spring and hit a first-grade girl in the head.

"Izzy, that redhead over there on the swing is Susan Flannagan. She is Sister's pet and a tattletale. Just be careful. She might use things you say or do as a weapon later to get us in trouble. She calls me Francis in front of the nuns but Four-eyes in front of her girlfriends."

Susan jumped off the swing and glared at us for a moment, and then she stuck out her tongue before heading back toward the building.

Izzy spit in her direction as he removed a small, clear, crystal perfume spritzer from the pocket of his corduroy pants. It was filled with a clear liquid. He sprayed it toward her swing, then at himself, and finally at me.

"What are you doing?" I asked.

"It's holy water. I'm baptizing her Suck-Up Sue, teacher's pet, me Saint Izzy the Great, and you are now Sir Saint Francis."

With Izzy now in her class, Sister would soon start using vodka, not holy water, and praying the Rosary until her fingers bled.

The bell rang, breaking up our introductions. I kept focusing on Izzy's crooked finger. It was bigger than the rest, about the size of my big toe, had no nail, and looked like it still hurt.

"I don't mean to pry, Izzy, but what happened to your finger?"

Izzy took out his spritzer like he was going to spray me again, but then he put it, along with both his hands, into his pockets. Looking down at his new, shiny-black, untied uniform shoes, he turned his back, walked away, and mumbled, "No big deal. I just got punched in the face while picking my nose."

The second week of fifth grade we had a duck-and-cover drill for when the Russians dropped an atom bomb on us. When the tornado sirens sounded, we were to crawl under our desks and cover our heads with Bibles. It was the fattest book we Catholic kids had. The public schools did duck and cover too, but they used thick geography books.

Suck-Up Sue cornered Izzy and me in the cloakroom before school. She gathered her long red hair with one hand, and when she turned around, her newly made ponytail brushed my face. Izzy and I ignored her, so she opened her blab-master.

"Just so you boys know, I started going to confession every week now. Just in case Khrushchev drops the A-bomb on us. My soul will be pure when I die, but what about yours?"

That was Izzy's cue to flip the stage and corner her like he was a cat and she was the mouse.

"Susan, that's a super idea! I mean, to cover all your sins. Do not pass go. Use your get-out-of-Hell-free card. When you croak, just walk up to the Pearly Gates with your pure lily-white Susan soul and kiss Saint Peter on the lips while showing him your latest hairdo."

Susan's face flushed, and pushing between the two of us, she tried to get to her desk, but Izzy put out his foot to slow her down. "By the way, what was your biggest sin last week? Did you rob a bank? Try to murder the person that just made your face turn red?"

She hopped over Izzy's foot and said, "You boys are both mean and so very immature."

The nuke drill was on time, and all my classmates except Izzy dove under their desks. Izzy refused to scamper and hide like a scared mouse. He simply ignored the sirens' blasts, walked to the window, opened the shade, and looked across the playground at the steeple on our church.

When the drill ended, I crawled from under my shelter and brushed the dust off my uniform trousers. When I did, a jaw-breaker freed itself from a hole in my pocket and rolled all the way under Sister's desk. She did not see it because her eyes were focused on Izzy.

"Nice job, class. And, Isadore, you are excused to go to Sister Maria Goretti's office."

Sister Maria Goretti was our principal. All the older boys called her the G-Man because they said that she worked for the FBI and was really a man in nun's clothing, and that her long black-and-white penguin outfit hid her muscles, tattoos, and pistols. Duke, our lead altar boy and football quarterback, insisted it was really Sister Goretti's three long chin hairs that were the dead giveaway that she was a man.

When Izzy came back from the G-Man's office, Sister Ann Margarite adjusted her white chin guard, then grabbed her pointer, making Izzy squirm before he apologized and taught us all a lesson about misbehaving.

"Isadore, what did you tell our principal about your disobedience?"

Izzy stood straight, speaking loudly as if he were responding to a marine drill sergeant. "I told Sister that if it was a real bomb, I wanted to see it with my eyes wide open, not closed while hiding under our Lord's Good Book."

Izzy took that whack on his palm like a martyred saint. Grinning, Suck-Up Sue turned to me, rolled her eyes, and whispered, "Your little friend deserved it."

Izzy heard her whispers, so he peeled off all the used chewing gum from the underside of his desk, warmed the large wad in his palms, and when Sister was not watching, flicked it at Susan. Izzy flashed me a wide smile and gave a thumbs-up when the gum stuck in her ponytail.

Unlike Izzy, I was a pleaser. For the most part, I always attempted to keep my nose clean. But during the past year at Holy Family and even in my own home, I think Izzy was becoming sort of a teacher, maybe even sort of like a prophet to me and I began wondering who I was and where I was going. Izzy was fearless and confident about questioning anything and everything. Something I could not do, at least not just yet.

I still enjoyed praise and followed most of the rules at home, church, and school. I pretended to slurp religion like it was chocolate milk, gulping loud, fast, and hard, and I always got As. I was a Boy Scout and the youngest altar boy to learn Latin at Holy Family. When I did mess up, I tried my best to hide it from my parents so as not to disappoint them.

Izzy stuck to his own beliefs and challenged anyone about anything. He feared no nun nor priest, not even his drunk old man. He swung at every pitch, getting in trouble with everyone in authority and also often with his archenemy, Susan Flannagan.

I admired my friend's convictions, but he really worried me when we entered eighth grade. His older brother, Jack, had died a little over a year before. Izzy's protests and rants increased, and he trusted only me and my seven-year-old sister with even small doses of who he really was.

My sister's name is Mandy, though Izzy called her the Worm because she was always squirming into our business. Mandy loved the nickname, giggling whenever Izzy used it. Mandy became my responsibility after Grandma Rose fell ill because, without Grandma's help, Mom and Dad had to focus more on keeping our struggling candy factory going.

Izzy didn't mind my sister always hanging out with us. He treated her like she was his sister too. He tried to protect her before I even knew she needed protection.

5

Mississippi River

SUMMER 1967

When you pass through the waters,
I will be with you; through the rivers,
you shall not be swept away.

—ISAIAH 43:2

The three of us rode our bikes to the Mississippi after breakfast. Mandy side-saddled with me. She was just getting used to riding without training wheels, and she couldn't handle the distance yet. Besides, she was small for her age, so I did not mind.

As I was pedaling, I kept thinking about a moneymaking scheme to get Izzy back to the St. Croix River where his brother died. After Jack's death last June, Izzy stayed away from all water except swimming pools. He avoided lakes and rivers and refused to climb into a boat or canoe with me.

I started thinking that if I could pull off my idea for a canoe trip with Izzy next summer, maybe it would help Izzy find peace and get him back to normal again, if there ever was a normal for Izzy.

The hot day of Jack's tragedy, Izzy's old man was tossing back happy juice at the VFW in St. Croix Falls, Wisconsin, too drunk to join his sons on their day canoe trip. After Jack's funeral, Izzy's old man started drinking more and giving Izzy frequent verbal beatdowns, but he rarely resorted to physical violence after that time he wounded Izzy in fifth grade.

Eventually Izzy confided in me and told me what had happened to his finger back when we'd first met. Izzy's mom was not home, and when Izzy threw a tantrum about going to Holy Family School, his old man took off his brass-buckled belt and bruised Izzy's back and bottom, making him bleed. After it ended, Izzy thought his old man's back was turned, so Izzy flashed him the middle finger.

Izzy said, "Hell, Francis, I didn't know what it meant except my brother Jack and his friends always did it when they messed with each other."

Izzy's old man saw the gesture in a mirror and came at him like a madman.

"He caught me, forced my hand down on our kitchen's wood cutting board, and whacked it with his buckle. Crazy animal broke my finger."

All I could think to say was, "I'm so sorry, Izzy."

Even today, at Cherokee Park's Mississippi River caves, Izzy stayed over twenty-five feet from the river's edge and refused to help spear carp, a skill he had taught me after we tired of hopping the trains last year. Izzy thought we could save our river from the infestation of rough fish forcing out the good fish.

Mandy was tagging along, dragging her short, fat walking stick behind her. It was fashioned out of a smooth piece of pine that Izzy had stripped. He carved a skull handle out of a huge knot at the top. He even varnished it and had given it to Mandy so she could poke around in the caves. He also gave her a cheap flashlight that rarely worked. Mandy would sometimes hide them, even bury them in the sand in the cave, and then dig them up on her next visit.

Izzy was watching her. He took out his new Zippo cigarette

lighter, lit a Lucky Strike, and then, looking first at Mandy and then at me, blew a perfect smoke ring. Then he complained again about the carp.

"Those slimy sons of bitches are wrecking the fishing, squeezing out the bass and walleye. I'll whittle willows and start the fire for the wieners. You and the Worm can pitchfork them to death. I'll dig the pit for their funeral."

I gave him a dirty look for swearing in front of Mandy and started dragging the large empty burlap candy factory bag and my fishing fork to the river's edge. My little sister followed like a happy puppy.

When the burlap was full of raw Spanish peanuts, it weighed one hundred pounds. On that summer day, the heat and humidity created a peanut-juice stench worse than ever. I wondered if the wounded fish would despise the stink as much as I did. The bag usually reminded me of our factory and the good aromas of roasting nuts, not bagging dead fish.

When Frank, our lead candymaker, perfectly parched the nuts, they gave off an aroma better than movie-theater popcorn. However, the hot oil was extremely dangerous and never to be left alone, not even for a second. Frank watched his copper thermometer like a hawk. If unattended, the oil could smoke and catch fire. The kitchen would then become an inferno worse than Hell. Water would not help; with all that peanut oil, it would only spread the flames.

The fire-extinguisher sales guy scammed my father into buying two large red extinguishers to prevent disasters like oil fires. Dad mounted them on the wall behind the round cast-iron candy-kettle furnaces. The extinguishers would probably never be used but functioned quite nicely as a coatrack for soiled employee aprons.

My dad complained because he had to spend a few bucks on the new equipment and had to follow both state and city safety regulations.

"Son, it's a racket," he said while adjusting one of the extinguishers on the wall's mount. "They sell me this junk, then sock me with fees to recharge and inspect it each year! I don't have money to burn!" My father chuckled at his pun.

Every January, Dad made me take a black marker and initial each unit's tag to prove they had been serviced.

"Isn't that forgery?" I asked.

"Francis, it's not forgery if you write your own initials. Now go make us some money as that pretend writer or journalist you say you want to be someday and put your initials on the service log."

I wrote FMP for Francis Michael Paulson. If the St. Paul fire inspector ever asked, we were supposed to say the FMP guy died or retired.

My secret fishing hole for carp was a backwater slough from which I could see the old iron High Bridge. It was the bridge Izzy and I often raced our bikes across. I hated the clacking of the weather-beaten wood planks, but Izzy didn't seem to mind. He always edged me out at a dangerous speed.

I coasted, scared shitless, but Izzy pedaled full force like he was the Wicked Witch stealing Toto in *The Wizard of Oz*. One time he stopped abruptly and let me win. I walked my bike back to where he was standing. He was peeing over the rail. "I was going to jump," he said, "but I needed to take a whiz first."

That's Isadore: always pushing, challenging the universe, trying to make life go faster. The nuns at Holy Family tried to rein him in with detentions, chores, and chapel time. Once, after he'd hidden Suck-Up Sue's fancy heirloom chapel veil, they even made him write out the whole book of Job in cursive. The veil was from Suck-Up's dead Irish great-grandma, and she wore it to every Mass.

"Francis, it was too funny. All the girls had their tidy, white, lacy veils, and there was Suck-Up with a brown paper towel from the girls' lavatory that Sister had bobby-pinned to her hair."

Susan caught Izzy when he pretended to blow his nose in it as he walked to the Communion rail.

I knew the bridge's history well. I got an A on a report about it from Sister Agnes Marie in fifth grade. The bridge had haunted St. Paul since it was built in 1889. It was called the Suicide Bridge. On Halloween, pranksters tossed pumpkins and pretend bodies off the bridge. They'd throw them from their moving cars. Once, someone even launched a stick of dynamite that exploded before it hit the water. Suicide Bridge kept the police busy, especially in October.

The bridge was a mile long and towered 190 feet above the water. It boasted great views of downtown St. Paul, the river bluffs, and the many sand caves lurking below. These were the same caves that brewers once used to store beer. Now, the caves were mostly used by train hobos, or by teenagers looking for a place to smoke, make out, sniff glue, and bump uglies.

The suicides were the buzz at Holy Family School. They spooked me too. I had nightmares that I would reach my bike's top speed, hit a missing wood sidewalk plank, and get hurtled over the rail.

I blame Mom and Dad for the nightmares, as my mother put the image in my head whenever I pled for some exception or privilege. "Yes, Francis, I know Izzy stays out after dark, but you cannot. After all, if Izzy jumped off the High Bridge, would you?"

Dad invoked the bridge when he was ticked off, usually after a lousy bowling night.

"That damn son-of-a-Lutheran Omar cheated on his bowling card again. Next time, I'm kicking his fat heathen ass over the High Bridge and upriver to Lake Itasca!"

Benjamin Harrison was the president when the bridge was built, but he missed the ribbon cutting due to the Pan-American Conference. The first suicide came shortly after. Purportedly, a well-dressed gentleman had asked a young man to hold his horses while he checked his carriage. The gentleman handed the guy his leather fedora and jumped. They say hitting the water from that high is like hitting cement. No survivors.

Over the years, there were more newspaper accounts of suicides, all similar, with just the names of the dead changing. More men than women jumped. Each time, traffic was disrupted as boats combed the river for the body. The curious used binoculars to spy from the Wabasha Bridge when the High Bridge was blocked by cop cars whose flashing red lights advertised the spectacle.

After last May's jumper, we all got the Jesus/Judas-suicide Bible lesson. We heard how Judas, and any of God's children who offed themselves, would burn in Hell.

The day of the fishing trip, a group of high school girls were on the bridge, dropping rocks into the water below. They were giving Mandy and me a good look-over.

I picked up my spear with one hand and scooped a fistful of chum with the other. I had gobs of rancid meat chunks that Joe had saved for us from his general store.

"Let's put on a good show, Mandy. I think we got ourselves an audience."

I tossed my chum out over the water. As soon as it hit the surface, the water foamed with large carp lurching for the stink bait. I chucked my pitchfork like a madman. Sometimes it took three tosses, but I never lost my weapon because I had tied twenty-five feet of twine through a hole I had drilled through the handle. Today my first throw was a bull's-eye. Reeling in my prey, I took off my T-shirt, looked up at the cute girls, and flexed my muscles.

"Stay out of my way!" I yelled at Mandy when I threw my fishing fork again.

I kept going until the girls on the bridge got bored and walked away. I was exhausted, standing over a pile of bloodied carcasses with several flies encircling my bare feet. Mandy held the burlap bag open as I plopped each bloodied carcass inside. The wounded stared at me with translucent eyes.

Back at camp, Izzy had the hot dogs on sticks. Mandy tried to convince him that we should burn the carcasses, not bury them, insisting that if the campfire was bigger and hotter it would work.

My best friend scolded her.

"No way, Worm! That's not kosher!"

Mandy frowned. "What's kosher, Izzy?"

"Kosher is like a mortal sin. It means wrong, illegal. The stuff they send people to Purgatory or the Ramsey County Jail for. You don't want to end up there, do you?"

Mandy shrugged. "Guess not," she said. "What is Purgatory?"

"Do I look like your ma or a nun, little miss fisherwoman? Go ask a priest. That's what they get paid for. To scare little kids into being good."

Izzy then started carving out a half dozen fish eyeballs and placing them in a small glass jar.

"What's that for?" Mandy demanded.

"That's for me to know, and for you to find out, Worm."

"Tell me. Please tell me, Izzy!"

"Let's just say it is a gift for a goodie-two-shoed ugly red-head. Now go burn your weenie, and quit asking me questions."

My sister named each fish after cartoon characters as she poked them with her stick. She counted them one by one as I tossed them into Izzy's deep open-pit grave.

"That one is Mighty Mouse," she giggled.

"There goes Tweety Bird and Felix. Yuck! Yogi is missing his eyeballs!" She then asked me which ones were boys and which were girls.

"I think this one is a girl, Mandy. You'd better name her Olive Oyl."

"How do you know it's a lady, Francis?"

I playfully grabbed my sister by her bare feet and held her upside down, nose to nose with the fish in question. "Because look—she's wearing lipstick!"

Just before we laid the last fish to rest, Travis, one of our classmates, came out of the cave with his girlfriend. They were passing a smoke between them.

Travis was quiet, but cool. He loved playing marbles with Izzy and me, and he was good at it. His girlfriend went to public school. She was Mexican and spoke Spanish. She taught Travis how to cuss in Mexican, and Travis taught us.

When he saw Mandy, he ground the cigarette out in the dirt before she noticed it.

"I sure hope you ain't wasting them good fish," he said. "This here is my friend Maria."

Izzy responded, "Good fish? Hell, Travis, do we look like carp eaters? Sure as shit not gonna eat 'em. Crap tastes better than carp. Just ask Francis. He's tried both!"

Travis and Maria sat on the large smooth elm stump next to our fire ring. Izzy slapped two hot dogs in buns and gave them each one.

"You know, my father works at the stockyards in South St. Paul, and he knows a guy that pays money for fish, dead or alive," said Travis. "It don't matter what kind."

Travis claimed he could get us 4.50 per hundred pounds of fish, and slightly less than that for any leftover candy from our factory, like stale pecans, rancid corn syrup, burnt batches, and the like. He said the people he knew would even pay for rats if we had any. It was all cheap hog food that kept pigs fattened when their holding pens were backed up a day or two before slaughter.

My smile almost stretched across the river. Finally, there was a way to earn money and advance my plan for that canoe trip with Izzy. Travis said that in his proposal, he'd figured a small cut for himself. He did not divulge how much, and I did not care.

He said his father was teaching him to start saving money now so he could go to the university in Duluth and study forestry after high school. So every Saturday, Travis's father drove him to butcher shops and bakeries, and Travis asked the owners for leftovers and clean garbage. "You know, plain garbage with no coffee grounds, paper, and the like. Just food waste that you might eat if you were a pig."

Travis said fish was top dollar because pigs could eat the heads, guts, bones . . . everything. And it was all high-protein.

We agreed that every Saturday afternoon at five o'clock, Travis and his father would meet me under the bridge, and I would get paid cash after they dumped my fish into a garbage can and weighed it on a grain scale in the truck bed.

We shook on the plan, and Travis and his girl went back into the cave to hide their pack of Lucky Strikes for next time. When they emerged to say goodbye, her hair was all mussed up and Travis had a big red spot on his neck. Then they climbed up the river bluffs so he could walk her home.

I knew I needed more than fish money for my trip, so I tried convincing my father that I was old enough to help with our candy store's large wholesale peanut brittle order that Minnesota Mining placed each Christmas. They needed a full ton of brittle for their employees' holiday gifts.

I was grinning inside and out. The sun was shining. It felt like one of those perfect days you never forget. I was enjoying time with my little sister and Izzy, and then, thanks to Travis, I had a new moneymaking scheme.

It was as good a time as riding the Ferris wheel at the state fair every August. I did not know it then, but my Ferris wheel would soon turn into a backward roller-coaster ride for all of us.

6

"Rock-a-Bye Baby"

AUGUST 1967

Grandchildren are the crown of old men,
And the glory of sons is their fathers.
—PROVERBS 17:6

Grandma Rose ran our candy factory after Grandpa died. That was before Mandy arrived. My classmates said I was the luckiest kid in St. Paul because my grandma owned a sweetshop and I could eat all the candy I wanted for free.

Grandma loved to dance, especially the polka. After she indulged in a couple of adult beverages, she would get loud, sing, and tell jokes, making everyone laugh, especially at our factory's annual New Year's Eve employee celebration.

Mandy and I loved spending overnights at Grandma's big two-story house. It had three porches—one out front, one in back, and another upstairs, where we would sit out at night and watch the stars.

Once, when I slept overnight, I busted my eyeglasses. I did not put them in the hard case when I went to bed. When I woke up, they were on the floor. I stepped on them and cried like a baby, too afraid to call my father. Grandma went to her nightstand, pulled out a pair of her old eyeglasses, came into my room, dropped them, and crushed them with her foot. "Francis, now we are both in the doghouse together," she'd said.

Years later, Mandy's psychologist told Mother that in my sister's young brain, she held herself responsible for sending Grandma to the hospital, and she thought it was her fault we lost her twin sister, Shannon.

Rich Grandma Rose's illness came a few years after Shannon was gone. Shannon was the one thing no one talked about in our house anymore. I guess my folks figured we could just erase her from our memories. I sang to Shannon and Mandy when they were little. I was ten, going on eleven, and Mandy was three on that dreadful Saturday morning when Shannon never came back home.

Neither the tragedy with Shannon nor Grandma Rose's illness was anyone's fault, but Mandy blamed herself.

The fiasco started out as great fun at first. Izzy, Grandma, and I were watching *Bonanza* on her black-and-white Philco television set.

Izzy had been spending more time with me and Mandy because he was trying to keep his distance from his angry old man. Like my mom did at our home, my grandma made him feel welcome in hers.

Mandy was working on her Minnie Mouse coloring book in Grandma's kitchen when she snuck Oreo cookies and washed them down with the brandy-and-Tang mixture that Grandma kept in her refrigerator. Afterward, my sister rushed out to the living room and surprised Grandma by jumping on her lap while she was sitting in her favorite chair.

Mandy called it the Tilt-A-Whirl "Rock-a-Bye Baby" chair. It was huge, well worn, and poorly reupholstered in an ugly red-and-black plaid cloth.

It rocked back and forth but also swiveled in circles like the steel merry-go-round on Holy Family's playground. The bottom springs were gigantic. Dad kept them lubed with Crisco, tightening the bolts when they came loose.

When I was younger, Grandma did not rock me to sleep; instead, she rocked me dizzy and silly in that chair like it was a carnival ride. I was too old for the game now, but on that night, after eating and drinking the juice, Mandy wrapped her arms around Grandma's neck and begged her. "Play 'Rock-a-Bye' Tilt. Please, Grandma!"

Grandma obeyed and started her ride twirling clockwise, the springs creaking and her forehead sweating. Mandy was squealing with delight, so Izzy and I turned away from the TV, more amused by the chair-ride sideshow.

Grandma tired, so she slammed on the brakes by stopping the chair with her feet. Mandy jumped off, stumbling around like a drunk. Then she jumped back on Grandma Rose's lap and started coughing orange-brown sludge all over our grandmother's face and neck.

The vomit creek flowed down Grandma's body to her skinny legs and finally dribbled into her pink knit booties. With one last heave, my sister's head slammed into Grandma's breast. Grandma Rose's eyes closed. She clenched her jaw and pounded her chest, hollering, "Jesus, Mary, and Joseph!"

Grandma shoved my sister at me and grabbed the stair railing, pulling herself up toward her home's only bathroom. I followed with Mandy strangling my neck. I was about to lose my own dinner too; the Oreo cookie sludge was wicked, and the brandied Tang gave off a dreadful, rancid skunky stink.

Izzy did not know what to do, so he went to the kitchen, filled a bucket with hot water and some dish detergent, plugged his nose, and started cleaning up the puke.

Upstairs, turning on the shower with one hand, still clutching her chest with the other, Grandma wheezed. "Francis, have Izzy lock Kevin on the back porch."

Kevin was her Mexican Chihuahua. He was going batshit

crazy with the ruckus. Izzy had already separated the dog from the meal he was making of Mandy's hurl, but the beast was howling like a wounded hyena. I shut the bathroom door but could still hear Grandma and Mandy talking over the running water. She was speaking ever so gently with my sick sister.

"Mandy, I'm OK. Does your tummy hurt? Let's pretend we are in the rain, getting fresh and clean. I'll wash our clothes after we are finished. You just surprised me and hurt my big ole boob with your noggin. I'm better now, and so are you. I love you, but no more cookies tonight."

When Grandma and Mandy came back downstairs, they both were wearing pajamas. Grandma Rose's face was pale as a ghost's, and she was holding one hand over her heart. Izzy and I had cleaned up the mess as best we could, but her favorite chair was now sopping wet.

Izzy pushed her other chair next to the carnival rocker and helped ease her into it. It was a solid-oak spindled rocker that she'd lined with her handmade quilt.

"You sit here, Grandma," he said, covering her with a wool blanket. "Can Francis or I make you some tea?"

While Izzy was taking charge and being kind to my grandma, I went into the kitchen and called my father to pick us all up and check on his mother. When he got there, Rose was sleeping, still clutching her chest. I did not even get to kiss her goodbye.

Izzy and I rode bikes every Saturday to go play poker with Grandma during her stay at the Little Sisters of the Poor hospital. She loved cards and taught us both how to cheat like gangsters. Before she got ill, Rose took her "nip of brandy" before bed, mixing it with Tang for the vitamin C. She said it was medicine for her heart. One Saturday, before we left, I asked if I could bring her anything the next morning when we came to visit after Sunday Mass.

"Francis, have your dad bring me a pint of Christian Brothers Brandy. The painkillers are not working anymore."

After we left her, Izzy and I unchained our bikes.

"Damn it, Francis, if your granny cheated in the back rooms at the Belfort Club like she did today, she'd be dead already. The Mafia would dump her body next door in Mr. Wong's trash can with the cockroaches and his sweet and sour chicken."

I know Izzy did not mean any harm by his remark, but the word *already* stuck to me like glue. Already? Death? Two simple words that hit the center of my heart like poison darts. No! God will save his best miracle for her. I wondered how much time Grandma had left. How many days did I still have with her?

"Izzy, leave her friend Duc Wong out of it. She likes him, and all the times we've been there, we found a cockroach only once. It was dead, and it wasn't in the food. Just under my napkin. She still tipped him with a quarter pound of her cherry cordials."

"Well, cherry cordial this, dick breath. My brother Jack said those crooks at the illegal backroom joints own all the Twins and Vikings number-boards that our dads buy at the bowling alley from Cigar Ron."

I motioned for Izzy to hurry up and wrap his chain around his seat. We needed to ride fast to beat the dark so he would not get punished again by his drunk old man. He ignored me and just kept on jabbering.

"My brother said that Ron is just a small-time bookie but carries around a wad of cash bigger than a roll of ass-wipe, and that he puffs Cuban cigars longer and darker than his turds just to look tough."

Izzy told me Jack claimed that one family, the Parinos, owned all the liquor stores in St. Paul and that they ran an after-hours jazz and blues bar and billiard joint. Supposedly, it was all a cover for illegal dope and Mafia stuff. Jack promised he would take Izzy there before early Mass some Sunday, and the joint would still be full of hookers, dope smokers, and crooked St. Paul cops who should have been out keeping St. Paul safe from the riffraff and punks coming over from Minneapolis.

"Jack told me that St. Paul cops should not be dancing with Minneapolis whores, but Jack never had time to keep his promise."

"I'm so sorry about Jack, Izzy." It was all I could ever think to say.

Izzy stopped talking. Before we pedaled away, he flipped his Minnesota Twins cap backward and got really serious, a rarity for Izzy. He spoke so softly I could barely hear him.

"Grandma Rose is way cool, Francis. She loves you and the Worm a lot. Probably more even than she loves her plastic Jesus and ceramic saints all put together. I wish she were my granny. I'd trade your grandma for my old man any day."

I wanted to hug Izzy like I'd hugged Mandy after our other sister, Shannon, was gone.

But before I could respond, Izzy said, "Your ole granny is smart as a whip, too. She cheats me out of my M&M poker chips, then she bows her head and starts praying with all them nuns like she's got one foot in Heaven already. Yep, I'd trade any day. Since Jack died, my old man hardly even looks at me."

I had a plan to save Izzy but not Grandma Rose.

7

Rose's Hand-Dipped Chocolates

Remember the Sabbath day, to keep it holy. For six days you shall labor and do all your work, but the seventh day is a Sabbath of the Lord your God; on it you shall not do any work, you, or your son, or your daughter, your male slave or your female slave, or your resident who stays with you. For in six days the Lord made the heavens and the earth, the sea and everything that is in them, and He rested on the seventh day; for that reason the Lord blessed the Sabbath day and made it holy.

—Exodus 20:8-11

Izzy was consuming too much of my time and energy, but in an odd way, I welcomed it. It gave me purpose to try and help another person, to be a real saint. However, I needed to be there for Grandma Rose too.

I started making changes that my parents and school would not notice so I could spend more time with her. I told Sister I could serve Mass only one morning per week, no more Sundays or evening devotions. I let my homework slide to be at the hospital after school. Sometimes, when the morphine eased her pain and she dozed, I did my studies and tried to catch up.

I treasured my alone time with Grandma at Little Sisters. I wrote about our time together in my journal so I would never forget.

Grandma encouraged me. "Francis, tell me if you want me to talk slower. You need to get your family history accurate."

I started keeping a journal the same year I won a contest for young writers and had my article published in the St. Paul Pioneer Press. The story was about a blizzard, "the storm of the century," that shut down the Twin Cities for two days the previous April. I didn't get paid, but I won eight free movie tickets for the World Theater in downtown St. Paul.

I got hooked and decided I might want to be a writer or journalist someday when I saw my own byline and photo in the paper.

During that blizzard, Grandma Rose and I were snowed in for two days. We played cards and checkers by candlelight the first night. We slept near the oven in her kitchen on camping cots, using her gas stove for heat until power was restored. I got to drink hot cocoa, eat junk food, build snow forts, and jump off her upstairs porch into piles of snow taller than the neighbor's garage.

They even shut down the airport, train, and bus depots. For two days, nothing except snowplows were moving in Minneapolis or St. Paul. Babies were born in tow trucks. Twenty-three people died. Some from heart attacks while shoveling snow. An older couple that belonged to our church died when the roof on their home collapsed. They'd been living on the river flats below Cherokee Park. Others froze to death, like the four teenagers who'd been stranded in an ice-fishing shack on Lake Phalen. The two girls and two boys were from Henry Sibley High School. They'd gone there to smoke, drink beer, and make out. A Ramsey County deputy sheriff found them buried in a thirteen-foot drift two days later. They were frozen stiff as boards.

I filled up four notebooks while Grandma was suffering in the hospital. I hid them, along with the rock albums she gave me on my birthday, in the false ceiling of our back porch. I did not want anyone reading my innermost thoughts, poems, and stories unless I said to.

I put the sleek black vinyl albums there earlier because Mom threatened to burn my devil music. "Listening to that trash is like taking candy from Satan!"

One album was from the Rolling Stones, the other Herman's Hermits. They were both albums Grandma had gifted me.

Mom insisted "This Door Swings Both Ways" was a homosexual dance tune and "(I Can't Get No) Satisfaction" was about drugs and impure relationships.

Izzy had me hide his favorite album, too. It was the Doors' debut with "Light My Fire." When my folks were not home, we would put it on their hi-fi, and Izzy would crack me up by doing his Jim Morrison impression, playing air guitar and singing into a pretend microphone while wearing an old wig. One time, Mandy was home, and she chimed in next to Izzy, mimicking his gestures. She thought it was a hoot every time "light my fire" blasted out of the speakers because Izzy would take his Zippo lighter out and wave the flame above his head.

When she was awake, I asked my grandmother about her life. She said when she first met my grandfather, he teased her about her being Polish.

"That handsome Greek hired me as a teenager to work in his candy factory and trained me to dip cherry cordials with his secret fondant recipe. I wrote it down on the back of a holy card in my prayer book over there," she said, motioning to a small shelf on the wall. Grandma paused and smiled like she was reliving that day.

"He was much older than me and told me he needed to hold my hands to see if they were too warm to dip chocolates. After an uncomfortable amount of time, I asked him to let go. He said my fingers were too warm, but I could be the cherry-cordial girl because that job was done with a copper tool that had a wire prong on the end."

After my grandfather, George Paulson, died, Grandma started

working six days a week for ten hours each day to keep the candy factory running. She never drove a car and never pretended she was a big shot. She refused to join any clubs outside of her church. Everything revolved around her factory employees, her church, and her family—especially Mandy and me, her only two grandchildren.

She told me, "Francis, who needed a car then or now? On the farm, I'd walk or use the plow horse. Then, later, the streetcars in St. Paul got me downtown and to work. And now, the University Avenue number nine bus runs near my house and drops me off at the candy factory's corner. It goes all the way to Minneapolis so I can even see the Christmas lights and department store displays in December."

Grandma took the number nine to her factory at the crack of dawn each weekday morning right up until the doctor made her check into Little Sisters. She said Grandpa purchased a used car in 1941, but she never cared to drive it. It was a Ford coupe, and she said my grandfather used it to smuggle sugar to the factory. Sugar was rationed, and that is not good for a candy factory, so Grandpa bartered with one of the big department stores downtown. He gave them fudge, toffee, and peanut brittle in exchange for sugar that they got from their buyers out east. He saved the business doing that.

George Paulson died two Sundays before Christmas. On the day of his death, he'd attended his Greek Orthodox church and then went to work.

Grandma Rose winked at me. "He died because he went to work on the Lord's Day. He had a heart attack pulling a batch of candy canes on the big silver hook. Pulling and tossing candy works air into the hot clear sugary mixture, turning it a snowy white. It's hard work, and we did not know it then, but it was way too hard on his weak, aging heart."

I stood up and flexed my muscles for her. "I know, Grandma. Our candymaker Frank has strong arms and shoulders. He told me once that pulling candy would give me the strongest canoe-paddling arms in all of Minnesota. But no worries for me. My heart is young and strong."

Grandma reached for me and pulled me close to her bedside. "Francis, follow your dreams. If running a business and making candy makes you happy like it did for me, then do it. However, I think you might make for a great writer, poet, or newscaster someday. That could be your journey, your gift. But only you will know for sure."

"Thanks, Grandma." I kissed her warm cheek. "That's my dream, always has been. Tell me more about Grandpa."

"Well, the day he died, he needed to catch up on the candy order for the St. Paul First National Bank's Santa breakfast. Angelino, our regular hard-candy man, had taken a ship back to Greece to see his sick sister."

My grandmother asked me to pull a shoebox out from under her bed. She kept mementos in it. She searched through it until she found an old photograph. It was a picture of Angelino and my grandfather standing by the ship.

Grandma was smiling. "When I told your grandfather that Sunday was a day of rest, he kissed me on the cheek and said, 'Rose, I love you and the Lord, but we have to make hay while the sun shines.' I grew up on a farm, so he knew I would understand. That was the last time he kissed me."

I learned from my grandmother that Grandpa George was seventeen when he took the boat from Greece to America. At Ellis Island, they could pronounce George but not Papadopolous. Grandpa did not understand much English, so he nodded his head and accepted the papers and his new name, George Paulson. He hooked up with another Greek he'd met in New York who could pronounce his real name. Together, they took the train to St. Paul to work for Minnesota's railroad baron J. J. Hill.

Grandma Rose said Grandpa liked Mr. Hill because he paid a fair wage to any newcomers who were willing to work hard. Most of my grandfather's fellow crew workers were from Ireland and

Italy. He and his friend were the only two Greeks. They became good friends and even started pooling their savings. They vowed to someday open a sweetshop in downtown St. Paul.

Grandma said, "They both learned English and saved every dollar they could spare. Together, they opened Garden of Sweets Bakery and Candy Store. Initially it was downtown, but the rent was too high, so they closed the doors after two years and went their separate ways."

Six months later, George Paulson celebrated his new American citizenship by opening a small candy factory with low rent on University Avenue in St. Paul, not far from the Cathedral of St. Paul and the state capitol.

Grandma said my grandpa was always fascinated by the huge gold horses on top of the capitol building. Workers removed the horses for a week each spring so they could scrub and polish them. My grandfather would ask customers if they knew why the horses were missing, then he would tell them that the state employees took the horses down for a week each year so that they could poop.

Since the new shop was in St. Paul between the two cities of St. Paul and Minneapolis, Grandpa posted a freshly painted sign above the door. Its big, bold, blue letters read, CENTRAL CONFECTION CONNECTION. Later, after he married Grandma, the display window's canvas awning further defined the new shop's specialty. It read, *Featuring Rose's Hand-Dipped Chocolates.*

I thought that was funny since my grandmother's hands were too warm to dip chocolate by hand. The skilled dippers, not Rose, covered every morsel that passed through the front door. I guess it was no different than Colonel Sanders not frying every chicken himself.

After Grandpa died, Grandma had her Polish priest re-bless her factory. She told me that Grandpa had only let his Greek priest from St. George's Orthodox Church do the blessing. No Roman Catholic priest was allowed, even though St. Paul's archbishop was a regular customer.

Grandma said, "The first time Father Celeski blessed it for me, he went through a whole pint of holy water, sprinkled it everywhere. He doused the chocolate dippers' marble slabs and dribbled it into the kitchen's copper kettles, the peanut brittle cooling tables, and even the outer glass of the retail store's granite-and-marble display cases."

Grandma managed a weak laugh. "He got so carried away that he ruined a fresh batch of Grecian mints with his holy water."

My grandma then reached over to wet her fingers in the water glass by her bedside, and, opening the drawer in her nightstand, she flicked water on her Rosary and watch and said, "Father ended his rainstorm blessings by opening our cash register's main drawer and dousing it. He told me that is where I would need God's help the most."

I noticed her hand trembling as she opened her drawer, pretending it was a cash register.

My grandmother now needed more than holy water to help her. I wanted to stop her suffering, but my prayers were not eliciting any response from God.

I kissed her cheek to say goodbye. She reached out, squeezed my hand, and said, "I love you." Then she closed her eyes, put her right hand on her heart, and rolled onto her side. Jesus was watching her from the crucifix on the room's pale wall. I looked up at it, made the sign of the cross, and left her to rest.

I wrote one sentence in my journal before bed that night. It read, *If you care, please come down from your dead tree and help her heal.*

8

Limbo Soup

SEPTEMBER 1964

*Jesus answered, "Truly, truly, I say to you, unless one is born of
water and the Spirit, he cannot enter the kingdom of God."*
—JOHN 3:5

I thought Limbo was what people did in our basement on New
Year's Eve. Dad and I held a broomstick, and the chocolate dippers, candymakers, clerks, and packers shimmied underneath
the pole to Chubby Checker's "Limbo Rock." The winners of the
limbo contest got a case of Hamm's Beer or a bottle of Christian
Brothers Brandy as their prize.

Anna, our best chocolate dipper, usually won and chose the
brandy. She was tall, skinny, and flexible. She shared her winnings
with Jenna, who oversaw the caramel cut-and-wrap tables. Jenna
laughed her way under the pole but was top heavy with enormous
boobs and usually fell on her rump. It was my job to put down the
broom and help her up. One time after sampling their winnings,
both dippers fell asleep on my bunk and upchucked brandy all
over my Minnesota Twins bedspread.

The first time I heard about the other kind of Limbo was the
day I met Izzy. I asked my mom if he could come over for supper

and hang out sometime.

"Of course, Francis. I'm proud of how easily you made a new friend. I look forward to meeting Isadore. Just find out what day works for him and have him clear it with his folks."

"He hates being called Isadore, Mom. Please just call him Izzy."

"Well then, Izzy it is. I'll ask your father to put some burgers on the grill, and I'll make hot-fudge sundaes for dessert. We can use the candy store fudge. Maybe you can invite him to tour the candy factory sometime too?"

Things sometimes change in a single moment and not always for the better. Minutes after our chat, Mom fell down the basement stairs while carrying a load of laundry. Unfortunately, the baby inside my mother never recovered from that fall.

I grabbed the phone and called Dad at work. Our black rotary phone was on a party line, and our neighbor was on the shared line, but she hung up right away so I could call. My father hurried home and rushed Mom to St. Joseph's Hospital, where she stayed for several days.

Mom was shaking when my father brought her home a week later.

Sister had all my classmates craft her a giant card, which was waiting for Mom on our kitchen table. Next to it was an expensive vase of lilies that Dad had purchased for her. They were not in season, but they were Mom's favorite flower because they reminded her of Easter. She started crying when she saw me, so I hugged her.

More than anything, my mother wanted everyone she loved to go to Heaven, especially her husband and us kids. But God did not give my new sister enough time to get baptized. The baby died at the hospital. Stillborn is just a nice word for dead baby. My parents named her Cynthia.

Five weeks later, on a Saturday afternoon, there was a knock on our door. Dad was at bowling practice. Father Joseph, the young new assistant pastor, came to visit Mom.

Mom was barefoot and still wearing her white terry-cloth bathrobe when she opened the front door. She was not expecting anyone, especially a priest, but she tried to make him feel welcome.

"Good morning, Father. I'm sorry. I mean afternoon. It is afternoon, right? Please come inside."

"Yes, it is afternoon, Mrs. Paulson. I should have called first, but our parish secretary is off on Saturdays, and I could not find your number."

I heard Father clear his throat, buying time, searching for the right words. "I just came from the cemetery and was in the neighborhood."

"Who died, Father?"

"Darrin Hawley."

"Oh no. He was so young."

"Passed on Wednesday. Massive stroke. He was walking his mail route just a few blocks from the rectory."

"Can I get you tea or coffee, Father?"

"No thanks, Eleanor. I had my fill already."

"OK, then."

"Eleanor, last week, your husband called the church office and got put through to me. Antonio is concerned for your well-being."

"I'm worried too, Father. I feel tired, sad, and helpless most days, and I have awful night dreams about my baby."

"Mrs. Paulson, I'm here to listen. Please take this Rosary. Our Blessed Lady will help too."

"OK."

"May I sit down, Mrs. Paulson? Here, by your dog, on the sofa?"

"Kevin, get off the couch! Sorry, Father. Francis dog-sits for his grandmother on Saturdays when she works a long shift at the candy factory."

"Well, Eleanor, I see little Kevin minds you." Father let out a short, genuine laugh. "I would, too, if you yelled at me like that."

"I'll put him in Francis's room, Father."

I jumped onto my bed and pretended I was napping. Mom opened my door, shooed the dog in, then shut it tight. Kevin jumped on my bed and started annoying me, licking my face. I shoved him off and cracked the door so I could better hear their conversation.

Mother probably should have changed into a house dress. It seemed odd for a lady to sit on a couch in her pajamas with another man when her husband was not home. But a priest must be different than a real man. Father spoke again.

"Eleanor, how about we bow our heads and start with a prayer?"

"OK, Father."

"Almighty Heavenly Father, Jesus said that whenever two or more are gathered in his name, there is nothing he will not grant them. We ask your intersession in helping Eleanor find peace and healing after her sudden loss. We ask this in Jesus's name. In the name of the Father, Son, and Holy Ghost, amen."

There was a long silence. Then Mom finally mumbled, "Amen."

Father continued his cheerleading Bible lessons.

"Eleanor, I think your sadness is hurting your ability to be a good wife and mother, like you just acknowledged. Feelings of shock and sorrow, like yours, are common in these situations, but they can be overcome with our Lord and the Virgin Mary's help."

"Father, it's not only about losing my baby. That was hard. It's hard every minute of every day. I cry for her, and I pray the Rosary night and day, but my pain never goes away."

"And Our Blessed Lady hears your petitions, Eleanor. She is not deaf to your anguish."

"Father, it was not baby Cynthia's fault she died that way. Me carrying laundry. Tripping down the basement stairs to the cement floor. A few hours later, I was numb all over, holding her tiny blue bloody body and watching Antonio weep. I did not know what to do, so I grabbed him too, our dead baby between us. This pain is more than Jesus, Mary, or you can assist me with."

Father was silent for a long time. I opened the door wider. Finally, he cleared his throat again.

"Eleanor, remember, the Virgin Mary understands your heartaches. She lost her only son on that cross when he died for our sins to give us eternal life."

"Yes, of course, Father. Her son. Must have been awful. But what about my daughter? She had no time to be baptized and earn eternal life. She will never experience Heaven. What about Cynthia?"

I was proud of Mom for asking the same questions I wanted to grill Father on.

"Eleanor, your stillborn baby's soul is still safe in Limbo. All souls in Limbo are spared the purging of Purgatory before Heaven. They just will not experience the glory of Heaven. However, she will never be aware of that loss."

"Not be aware, Father? How so? In what way?"

It sounded like Father Joseph was now panicking, grasping, struggling for words. "Ah. Ah . . . well, let's think of it in terms of a Thanksgiving feast."

"OK, Father. Pumpkin pie is my favorite."

"If you have never been to a splendid Thanksgiving surrounded by family, fancy linens, and fine china, if you've never smelled the wonderful aromas of turkey, sage stuffing, cranberries, and pumpkin pie—you would not know enough to miss it. You could be happy with potato soup as it is a hearty and filling meal in itself."

"Really, soup? Yes, I suppose one can survive on soup . . ."

"Yes. Now dab those tears, Eleanor. Take my hand and let us pray."

"Yes, Father. Let's pray for Cynthia and her Limbo soup."

I closed my door, shutting off the conversation. Now my

sister had to eat soup with no pie. They must have taught Father to say that when he went to Moses, Jesus, Pope, and priest school.

When Father left, Mother went into her bedroom. I could hear her sobbing. I knocked on her door.

"Antonio?"

"No, Mom. It's me, Francis."

When I opened the door, she sat up, moved to the edge of the bed, and motioned for me to sit beside her.

"Are you OK, Mom?"

She hugged me. I squeezed her back hard. She managed a weak smile. "Now that you are here, I'm fine, honey. Your hug makes it much better."

Neither of us said anything more. I eased my way toward the door. Before I closed it, I told her I loved her.

I knew my mother would still find some way to pray us all into Heaven regardless of what she heard from Father Joe. I finished writing my own questions about God's second-class playground, a dead-baby safety net called Limbo.

I fell asleep before dark. I dreamed big and in color. In my nightmare, my dead sister had brown hair and matching big brown puppy-dog eyes. She was locked in our garage, sipping potato soup out of a tin cup like prisoners do in jail. She looked up, smiling at me. I could see she had lost her two front baby teeth. I bashed in the garage window with a sledgehammer and slipped her my piece of pumpkin pie.

9

Shannon and Mandy

OCTOBER 1964

For this child I prayed, and the Lord has granted me my request.
—1 SAMUEL 1:27

There was an ice cream party for our school's candy fundraiser. I stayed after school to get my fill of ice cream and sprinkles. I was always the top candy bar seller, but Dad never allowed me to claim my prize since it was Grandma Rose's candy bars that we sold. This year, the prize was a Timex watch. That trophy went to Travis, the second-place seller.

Grandma always rewarded me anyway, under the table, after the fundraiser was over. Last year, she gave me the same Boy Scout jackknife the school awarded to the runner-up boy. It was on October 4, St. Francis of Assisi's feast day.

"Happy feast day, Francis." She handed me the gift-wrapped knife.

Dad had come home early that day and was waiting for me after my party. Mom had placed homemade chocolate-chip oatmeal cookies on the table.

Dad pointed to my regular chair at our kitchen table and said, "Francis, you know how hard it's been on your mother since the accident."

"Yes, sir."

Mom poured me a glass of milk and handed me the cookie platter. I was full from eating so much ice cream, but she had made the cookies specially for me, so I took one.

Mom said, "Honey, after much praying, I decided—and your father agreed—that we should have another baby, but not the same way you came to us."

They had decided to adopt, and I was about to gain two sisters who, for whatever reason, couldn't stay with their real mother. They were identical twins, just over three years old. Dad told me I would need to be responsible and set a good example. Mom said I could teach them games and prayers. All I wanted was my old mom back, and if this would help her and make her happy, then that would also help my dad. I would do anything to get back the Mom I used to know, so I figured this would probably make me happy too.

The following week we drove to the agency. My folks signed a bunch of papers, and that was it. We left with Shannon and Mandy. Miranda was her official saint namesake, but we all preferred the nickname Mandy that her real mom had given her.

On the ride home, I sat in the back seat between the girls and made sure they did not jump around. I had an arm ready to hold each of them down in case Dad needed to slam on the brakes. I started singing "Found a Peanut" to them. Mandy was looking at me, amused, and I could tell she liked it. Mom was humming along. Shannon must have been tired; she just stared up at our car's ceiling.

I remember that day: our new car, the drive, the joy that surrounded me. Mom was laughing again. Dad was proud that he had just filled up the back seat with three kids. He even stopped by Dairy Queen and let all of us eat ice cream in his new car without worrying about the ice cream dripping on the seats.

The station wagon still had its fresh new-car smell. I liked the radio, a shiny silver knob with a red needle that tuned into each station. The inside doors sported chrome window cranks and latches with big push buttons to let you in from the outside. The dashboard was fake wood-grain that matched the exterior panels.

Grandma Rose liked the "Jesus straps" the best. They were strong leather loops that hung above each of the four doors. Once, when my father took a fast turn on our way to church, she whispered that they were there for me to grab onto and pray, "Oh Jesus!"

My father paid seven extra dollars for whitewall tires like the race cars had. If they made wood-grain tires, he would have picked those instead.

Dad bought the Ford wagon in spring. I liked the red-and-white vinyl bench seats. When I spit into my hand and rubbed just right, they'd make a fart sound.

Dad loved his new daughters, and that justified the twenty-two hundred dollars he spent on our car. He told Mom he could now fill up the back seat with me and the girls and still have room in the way back for his outboard motor and luggage when we went to Jacobson's Peaceful Pines Lake Resort for our annual August vacation.

"No need to strap down that big canvas Sears cartopper anymore," he bragged.

Then he looked at me in his rearview mirror and asked, "Francis, why do they call it a Ranch Wagon? There are no ranches in Minnesota, just farms and ten thousand lakes."

I stopped singing to answer. "Maybe Mr. Ford is from Texas," I said. "If he were from Minnesota, he would have named it a Lake Wagon."

Mom laughed, turned around, and, kneeling on her seat, wiped the ice-cream mustaches from the twins' faces.

"I think family wagon is the perfect name for our new vehicle," she said.

10

Gone!

OCTOBER 1964 - MARCH 1965

Then the Lord said to Cain, "Where is Abel your brother?"
And he said, "I do not know, am I my brother's keeper?"
—GENESIS 4:9

I noticed Shannon was not speaking like Mandy when I played with them. They often ran into my bedroom like a tag team, encouraging me to play with them. Shannon loved my drop-the-cup game the most. Their favorite toys were the engraved sterling silver drinking cups Poor Grandma Patricia gave to them. She also gave them their own name-embroidered blankets for their christening.

They were expensive gifts that Grandma Patricia insisted were meant to be used, not hidden away in a curio case. The girls loved the cups and even used them like a mirror, reflecting their distorted faces. The twins rarely let them out of their sight.

The girls would stand on my bedroom desk chair and hold their cups above their heads. I made them close their eyes and drop them. Then, I retrieved the treasures and hid them some-where on me or nearby. They thought it was hilarious when I tried to hide them under my butt or armpits.

Izzy got a kick out of the girls' antics, too. Mandy worshipped him, hugging his leg every time he visited. Izzy knew they loved their engraved drinkware, so he gave them each a cheap dime-store steel harmonica. Mandy spit more than she actually blew, but she got out some notes. Izzy thought that was hilarious.

Shannon ignored her instrument. She was really slow to speak, too. Usually, she just made gestures, nodding her head vigorously, but she giggled endlessly when we played our games.

It made Grandma Patricia happy when she visited and watched her granddaughters enjoying her gifts. Grandma hit a home run with that sterling silver.

The first time I heard Mandy really scream, it was directed at Kevin on one of the Saturdays I was dog-sitting for Grandma Rose. Mandy usually ignored him, and she pushed him away when he annoyed the twins, but Shannon feared Kevin. He'd nipped at her once when trying to steal her doll.

When Mandy caught Kevin tugging Shannon's doll by the hair, Mandy screamed, "Bad dog! No!" He let go and ran like the wind. Shannon was crying but said nothing.

My mother later told me that she took Shannon to Grandma Rose's Polish doctor about a month after the adoption. Mom was worried that Shannon might be "mentally challenged" because she was not speaking like her sister. Mom was furious with the doctor's comments, so she deepened her voice to mimic him for me.

"Not to worry, Mrs. Paulson. I've seen teenagers that still can't talk worth a hill full of beans. Your daughter will be speaking soon, and if being quiet is her nature, she'll make for a good wife someday."

My father never really listened to Mom's worries and concerns. I don't think he did it to be neglectful. He just figured things would work themselves out in time, without him having to spend money on the problems. He'd always seen his number-one job as being a provider, for us and for our employees, so his head was usually focused on keeping the business going.

I made it my job to listen to Mom, and I even wrote in my journal one night: *I think no one hears my mother but me, and I'm still just a kid. Maybe that's all I can do for now. Just listen.*

I still have nightmares about fire but never about the fire that changed all of us forever. In my fire dreams, I'm always running and tripping, about to be burned alive. I wake up in a fierce sweat before the flames can engulf me. I have never had night terrors about that awful March morning, though. Maybe I blocked it from my inner brain, as though it did not really happen.

I only left them for seconds. Dad was at Joe's General having coffee with Cigar Ron. They were working on the upcoming gambling boards for the Minnesota Twins. Mom was door knocking with the Rosary Society, collecting for the March of Dimes.

I was in charge of the twins. It was only to be for a few minutes, between when Dad left and Mom got back. But she got delayed.

Mom trusted me with the girls. I felt good when she told me, "Francis, they love you and mind you better than they do me sometimes. You are very mature for your age."

I was singing and making them chocolate-chip pancakes, their favorite. Kevin started yapping, so I ran to the back porch to see if someone was there, but it was just the wind rattling a window. I returned in seconds. I think they were both standing on a single chair, probably reaching for the pancakes, when Shannon lost her footing and fell into the burner's flames.

I screamed, "Stop!"

Mandy froze and then started wailing. It was too late for Shannon; her pajama sleeve was already on fire, then the lace on her collar, then her hair.

As she tried to scamper from the fire, I grabbed the milk jug and emptied the liquid on her head and pajama top. I tossed her over my shoulder and ran to our neighbor's house. Mandy followed barefoot, still crying. Jim Stockman told his wife, Kathy, to go find our mom. Then he drove his red Ford Mustang, like the race car that it is, to the hospital. Susan's father, Dr. Flannagan, was the chief surgeon at the burn center. He and his team worked on Shannon.

That was the last time Mandy and I saw our sister.

11

Silence

MARCH 1965

For God said, "Honor your father and mother," and, "The one who speaks evil of father or mother is to be put to death."
—MATTHEW 15:4

The Friday after the fire, my parents called me into their bedroom. I sat on the edge of their bed. Mandy was napping. Dad shut the door and told me the dreadful news about my other sister.

"Francis, the fire was not your fault. Shannon could have died, and you saved her life with your quick thinking and action. She will be in the hospital for at least another month. However, when they release her, she will not be able to live with us anymore."

Mom sat there like a zombie.

"They say Dr. Flannagan is the best burn specialist in the Midwest," my father continued. "He told us that after he completes her skin grafts, Shannon will recover. With the right help, she'll lead a good life."

I went numb on my insides. My heart was trying to jump out of my chest. "Not live with us?" I asked. "Skin grafts?"

"Correct," my father said. He turned away from me, looking out the window. "She will have scars on her right arm, neck, and backside, as well as on her scalp where her hair caught fire. Shannon now has more issues than we, as a family, can help her with. Financially, and in other ways too. Your mother and I met with Father O'Malley at the adoption agency yesterday."

Mom was not looking out the window. She was focused on me. Her eyes were bloodshot, her face ashen gray.

Her voice was flat and feeble. "Francis, I've been praying day and night. This might be for the best, honey. The agency already found a new home for Shannon when she is ready to leave the hospital. One that can give her things we cannot."

Dad stood up. He hovered over me and said the doctors also told them our sister was not mentally slow. She was smart and brave. She just could not hear. Shannon was deaf.

My parents, the adoption agency, and our priest all met behind my back and decided that Shannon should be taken in by a rich Catholic family with the resources to cover her medical bills. That family lived in Faribault, Minnesota, a small town where there was a well-respected academy for children with hearing loss.

Mom's silent tears were now visible. She looked like she might faint.

"Shannon is so young, Francis. She will be getting all the attention and resources she needs to lead a long, happy life, something we cannot give her, especially since Grandma's factory is having money troubles again. Your father has not had a raise in two years. I'm sure Shannon's new family will love and care for her as much as we did."

My father read my hateful face like a book. He glared back at me, the rage making his face red.

"Goddamn it! Yes, Francis! Everything, including money! These things cost more than I can provide! It is best for Shannon and also for you and Mandy!"

I could not believe my ears. My face was flushed, my mouth dry, and I was sweating all over. I had to save my sister.

"Mom, Dad, I will help! I'll cut grass, shovel snow. I'll work at the factory for free, and Joe will hire me to do odd jobs in a few years. He hires others my age and pays cash. They even get free food for working there. I'll get a paper route, and I'll learn to caddie at the Mendota Club. I can transfer to public school. That will save us lots."

Mom dropped her Rosary, ran to the bathroom, and locked the door. An even more intense rage overtook my father's face, and it was all focused on me. He bent over me and grabbed both of my shoulders, his eyes burning into mine. I looked away, down at my feet. Everything was a blur of tears.

"Francis, that's enough! It is done. Be strong for your mom and Mandy. No need to ever discuss this again!"

Be strong? In that moment I felt weak trying to relate to my father, like Izzy probably did toward his old man. Strong. I will never forget the strong odor of Shannon's burning scalp and hair. I could not save Shannon, but perhaps I could redeem myself and still be strong for Mom, Mandy, and my best friend, Izzy.

Soon after Shannon left us, Mandy kept leaving her bed and sneaking into my room to sleep with me. I think she was afraid that if she lost Shannon, I might be next. Mom let it go on for a couple of weeks and then said, "Francis, I know you are trying to help her, but it is not appropriate. She has her own room."

The next day, Dad took down both girls' old bargain twin beds and surprised Mandy with a fancy new one. It had a pink canopy on top. It came with a nightstand and three drawers for all the little things she liked to collect. How could my father afford expensive furniture but not provide for my absent sister?

Mandy kept sneaking into my room until Dad threatened to put a lock on her door from the outside. Shannon had her one fire, but Mandy's dance with danger was just beginning.

12

Killing Grandma

SEPTEMBER 1967

The last enemy to be abolished is death.
—1 CORINTHIANS 15:26

"Malignant" is what the Polish doctor from her church called it. Then he sliced off my grandma's right breast. Grandma Rose's well-being was in danger.

On Grandma Rose's last Saturday alive, Izzy and Mandy joined me to visit her. Mom and Dad had to go to our factory early, clean it up real nice, and then meet a reporter from the *St. Paul Pioneer Press*. The paper was doing a Sunday feature about Rose's Fine Chocolates and all the varieties of holiday candies we made, including some novelties, like a four-foot-tall solid-chocolate Santa and six-foot-long candy canes.

After Grandma Rose fell ill, Mom started pitching in every Saturday to help keep the business going. My father was struggling to handle Grandma Rose's medical bills, her business debts, and payroll for his employees. The good news was that the free publicity we were about to receive would give us a needed boost for our Halloween, Thanksgiving, and Christmas candy orders.

Mom insisted I had to babysit rather than meet the writer. It was not real babysitting, as I never got a quarter. It was what a big brother was supposed to do for free.

"But, Mom, I need to go. And besides, Izzy and I were planning on going to Cherokee Park before visiting Grandma Rose. Mandy can't keep up with us on her kid bike."

"No buts about it, Francis, offer it up. Ride slow or take her sidesaddle. Be a nice brother and a soldier for Christ. Mandy will be no bother. A special adventure with her big brother will be good for both of you, and Izzy too."

I so wanted to go to the candy shop to meet the big-shot writer.

Instead, I drove my sister sidesaddle on my bike to Izzy's. Mandy annoyed me the whole way by singing the theme song from *The Wizard of Oz* but changing the lyrics to "We're off to see the Izzy, the wonderful Izzy of Oz."

When we reached his yard, she jumped on my friend's back, tossing his Twins baseball cap into the rhubarb patch. Izzy's mom saw us from her kitchen window, rushed outside, and one-arm-hugged me. She had Izzy's yellow rain slicker in the other arm.

"Oh, Francis, please tell your mother and father we are praying for your grandmother every day."

It was drizzling as Izzy eased Jack's bike from the garage.

"Isadore, where are you and Francis taking Mandy in this rain?"

Izzy hopped on his brother's three-speed Schwinn and shouted, "Going to Joe's General to buy stale wieners from his bargain barrel, then riding to the Cherokee Park caves where we'll wait out the rain while smoking cigarettes and looking at Francis's dad's new *Playboy*. I love you, Ma. Bye!"

"If you say so, honey. Have a good time and be home before dark. And take your rain poncho!" Izzy's mom waved us off.

We were already pedaling away as Izzy got in the last word. "I'm good, Ma. I'm not sugar, won't melt!"

We stopped at the park every Saturday afternoon before

riding to the Little Sisters of the Poor hospital. Once we settled around our fire, Mandy played with her Barbie and sucked on a Tootsie Pop, taking in every word of our conversation.

We usually talked baseball, arguing about whose cards were worth more—Izzy's Harmon Killebrew or my Rod Carew. Neither of us had any real Twins autographs. I did get Rich Rollins's wife's autograph on the back of a Wrigley gum wrapper when I sat by her at a bowling fundraiser.

Rollins was an OK Twins third baseman, but his wife was pretty, smelled good, and talked with me. I figured later on that her signature, Lynn Maher Rollins, would probably never be worth anything unless she became a movie star or a serial killer.

Inside the privacy of our cave, Izzy was jabbering about which girls at Holy Family had the prettiest hair and best breasts. He mostly went on about how much he hated Suck-Up Sue and how I should help him pull pranks on her. That day, we talked about serious stuff, too, like the Vietnam War, the commies, and NASA. Izzy then drifted into making fun of the nuns he did not like. I switched the subject to our head priest's reputation with liquor. I told Izzy I heard it from Father himself.

"Last Sunday, during his sermon, Father was talking about how gossip is a sin, and then he said he overheard a group of the Rosary Society ladies whispering that the owner of the Black Derby, the bar just two blocks from the rectory, had to walk Father home after midnight when he tipped one too many pints." To demonstrate, I stood up, put my Orange Crush to my mouth, and guzzled the remains, saying, "Father then yelled at all of us while spitting into the microphone: 'And all I say to all of you is, don't do what I do, do what I say!'"

Izzy whipped out his Zippo and lit a cigarette he'd snuck from his old man's pack of Camel Straights. He pretended to pass it to Mandy. She looked at him and giggled.

"How do you do it, Izzy?" I asked. "You had Sampson balls talking to your mom like that, and for once you were telling the truth."

Mandy tugged my arm. "What are *Sampson balls*, Francis?"

Izzy handed her another sucker. "That is for us to know, and for you to find out, Little Miss Nosy Worm."

Then he addressed me. "Francis, I keep telling you that it is all about my system. It is just one of my "Isadore Principles." Principle number twenty-four: Tell adults the truth, and they will never believe you."

Izzy always spoke with passion and certainty. For a while, even the nuns swallowed his tales, not catching the exaggerations. That was the power of Izzy and his Principles.

He was serious as a heart attack about his system. He wrote a book about it, and it contained fifty beliefs about life, family, and religion. He borrowed my Boy Scout wood-burning tool and took an hour carefully binding the book and then engraving the book's title—*The Isadore Principles*—on the brown leather cover. Suck-Up Sue called it "Satan's Principles."

Mandy held out her hand toward Izzy for another Tootsie Pop and then moved closer to the cave entrance to bury her doll and newly found agates in a big white pile of sand she'd gathered there. On her next visit, she would dig them up and pretend to find treasure. Early that summer, Izzy removed her prizes, hid them elsewhere, and in their place buried a big rubber rat with a dollar bill tied around its neck.

My friend continued to try to persuade me. "Francis, if you master my Principles, 80 percent of the morons in the world will believe you too. Just like Jesus convincing all those losers at Cain and Abel's wedding that water was wine. That is Isadore Principle number eighteen: Don't believe all the magic in the Bible."

"It's called 'The Wedding at Cana,' bigger moron. Not Cain and Abel's wedding."

Izzy shot back, "My point, Mr. I-kiss-Sister's-ass-in-religion-all-day-and-twice-on-Sunday, is that Jesus communicated with passion and preached with confidence, and that, along with a spot of red clay food coloring, went a long way in scamming the locals and those wedding guests, and no one fell off their camel driving home drunk."

I flicked a twig at his head. It landed on his baseball cap. "Don't you mean donkey?"

He removed his hat, filled it with sand, and fired it back at me. "Camel, jackass, or on a pus-infested leper's back. That Bible BS keeps Catholics under control. All pie-in-the-sky hocus-pocus. Create the world in seven days, walk on water, change water into wine. Don't get me wrong: Jesus was cool. I would hang with him, even share my smokes, look at a *Playboy*. Hell, if the Jeezter hung with that hooker Mary Monroe, he would hang with us."

"It's Mary Magdalene, not Monroe, Bible Breath."

"OK. Whatever. I'm just saying people need something to believe in. They don't want to think their lives are all shit except for baseball, Santa Claus, the Easter Bunny, and ten-cent Dairy Queen on a hot afternoon. Then, they get really sick like your granny, or disappear like Shannon, or even die like my brother, Jack."

I shook the sand out and gave his hat back to him. "And you learned all of that from *The Three Stooges*."

Izzy dropped his smoke in a puddle, and without missing a beat, he withdrew another, lit it, and blew a smoke ring in my face. Then he continued his rant.

"I'm telling you, Saint Franny, master the Isadore Principles and you'll be Pope someday. I'll be the first one to polish your halo. You can hang up your altar-boy cassock for good, and maybe Suck-Up will drop her drawers for you. There's never been a Pope Francis. Pope Francis, my best friend, eighty years old and still a virgin because he never used my Isadore Principles to talk a girl into his pants."

When we arrived at the hospital, my grandmother was groggy from morphine. The only game she could manage was Blind

Man's Bluff. We all held a card to our foreheads. Grandma Rose was feverish and clammy, and I held her card for her. It was the six of spades. Mandy's was the six of diamonds. Izzy held the ace of hearts. Mine ended up being the six of clubs.

The nuns had left us alone after they lit a large Jesus candle that was put on a small table next to Grandma Rose's bed. The room reeked of holy incense that the priest had set afire after giving Grandma the sacrament of Extreme Unction—her anointing and last rites—before we arrived. The holy water, anointing oil, and incense were supposed to make the cancer go away, or at least send her on a faster yellow-brick road through Purgatory and into Heaven.

Grandma liked gambling, so I'm sure she was covering all her bets when she let the priest do his hocus-pocus rituals.

The candle kept flickering, reacting to the fan the nuns had brought in to help cool Grandma down. It was casting eerie shadows on the ceiling. Grandma Rose was struggling to open her eyes and acknowledge us.

Izzy was having a meltdown. He whispered to me, "Holy shit, Francis. All three of you got sixes. Six-six-six. That is the mark of the Devil. Blow out the candle. They are death cards along with that death candle. Blow it out now."

We were crowded in her small room. She held a starched white sheet to her chin, and our shadows danced on the pale-yellow walls. The odor of melting wax was mingling with the incense, the same incense that made me wheeze when I served funeral Masses. She knew I was there, because when I reached out, she gave my hand a feeble squeeze.

Grandma tried to speak. I leaned my ear next to her lips to hear her faint voice.

"Children, I let you win again. You all have happy, kind hearts. Should not be fussing after me. Best leave. Go outside, and run around."

Letting go of my hand, she tried to extend her arms as far as she could like she used to when she was showing Mandy and me how much she loved us, but they fell limp to her sides.

"I love you this much," she murmured. "Isadore, too. You make me smile. Sly as a fox, but inside, you are gentle as a dove. You have a kind heart too. You are all aces."

She nodded toward a glass of ice chips and my grandfather's small brass crucifix on her nightstand. Izzy whispered, "She wants a drink and her Jesus, Francis. For Christ's sake, blow out the damn candle."

Izzy placed the crucifix into her palm. Mandy held the glass to Grandma's lips, but her chin was in the way. The ice spilled out and slid down our grandmother's neck. She started gasping when it hit her chest and heart. She was struggling for air. Mandy was wailing, watching helplessly as the ice soaked through her hospital gown. Grandma kept grasping her Jesus, trying to catch air. I ran out of the room, hollering for a nun, a nurse, anyone.

13

Rose's Last Party

OCTOBER 1967

Blessed are those who mourn, for they will be comforted.
—MATTHEW 5:4

The *Pioneer Press* obituary read, "Rose Paulson died peacefully with family at her side." That's what I told everyone. But Izzy, Mandy, and I knew the truth. Grandma Rose left us inhaling bad incense and tightening her grip around her brass Jesus with the ace of spades lying on her bed.

It was my first wake. Mandy hid in the funeral home's cloakroom. Izzy heard her sobs, put his arm around Mandy's shoulder, and gave her a box of animal crackers. She fell asleep, so he put a coat under her head and shut the curtain of the cloakroom. I could not sob. I was angry. Angry at God for taking Grandma Rose and for making her suffer.

At the funeral home, I overheard my dad telling a group of our employees that Grandma had wanted the Jazinski brothers, the undertakers that went to her church, to make her up.

"They did good. She looks real nice," Dad said.

Izzy knelt with me by the casket. Grandma wore her royal-blue dress, the same one she wore at my confirmation. A Rosary was wrapped around her hands, and a cameo of the Blessed Lady was pinned to her chest. I thought it odd that she still wore her glasses. Who needs those when they're dead?

Flowers from our customers were everywhere. They helped mask the room's smoky stench. Even Mr. Wong sent plastic flowers that he had delivered from Chicago's Chinatown. The funeral home was haunting. Ugly gold drapes dropped to the floor's puke-olive carpeting. There were no windows behind the curtains. How dumb was that? Dimly lit table lamps highlighted their dusty lampshades.

The Polish church women kept hugging me. They reeked of cheap Golden Rule department-store perfume. Izzy noticed and announced it a bit too loudly.

"Jesus H. Christ, Francis! If you had warned me those ladies would smell this bad, I woulda brought more of my own BO!"

When Izzy and I were not paying attention, Mandy left the cloakroom to pee. She was gone a long time before anyone noticed. Sal Jazinski brought her back, holding her firmly by her wrist, and summoned Mom and me to his office. Dad was busy talking with Cigar Ron and his bowling team near the coffin.

It was hard to tell Sal and Nick Jazinski apart, if not for the name badges above their suit-coat pockets. They both had slick, greasy black hair, pencil mustaches, and Groucho Marx eyebrows. They sported identical black horn-rimmed glasses with lenses thicker than pop bottles.

Mom and I were standing. Sal released Mandy into Mom's custody, giving her a push our way. He sat on his desk facing us, probably trying to figure out how to up Dad's bill.

"Mrs. Paulson, we need to have a serious chat about what your daughter did."

On her way to the bathroom, my sister had decided to take a full tour of the mortuary, and she had lit every candle she could find using a lighter she had swiped from Cigar Ron's coat pocket. It was in the shape of a Playboy Bunny, so later she gave it to Izzy.

In the basement, she even emptied two dozen supersized sancti-fied votive candles out of their cases and lit those too.

Later, at school, I heard gossip that the Jazinskis blamed us for the charred toilet paper roll they found in the women's toilet along with a stack of Grandma's half-burnt holy cards.

Mom was exhausted and did the only thing she could do on such a piss-poor night. She held Mandy tight. My sister buried her face in Mom's shoulder, tears dampening both of their new dresses.

Grandma's priest, Father Celeski, slammed a couple of free whiskey shots and then gathered us around the casket for the Rosary. He prayed so slowly that I'm sure even God fell asleep. I kept staring at the big zit under Father Celeski's fat, blue-veined, red nose. I wanted to pop the pimple with a tweezers.

When Father finished, the adults went into the next room for smokes, food, liquor, and Rose stories. I never would have guessed they threw parties like this for dead folks. The room was hazy. Smoke mixed with the scent of beer and Grandma Rose's favorite, Christian Brothers Brandy. They had animal crackers and Hawaiian Punch for us kids.

Grandma was all alone in the next room with her eyeglasses, a truckload of real flowers, Wong's plastic bouquet, and over a dozen holy candles nearing the end of their wicks.

Father Celeski stuck around for more free booze. The room got rowdy as people kept drinking and toasting Grandma. Two of the Polish church ladies brought their husbands' concertinas and made their men play my grandmother's favorite polka tunes. If there had been room to dance, there would have been dancing.

The festivities went on for over two hours before the Jazins-kis pushed people out. Sal had to drive Father Celeski's car back to the rectory while Nick drove Father.

After all the adults left the party room, Izzy finished off the liquor remaining in the bottom of everyone's cocktail glasses. Before swallowing the last one, he raised it in a toast to the ceiling and said, "Francis, the Worm rocked it tonight by lighting all those candles for your grandma. Your granny is up there laughing so hard she is crying. That's why it's raining now. She said it right, Francis. You are an ace."

I took the glass from his hand, set it on a small end table, and said, "She's your grandma too, Izzy. You made her happy. She said you have a gentle heart. You were also an ace, remember? I read that we Catholics call it 'the Community of Saints.' It means we are always connected with those we love who have died before us."

It seemed Izzy liked that because he did not have a smart-ass comeback, even after sipping all that liquor.

On the way home, Mandy sat between Izzy and me and held my hand. Her other hand was holding Cigar Ron's Playboy Bunny lighter. She was sound asleep when we got to Izzy's house.

When my dad pulled up to Izzy's house, Izzy chucked me on the shoulder and slid me two envelopes, one small, one larger.

"Hide these," he said. "The big one is from the Worm. The other is a gift I'd like to give my old man someday."

He opened the car door and got out. "Thank you for the ride, Mr. Paulson. I'm sorry about your mother. Someone will drop me off for the funeral tomorrow."

Before I went to bed, I opened both envelopes. The Worm's contained two of Cigar Ron's Cuban cigars and his Playboy Bunny lighter. Izzy's envelope had a black-and-white photo of his old man swigging a beer with three bullets taped to the back side of the picture.

14

Mary's Finger

OCTOBER 1967

And he said to them, "It is written, My house shall be called a
house of prayer; but ye make it a den of robbers."
—MATTHEW 21:13

I was sickly during the funeral. St. Stanislaus, Grandma Rose's
church and cemetery, was on St. Paul's north end, near Frogtown.
Frog was slang for *French*. My other grandmother, Grandma Patricia, sat by Izzy, Mandy, and me. She was holding Mandy's hand
through most of the service.

Grandma Patricia went to St. Joan of Arc, the Frog church just
a few blocks away. Grandma was French Canadian, from Quebec.
Poor Grandpa was German, but he died before I was born and just
went to Mass wherever Grandma Patricia told him to go. I would
have picked St. Stanislaus, a Polish church, over Holy Family, as
it sounded like *St. Santa Claus* if you said the name real fast like I
did when goofing off sometimes.

There was a huge statue of St. Joan staring at the congrega-
tion from behind the Communion rail at St. Joan's. Mandy looked
forward to going to Mass at St. Joan's. She liked that St. Joan of
Arc dressed up like a boy to kill King Henry's armies. Mandy was

most interested in how she was burned alive to become a saint. Mandy insisted that when she got confirmed, Joan was to be her namesake.

I think Mom had Grandma Rose envy. Her mom did not own a factory, nor even a car. But her parents were proud when they finally paid off their home, and they kept adding more kids. They had twelve in all. My mom was the youngest, and she said my grandfather always joked that he wanted one more so he could tell everyone he had a baker's dozen. His father, back in the old country, was a baker.

My mom's father was active in the Minnesota DFL; he was a die-hard union man. He worked his butt off as a volunteer campaigner for Franklin Roosevelt, and when Grandpa lost his job, like many did in those times, he got a new job with the WPA building rock walls at Como Lake and Como Park.

Grandma Patricia was a practicing Catholic but was done having babies, so Mom told me Grandma created her own deterrent. She pinned a Wendell Willkie for President button on her nightdress.

Grandma took in mending and washed and ironed clothes for her priest, the wife of Grandpa's boss at the brewery, and some well-off uppity-ups on Summit Hill.

Grandpa started working as a night janitor at Hamm's Brewery after getting laid off from the American Can factory. He chose nights because the night shift was paid a nickel more per hour.

Grandpa did not even like beer. He drank a shot of bourbon on holidays, and even then only if someone offered it. When he was alive, Grandpa gave all his brewery's bonus free beer to my dad and others. If I were Grandpa, I would have sold it for half price and saved up to take Grandma on a vacation somewhere outside of St. Paul, like Duluth.

Every season, Grandma Patricia figured out Christmas gifts for her thirty-one grandchildren, including me. There was the Christmas of the socks. The Christmas of the knit scarves. The

Christmas of the crocheted mittens. And then there was the Christmas when she got her hand crushed in the wringer of her washing machine. That Christmas we all got a plastic Jesus from the St. Joan's Pagan Babies Fundraiser. The Christmas before my Grandma Rose died, Grandma Patricia gave us all hand-beaded Rosaries crafted with her crippled hands.

For my confirmation party, she gave me a holy scapular with a real relic from St. Francis of Assisi inside. She said it was a thread from a cloak that he wore way back then. I also got a prayer book, a box of homemade chocolate-chip oatmeal cookies, and two real silver dollars. Grandma did not trust banks but loved real silver coins. She collected them.

"That's real silver, Francis," she proudly told me. "And men that owned silver did not jump off tall buildings in 1929."

During Grandma Patricia's beaded Rosaries Christmas, my other grandma gave me a chemistry set, five dollars, a model airplane, and two rock and roll albums.

Dad dropped Izzy and me off at school after the funeral.

"Francis, it will be good for you to be with Isadore and your friends. You know, try to get back in the swing of normal again."

Once there, Izzy talked me into skipping the rest of the day by hiding in the stairwell next to the janitor's equipment room. I had never skipped school before, but I earned this one. Izzy started smoking a cigarette. The janitor smoked, so there was no risk of getting caught as the stairwell already smelled like stale tobacco.

Izzy was a jabberer most of the time but a good listener that day. I talked about the past weeks I had spent with Grandma Rose, and he said how he had liked getting to know her too. He shared a little bit about his old man and how he started beating on him after Jack died.

"He never whacks me if my mom is around, so I try to be gone if he is the only one there. That's why I hang with you and the Worm so much. When he beats on me, I refuse to cry, and not crying makes it worse."

It was after lunch, so the school was quiet with studies. Izzy suggested we move to the school's small prayer chapel, so he opened Janitor Jim's desk drawer and borrowed his keys along with a deck of cards. If we'd played cards instead of ball, Izzy probably would not have gotten into such trouble.

We settled in the small room's back pew. Izzy removed two small black rubber balls from his pocket.

"Look at these puppies, Francis. I saved up for them. They are made with compressed rubber and bounce ten times higher than any other ball will."

It started out as a simple game. We bet marbles to see if we could bounce the balls from the back pew into the flowerpot in front of the Virgin Mary statue.

"Izzy, our ass is grass if we get caught," I said.

"Won't happen, my friend. I have the key and locked the door from inside."

We got bored with the flowerpot challenge and started letting off steam by whipping the balls off the walls and ceiling, taking turns and counting how many ricochets we could each reach. I won on my ninth throw. I had thirteen solid hits. We stopped after we knocked off the Virgin Mary's pinky finger.

"Izzy, this is so bad. There is no way I can even confess to it," I said.

Izzy suggested I make up a substitute sin. "That's what I do. I make sure there is nothing about impure thoughts or saying *goddamn*. I just switch out my sins."

"How so?" I asked.

"I just say I sassed my ma once, skipped chores twice, did not finish homework three times, called Suck-Up butt ugly—stuff like that."

Izzy said eventually Father caught on to him, so instead of requiring him to say Hail Marys and a few Our Fathers, he made

Izzy do really hard stuff like extra chores and extra credit, plus he said Izzy had to be nice to Suck-Up Sue.

We decided that if we confessed to hacking off Mary's finger, Father would have called a huddle with the nuns, and we would be watched like hawks until our eighth-grade graduation in June. I also worried that Izzy's old man would whoop on him until Izzy was hospitalized.

Izzy unlocked the door of the chapel so I could go take a leak. When I snuck back, the door was open, and Izzy was not there. I walked home, killing time at Joe's General Store so I would not get to my house too early and get interrogated by my mother. No matter: Mom was sleeping, recovering from the horrendous week and Mandy's candle caper.

I, too, was recovering. I lay awake, staring at the moon out my window most of the night, reliving the awful events of the past month, and trying to figure things out. By keeping focused on helping Izzy and my mom and trying to be a great big brother, maybe I was ignoring other things that were spinning out of control. Or, perhaps, I was just trying to keep myself from going crazy. I did not know it then, but I was in for more torture the next morning.

15

POW

There is no fear in love; but perfect love casts out fear,
because fear involves punishment, and the one who fears
is not perfected in love.

—1 JOHN 4:18

The G-Man corralled me and beckoned me into her office after I served early morning Mass. I handled her interrogation like a Vietnam POW hero, even though she did not place electric wires on my testicles.

Izzy told me Jack had told him what the Viet Cong did to Americans in their POW camps. Nasty stuff like bamboo-shoot torture where they'd pour honey on the Americans' naked bodies and let fire ants chew on them in the blazing sun while sharp bamboo shoots pierced them to death unless they squealed. One soldier from northern Minnesota died when they electrocuted his private parts.

Before he died, Jack told Izzy he would not be going to college because he knew he would be drafted. Jack did not believe in our country getting deeper into the Vietnam War. He even marched and protested the war without his old man, a veteran, ever knowing about it. Jack's plan was to become a conscientious objector, escape to Canada, and hook up with a canoe outfitter because he loved paddling Minnesota and Wisconsin lakes and rivers.

Laughing, Izzy said, "My brother's first plan was to see if he could pop a boner at his army physical. You know, pretend he was homosexual so when the doctor touched him down yonder and asked him to cough, he would pop a big one." He said Jack told him that McNamara and President Johnson did not want those kinds in their foxholes.

One Friday night, when his old man was covering a night shift at the beer factory, Izzy's mom let us have a sleepover in his backyard tree house. We stayed up talking until dawn. Izzy told me he heard the word *fuck* for the first time when Jack summed up his take on the war.

Izzy said, "Jack said killing for peace was like fucking for chastity."

The G-Man closed her door and sat down behind her massive oak desk, leaving me standing. She started her inquisition by asking how my family was doing after Grandma's funeral. Next, she tried to put the fear of God in me, but I refused to look at her. I just kept staring at her black thumbnail and wondering what nunnery activity caused it.

When I finally did look at her, she made the sign of the cross with her thumbnail hand and spoke.

"Francis, a Holy Family student committed a grave sacrilege yesterday."

"What happened, Sister?"

I figured she was bluffing, since there was no witness except for Izzy and me when the Virgin Mary's finger went flying. She then grabbed a small ceramic statue from her desk and handed it to me.

"Do you know what a sacrilege is, Mr. Paulson?"

I cradled the gift in both palms, praying that her finger would not fall off too. After an uncomfortably long period of silence, I carefully set Mary back on the G-Man's desk next to her stapler.

"Sister, I think a sacrilege is a sin, like when a person makes fun of God's holy things."

"Yes, it's a very grave sin, Mr. Paulson," she said, twiddling her good thumb with the black one.

"You mean like a mortal sin, Sister? May I use the lavatory?"

I figured my question would expedite my release, but she ignored it. She was not done toying with me just yet.

She opened her top desk drawer, reached in, and then held out her good fist, opening it to reveal her treasure.

"Do you know what this is, Francis?"

"Looks like a small black ball, Sister."

"Yes, indeed it is, young man. A very hard small black rubber ball." She dropped the ball to the floor. "It's a super ball, Mr. Paulson."

"Wow!" I said when the ball hit the ceiling.

"Wow, indeed, Mr. Paulson." She handed me an envelope that read, *Read tonight and meet Sister again tomorrow after Mass.*

I went into the boy's bathroom, took the far stall, latched it, and opened her note. In big bold-printed black letters, it read, *Mr. Paulson, if you continue to hang out with a wolf, you will soon howl like a wolf.*

I flushed the note down the toilet and then went to find Izzy on the playground before the morning bell sounded. He filled me in on what had happened when I'd left to take a whiz.

"Francis, when you left to piss, I got glue from Janitor Jim's workbench and stuck Mary's finger back on. Hell, you can't even tell we hacked it off. But Suck-Up Sue had a hall pass to bring the 'Pennies for Pagan Babies' coins to the office. The chapel door was open, and she saw me by the Virgin Mary, so she tattled to the G-Man."

Just sixty seconds more and Izzy would have been clear, but Sister caught him locking up and saw a ball on the floor. Izzy jammed the other ball in his shorts. Sister made him call his old man at work to come get him.

Sister's punishment was to have him write out the first half of the book of Genesis in cursive. She also made him go to confession and grounded Izzy from the lunchroom for the rest of the month, which meant he had only thirty minutes to ride his bike home, eat lunch, and then return in time for afternoon geography.

His old man made him strip, and then, using his big, long-handled steel barbecue spatula, he whacked Izzy until bruises surfaced on his back and backside. Three hard whacks for each hour of work his old man missed. Six full windups.

He might have gotten more, but the cooking tool's handle broke off on the sixth whack. Izzy was grounded from TV, radio, and desserts for three weeks, except on Sundays. His mom got him that bonus.

Izzy had to reimburse his old man for the paint from Joe's General and repaint the chapel the next three Saturdays. My best friend was more peeved about his old man buying the cheap watery paint from Joe's bargain barrel than he was about anything else.

"My old man is a cheap son of a bitch. It's going to take me three Saturdays and three coats instead of one," he complained.

I felt awful. It was as much my fault as my best friend's, yet he took the full blame.

"I'm guilty, too, Izzy. You fell on your sword for me, and you did not have to. If they let me, I can help paint or at least cover your paper routes. You can't be in two places at once."

16

Halloween 1967

They were utterly astonished, saying, "He has done all things well;
He makes even the deaf to hear and the mute to speak."
—MARK 7:37

After Shannon was gone, Halloween was all upside down. I missed her so much that it still hurt my insides. I would have given up all the Halloween candy in the world to have Shannon back.

Even Dots, my favorite, never tasted sweet again. Shannon loved the red Dots best, while Mandy liked the green. When Shannon's hands would get sticky, she held them out to me, smiling. I pretended to lick her fingers clean before getting a washcloth and doing it right.

Mom tried to get me to go to Woolworth's with her to buy a premade costume. With Grandma Rose's illness, she hadn't had time to make them herself like she usually did. She'd been working more, and the funeral had consumed her.

I kissed her on her cheek. "No thanks, Mom. I'm all good."

She looked hurt. "OK, I'm not going to beg," she said while walking away.

I followed her. "Save your money, Mom. Izzy and I are making our own costumes. We're going as hippies. Mandy wants to be a mime, and we're helping her too. We just need a jar of your cold cream, your white bathing cap, and her white pajamas."

Izzy and I did my sister up for the big day. Her white face

77

almost glowed in the dark. Izzy swiped a tube of his mom's red lipstick and put a huge red clown-frown around Mandy's lips.

"There you go, Worm." Izzy stood back, admiring his handiwork. "Miss Mandy, your lips are now big enough to kiss a pig."

Mandy set a two-bagger candy record that night.

We all yelled "trick or treat" as loud as we could at our first house. Mr. and Mrs. Purfest opened their door, sized up the situation, and looked puzzled when they saw Mandy holding out two bags.

"Trick or treat! The girl can't speak," Izzy explained. "She's a mime and motioning you for two treats—one for her, and the other for her invisible friend. You can't see the friend—she's shy."

The night before Halloween, my sister practiced by not speaking with any of us. At dinner, her silence annoyed Dad. He refused to pass her a napkin when she motioned to him after pretending to get spaghetti sauce on her blouse. He glared at Mandy, but she just stared back.

"You think this is amusing, young lady?" Dad asked, raising his voice and pointing his finger inches away from her nose. "It is not. Your little act is quite rude."

Mandy brought along two pillowcases for her Halloween haul. They were the ones Poor Grandma Patricia had monogrammed for each of the twins. Mandy's pillowcase was wearing out, the red stitching now faded pink, but you could still read her name in cursive: *Miranda. Shannon* was stitched in purple. Each one had an angel with a halo needlepointed above the name.

Mandy kept both pillowcases in her nightstand's top drawer alongside her favorite treasures, like her artwork, Poor Grandma's beaded Rosary, and a photo of Mandy and Rich Grandma sticking out their tongues in the red-and-black rocker. Neither of us had a photo of Shannon. Our folks had destroyed or hidden all of them. Maybe they thought they could erase her from our memories.

The whole time we were running around the neighborhood, Izzy tried to make Mandy talk or laugh, but she held fast to her silence. He even took out his spritzer full of fake holy water and squirted her face.

"I baptize you Saint Mime of Jack-o'-lanterns, the patron saint of great pumpkins everywhere," he teased.

Mandy took the squirt on her nose without flinching or muttering a word, then she turned her back to Izzy. When she faced him again, she pointed to her eyes and made like she was crying.

People thought she was cute when they asked her a question and she nodded yes or no. One old codger with whiskey breath and slurred speech was a total jackalope, refusing all of us his stingy miniature Tootsie Roll.

He slammed his door yelling, "What the hell? Is that smart-assed little shit deaf and dumb?"

The next stop was much more fun. Mr. and Mrs. Baker recognized Mandy from church and put two bottles of Orange Crush in each of her bags on top of Mr. Baker's two Tootsie Pops.

"Don't drop your bag on the sidewalk, Miss Mime, or you'll have a real mess," Mr. Baker said.

Mandy flashed him a sad frown, blew a kiss, and winked. Mr. Baker thought that was hilarious. He called for his wife, Vicki, to come back with his camera and snap a Polaroid of the three of us.

When we got home, I traded all my Dots and Turkish Taffy for my sister's four bottles of Orange Crush. Mandy emptied her goods into a brown Piggly Wiggly grocery bag and weighed it on our bathroom scale. Then she folded up both pillowcases and went to bed without saying a word. The next day she was jabbering like normal.

17

JFK

NOVEMBER 22, 1967

Don't fear those who kill the body but are unable to kill the soul;
but rather fear Him who is able to destroy both soul and body
in Hell.
—MATTHEW 10:28

Duke, our quarterback, had to repeat eighth grade, so he always knew what was coming, having done it all once before. "All you numb nuts are going to get Sister Mary Kenneth's JFK lecture today."

Duke usually called Sister Mary Kenneth "Nun Kenny" or "Kennedy" behind her back. Sister was in love with all the Kennedys, especially our president, John, and his brother Bobby.

It was November 22, the fourth anniversary of our Catholic President Kennedy getting murdered in Dallas by Lee Harvey Oswald, the commie Russian traitor. Oswald got wasted by Jack Ruby, a big-shot Mafia guy, before the FBI had time to electrocute him.

Sister started social studies by making us all say a decade of the Rosary for the Kennedy family, especially for young Caroline and John-John, the former president's children.

"We lost a wonderful Catholic president, but they lost their father," she said, almost crying.

Sister then got to talking about how quickly Lyndon Johnson had taken over when the president's brains were sprayed all over First Lady Jackie's dress.

Suck-Up Sue shot her hand up, as if Izzy had just put another tack on her seat.

"Sister, what would've happened if Vice President Johnson had died in a plane crash on the way back to the White House after President Kennedy was shot and killed? Who would be our president then?"

Izzy fired a rubber band at the back of Suck-Up's head. It missed and almost hit Sister, but her back was turned.

Sister loved talking about the Kennedys so much that she was almost drooling. She said her ancestors had come over from Ireland during the potato famine. Every third summer, she visited to "see the most heavenly, beautiful place on God's green earth, the Emerald Isle, and especially the Cliffs of Moher."

According to Sister, every Catholic home in Ireland had four things you could see when you sat at its kitchen table: a crucifix, a painting of the Last Supper, a photo of the Pope, and a framed portrait of our thirty-fifth president.

Izzy raised his hand, urgently waving it at Sister.

"Yes, Isadore. What is so important?"

Izzy stood up, readying himself to exit the room. "Sister, only one president took the oath of office without his hand on the Holy Bible. Can I go to the lavatory, please? When I come back, I'll give our class the answer if you give me extra credit."

At the beginning of the school year, Izzy paid Duke fifty cents and his mint-condition Tony Oliva Minnesota Twins baseball card to forge a note from Izzy's family doctor claiming Izzy had to take a leak often and was being treated for a bed-wetting condition. Duke forged a lot of notes for others too. He had adult-looking penmanship and could vary it, so the nuns were clueless.

Sister responded, "Isadore, I'm sure you either dreamt that or read that in your *Mad* magazine, and I'm also sure you can go to the lavatory, but the proper grammar is 'May I go to the lavatory?' The answer is yes, and Francis will escort you, should you decide to take another detour to our Blessed Lady's Chapel."

Izzy entered the last stall, and I could smell him smoking the half-smoked Lucky Strike that he had found in the street on his way to school that morning. Izzy claimed he had tried more tobacco brands than anyone in the whole parish, but he refused to smoke a half-smoked cigarette if there was a trace of lipstick on it.

Then Izzy got to what he wanted to yak about.

"I think it is way funny when Sister gets caught up in that Irish-family fairy-tale BS, but she forgot to mention the fifth thing her family has in their house."

I took his bait. "What's that? And quit puffing, start pissing."

"The fifth thing is the five-gallon pail of homemade Irish whiskey in their root cellar!"

He laughed at his remark, then started coughing because he had inhaled. Recovering his voice, Izzy said, "Hey, Francis, how many Irish nuns does it take to change a light bulb?"

"Zip up and shut up. We gotta get back, Izzy."

"It takes twenty-five. One to hold the bulb and twenty-four to drink Sister's moonshine until the room spins."

"Izzy, you're lucky I'm your friend. I have so much dirt on you that you would not only get kicked out of Holy Family, but the Pope might excommunicate you. I know you can hold your piss all day and shoot a stream farther than a man with twice your gonads. Like the time I lost a dime when you arched it over Battle Creek, one bank to the other. Not a drop touched the water."

When we returned, Sister was still carrying on about the Kennedys. Izzy sat down and raised his hand again but did not even wait for Sister to acknowledge it.

"Sister, I also read two former presidents died from a diarrhea attack. It did not say if they died in or out of office. How would we find that out?"

"Isadore, I suppose you could find that out by excusing your-self, for a second time, but this time to our principal's office, and I will not give you extra credit about a president not swearing in with a Bible. That never happened in our America."

On the way home, Izzy bragged about his office visit. "Francis, I broke my record, doubled my average today."

"What record?"

"Last school year's record, dickwad. So far this year, in the three months since school started, I've been sent to the G-Man's office six times."

"What did she say? Did she call your old man? If so, your ass is grass."

"Not this time, but she said she will next time, and she'll also assign me a punishment. I noticed she was trying to hold back a smile after I explained myself."

Izzy said he convinced the G-Man that if she would go to the library with him, he would prove to her that Thomas Jefferson and James Polk both died from diarrhea attacks and that Lyndon Johnson, a Protestant, was actually sworn in on Air Force One using a Catholic Mass Missal because President Kennedy did not have a Bible on his plane, just his prayer book.

"I then told her that the encyclopedia called the other presidents' causes of death *infectious dysentery*. I told her most of my classmates would not know what that big word was, but everyone knows about diarrhea."

"Izzy, you are one heck of a great bullshit artist. You amaze me."

I pulled a Baby Ruth from my book bag and unwrapped it, just leaving a tiny bit of wrapper on one end so I could dangle it between my two fingers without touching the chocolate.

"Here," I said, dangling it in front of his face. "Eat this. Like Polk and Jefferson, you are full of crap too!"

18

Mime Game

In everything give thanks;
for this is the will of God for you in Jesus Christ.
—1 THESSALONIANS 5:18

If we had not had company, Mandy would have been spanked. She started playing her mime game again. Our guests were Poor Grandma and her neighbor-lady friend, who was also a widow, and Izzy. We had a massive crispy brown turkey. Mandy greeted Poor Grandma and her friend with a hug but refused to speak. Izzy showed up way too early.

"Hi, Mrs. Paulson! Smells delicious in here. Francis said I was invited for dessert!"

Mom pulled out a chair for him. "Oh, Isadore, we have a twenty-two-pound bird with your name on it. You are welcome to all the trimmings and pie you can handle. Would you like to lead our blessing?"

Mom set his place and lit the candles, and Izzy performed a Thanksgiving grace as only Izzy could.

He stood, crossing himself. "In the name of the Father, Son, and Holy Ghost, bless this turkey, but not its feathers and skin.

Now, let's open our mouths and cram it in."

I coughed trying to stifle my laugh. Mandy held fast in her silence, and then Dad took over.

"In the name of the Father, Son, and Holy Ghost—Bless us O Lord, and these, Thy gifts, which we are about to receive from Thy bounty. Through Christ, our Lord. Amen."

Our table was not big enough to set all the food in the middle, so Dad carved the bird, and then Mom dished individual servings onto her wedding china from a card table behind the kitchen table. She served her mother and her mother's friend first, then Dad. Izzy was next.

"Isadore what would you like, white or dark?"

Pointing to the small golden nub at the rear of the turkey, Izzy said, "I'll take the Pope's nose, Mrs. Paulson."

"What's that, Isadore?"

"You know, the turkey's butt. It is white meat and very juicy and moist."

Mom ignored him, slicing off the Pope's nose and hiding it under some stuffing. Then she sliced for him two slabs of breast meat.

I think Mandy pulled her mime stunt to entertain Izzy, but I was not sure. She even gave me the creeps. She did not put on her costume, but she refused to smile, and this time Dad sent her to bed without pie before everyone else was served dessert.

After the adults had coffee, Dad drove Izzy, Grandma, and her friend home. I helped with dishes. Mom fell asleep on the sofa, so I went to brush my teeth. Our bathroom smelled awful. There was burnt hair in the sink. The odor took me back to that day Shannon's hair caught fire. Burnt hair is an odor you never forget. I peeked into Mandy's room. She was sleeping with Shannon's pillowcase tucked under her cheek. I could see that she had cut her bangs and must have set them on fire in the sink.

I went back to the bathroom, cracked the window, and sprinkled my father's Old Spice cologne around the room to mask the odor. If Mom found out, she would have flipped and scolded Mandy for cutting her own hair. Then Dad would have to do the tough job and spank her when he got back home. That would be a not so pleasant end to Thanksgiving, one I wanted to, and did, avoid.

19

Playing with Matches

ADVENT 1967

And you will have joy and gladness,
and many will rejoice at his birth.

—LUKE 1:14

Sister Mary Kenneth's bad idea was to have us handcraft a foot-tall cross during Advent to give to our parents for Christmas. It turned out to be more fun than a backward toboggan ride down Suicide Hill, but it could have set one of us on fire.

When Izzy heard her plan, he said, "Sister's brain just farted big time. This will be out of control but more fun than watching Suck-Up Sue dancing in Hell on top of hot coals."

I also could not believe our eighth-grade project would involve fire.

Izzy continued, "I can't believe Sister Einstein is going to let us play with matches. What lunatic would trust us with them?" He tossed me Cigar Ron's Playboy Bunny lighter. "Maybe we will get a can of gasoline to torch too?"

All the nuns at Holy Family were big on having their students make crappy handmade Christmas gifts from kindergarten on. Mom had a shelf full of my Picassos in her curio and more ornaments on our tree: glittered pine cones, clothespins made into toy soldiers, sleds made from popsicle sticks, my third-grade photo of my mug framed in crayons. My only real masterpiece was a mason jar with a felt St. Nick on the lid and Christmas tree bulbs that I had carefully painted on the glass.

My first piece was Mom's favorite—a blue playdough pinch pot I'd made in kindergarten. I remember I could not wait until Christmas to give it to her. I licked the salt off the playdough while shaping it, then showed Mother my proud blue tongue. Eventually, I graduated to a ceramic ashtray that she would not let Dad use.

"Oh, Antonio, it's so exquisite. He put all his love into it. You certainly will not grind your cigarette butts into such a precious work of art."

Last year, Sister Peter Damian had us make wind chimes from old silverware and other noisy junk we brought to school and threw in a big pile before we started stringing our chimes. Izzy's was way cool. He used a tin snip and made his old man a chime out of beer cans. He rigged a small flashlight to the top, making it shimmer so it would cast shadows. Sister pulled the shades and shut off the lights so Izzy could demonstrate. Everyone applauded, except Suck-Up. She rolled her eyes at me and said, "Your friend is an immature smelly skunk."

I could tell Sister was not a big fan of beer-can art, but she thought she scored a spiritual victory as Izzy had put so much time and sweat into his creation. She encouraged him.

"Isadore, congratulations. Your piece of art is a brilliant sculpture, and it took a lot of effort."

I whispered back at Susan, "Ah, but what a sweet-smelling and brilliant skunk according to Sister."

Not only did we get to go play outside with matches, but Sister also invited our kindergarten buddies to help. Mandy was there. Susan Flannagan was her appointed buddy. The buddies couldn't strike matches like us big kids. They could only watch us play with fire. It gave them something to look forward to when they were our age.

There we were, sitting on the playground, lighting farmer matches. Each big, red-tipped wooden match was to be lit and burned for three seconds, then blown out. Afterward, we brought the charred sticks inside and glued them to a cardboard cutout of a cross.

Sister suggested that each time we blew out a match, we should say a Hail Mary. She broke us into groups of eight and separated the boys from the girls—a big mistake when fire was involved.

Izzy was in my group. We sat in a circle around a tin coffee can filled with snow. After each match was lit and its tip charred black, we blew it out and put the blackened tip in the snow can. Sister assigned captains. I was the captain for our team, which meant I would get blamed if someone caught fire.

I removed the little white paper bag filled with our candy store's red-hot cinnamon fireballs from my winter jacket pocket and passed it around to my team.

"I'm the captain, so I say we get to burn our mouths and make our tongues red while we are burning our fingers. Just don't go sucking on them once we go inside, or Sister will get mad."

Mandy took it all in, fascinated by the matches and the flickering flames. Izzy kept watching and mocking Suck-Up Sue's group by making his comical sign of the cross now and then as her team kept on lighting, blowing, and praying. But I liked how Susan was treating Mandy. She was keeping my little sister amused. She even gave her some tinfoil in which to keep the imperfectly burned matches.

My boy group just played with matches and flipped them at each other when Sister wasn't supervising. One bounced off my chin, leaving a black mark. I rubbed snow on it and gave the culprit the finger.

Izzy was wearing his favorite green-and-gold North Stars

hockey jacket that his mom found at the Goodwill. A flying match landed on it, melting a hole the size of a nickel right in the middle of the gold star.

Izzy yelled, "Bull's-eye for Travis!" He seemed amused, not angry.

Back in our warm classroom, we started gluing the matchsticks to the cardboard cross cutouts. Izzy told our team that it would be really awesome if we glued them with their red tips fresh and then had our families save them until Good Friday, when we would set them all on fire at once, right before Father started the Stations of the Cross.

"Hell's bells, a lot less suffering for Jesus than nailing him to a tree," he said.

When I got home, I emptied both Mandy's and my lunchboxes, putting them in the sink. Her lunch pail contained a partial box of farmer matches that she must have swiped from Susan's group. I scolded her and put them in the garage next to the lighter fluid and charcoal. Later in the month, Izzy and I went out to the garage so he could have a secret smoke out of the cold. The matches and fluid were both missing.

20

Lucifer

DECEMBER 1967

Be of sober spirit, be on the alert. Your adversary, the devil,
prowls around like an angry lion, seeking someone to devour.
—1 PETER 5:8

A nasty Doberman showed up by our candy-kitchen exhaust fan and chased the regular mutts away. I thought the dogs came for the sweet odors, but candymaker Frank said they liked the heat the fan put out. Frank named the Doberman Lucifer. The dog barked viciously and had no ID tag. One afternoon, when the animal refused to let two of our chocolate dippers exit to catch their bus, Frank called the city pound, but the beast took off before they arrived.

Dad called the cops after Lucifer tore the fly screen off our back door and busted the glass on the main door and the window next to it. The dog was trying to break in to eat what was cooking, and Dad thought it was a matter of time before he bit someone, an employee or a customer. I think the dog only tore the screen. Dad probably broke the glass on the door and window while trying to scare it off with his long-handled oak candy paddle.

My father told me later, "If I hadn't filed a police report on that vicious animal, my insurance could have refused to replace our damaged door and window."

The Friday night before I was going to start helping Frank, I was alone in the kitchen steam cleaning the giant nougat mixer while my father left to bank the day's receipts and pick up Mom and Mandy from the dentist.

Somehow, Grandma's Chihuahua, now our Chihuahua, got into the family wagon and escaped when Dad came to the factory to pick up the day's money.

Shortly after my father left, I heard a fierce ruckus out back by the exhaust fan. It was Lucifer and poor little Kevin. The Doberman had the little guy pinned under the grate in the window well, directly below the exhaust fan. Fortunately, one of the bars in the grate was bent, and the opening was just big enough for Kevin to hide out and escape death. Lucifer could not get at him but was hovering, yelping, drooling, and scaring the snot out of Kevin. I opened the back door, wielding a heavy steel snow shovel to rescue our pet.

Lucifer turned from Kevin and was about to charge me. I retreated inside. I then remembered seeing a *Dragnet* TV episode where Sergeant Friday did not want to shoot a mean dog with his gun, so he pointed a fire extinguisher at the threatening animal instead, and once the chemicals came out, the beast retreated.

I grabbed the extinguisher closest to me, pulled the pin, and went to rescue Kevin. I blasted Lucifer in the face, and when he turned to run away from the foam, I emptied the rest with a direct hit on his balls and poop chute.

Prying away the grate, I took our little shaking Kevin inside to safety and gave him a leftover hot dog and some water.

I knew Dad would be angry about me using the expensive equipment to save our dog instead of calling the cops, so I cleaned it up really well, put the pin back in, and hung the extinguisher back in its proper place.

I heard Dad tooting the horn out front, so I shut off the lights and locked the front and back doors. I hopped in the back seat. Kevin jumped on Mandy's lap and licked her face. My father had no clue that Kevin had escaped.

I think I made my grandmother proud by rescuing her pet, and I felt like a hero, but I could not tell anyone. I vowed to take my heroic actions to my grave.

I saved Kevin. I did not know it then, but saving Kevin also sabotaged my efforts to help save Izzy.

21

Hired

DECEMBER 1967

Whatever you do, do your work heartily,
as for the Lord and not the people.
—COLOSSIANS 3:23

Our factory's hard-candy room was Grandma Rose's favorite place. She never pulled candy canes on the silver hook like my grandpa or Frank, but she formed each warm, pliable peppermint stick's crook perfectly and then gently slid them in front of the big box fan so they could harden and shine. One day, I had to hang out after school, so Grandma showed me how to crook. She let me place the fragile striped treats onto silver trays for the store's showcase. She put all my deformed ones in a small white paper bag for me to give to my friends at school.

Everything was so perfect last Christmas. The candy store was filled with brittle, peppermint, and her love. Customers stepped behind the counter to give her hugs.

"They are not just customers," she told me. "They are family. Families with a sweet tooth."

Every December, our dentist from Grandma's church purchased a five-pound box of butter almond toffee. I thought that was a hoot—Dr. Belzuski buying candy. Grandma and her dentist also bartered with candy. Last time I went on the bus, Grandma gave me a one-pound (for a check-up) and a two-pound (if I had a filling) box of her chocolates, but she instructed me to leave them both regardless, cavity or no cavity. Everyone loved Rose, even the dentist.

I was just a young pup when my grandpa died. Grandma Rose quit dipping cherry cordials after that and spent most of her time keeping records and ordering supplies.

Occasionally, she worked with Frank making peanut brittle. She could tandem hoist the frothing hot kettles and spread the golden lavalike mixture on the marble cooling table better than most men. She worked quickly with her large pallet knife.

I was determined to get a job helping Frank this season so I could finish funding my trip to the St. Croix River with Izzy. The stockyard money would not be enough after I bought Christmas gifts for my family. I was now too old to give them the crap I made at school.

Dad shut down my pleas to work at the factory for weeks until Mom rescued me.

"Antonio, you should not discourage Francis's work ethic. Having him at the factory is much safer than having him running around in the dark delivering newspapers, getting jumped for his money, or hit by a car. I can't believe Isadore's parents put their only son at risk like that."

The first Saturday after Thanksgiving my father woke me at sunrise. "Come on, candymaker son of mine, get moving. That is if you want a job every Saturday from now until Christmas!"

Dad explained that I would get forty cents per hour but only twenty minutes for lunch. I could clock ten hours every Saturday, which meant four dollars per week. Counting the Saturdays before Christmas, I would earn twenty dollars. I needed six dollars to buy Mom, Dad, and Mandy real gifts, and Kevin a chew bone.

On the ride to the factory, I sat in the jump seat, Mom's regular spot, and tried to plant another idea in my father's head.

"Dad, I have a question. You don't have to answer it today, maybe just think about it, OK?"

"What's troubling you, Francis?"

"Well, ever since Izzy's father got laid off from his Saturday shift at the brewery, he has been hard on Izzy."

We were listening to Dad's favorite morning radio show, *Boone and Erickson*. He always had the first push-button set to WCCO AM, for talk, sports, and weather. He turned down the volume to answer me.

"OK, Francis, get to your point. What are you getting at?"

"Dad, it would mean a lot to me if we picked up Izzy on Saturdays and let him come and help too. He's a hard worker, and we would be done in time for his paper route."

"That's a tall request, Francis. Being around hot boiling kettles is not child's play. If you get burned, you can't sue me, but his folks could put me out of business."

"But, Dad, what if Izzy's mom says it's OK? Maybe just test it out next Saturday? I'd share my pay. It would cost you nothing. Just give him a Christmas card at the end with a fifty-cent tip in it. I'll take care of the rest."

Dad was chuckling.

"Son, you certainly drive a hard bargain, and I respect you for wanting to help Izzy with his situation."

He reached to turn the radio volume back up.

"I guess if both of your moms say yes, it's a go with me. I'll risk getting sued if you two should burn your buns off."

When we opened the shop, my father handed me a box of extralong matchsticks and showed me how to light the pilot light on the round open cast-iron stove. He shortened my apron, fitted me with a white paper hat, and gave me the rules.

I could measure and weigh ingredients, and I was responsible for keeping the paddles and other utensils clean and ready for

Frank. Each oak paddle was to be inspected after every batch and scrubbed clean to catch any splinters that might work their way into the finished brittle. Damaged paddles were to be tossed into the trash dumpster immediately. My father told me twice that under no circumstances was I to lift the bubbling mixture and tandem pour with Frank.

"Like I mentioned in the car, Francis, I don't need to pay for your skin grafts if you drop a batch and get burned. In a few years, you'll muscle up and will pour then. I'll make a candymaker out of you yet. Someone must run this place when I'm all wore out. That is, if you ever quit writing and want to earn a real living."

My father bringing up skin grafts gave me pause and saddened me, making me wonder where Shannon was, what she was up to, and whether she remembered me and even missed me, like I missed her.

I guess my dad thought making a living with hands that wrote or never got dirty was sissy, except for sports writers. I never knew he even read real books until I opened his nightstand drawer looking for a flashlight and Izzy and I discovered his paperback copy of *Valley of the Dolls*. The pages were worn, some marked with turned corners. Those were the ones Izzy and I read out loud to each other.

The movie versions of *Valley of the Dolls* and *Rosemary's Baby* would later be condemned by the Catholic Church, but nothing was mentioned about reading dirty books, so Izzy and I agreed not to open our copies of the *Baltimore Catechism* to find out if reading them was a grave sin.

Dad handed me Grandma Rose's handwritten recipe book, turning it to the sticky, stained peanut-brittle page. The writing was in her cursive, hard to read in places since the paper had yellowed and the fountain ink had faded.

"Frank will be punching in at seven thirty a.m. You listen to him. If you do, you will learn a lot about what it takes to be a professional candymaker. I'm going to meet Ron for coffee and football stuff, then make a couple deliveries."

Frank was seventy years old now, and he talked up a storm while working. I listened. He told me that he had retired from the big nut-roll factory down by the rail tracks years before Grandma Rose died. That factory was huge and owned by a large corporation in Chicago. Frank said the big shots there were all full of themselves and did not know a Brazil nut from an acorn.

"They came around with clipboards once a year in their three-piece suits, acting like their farts didn't stink, taking notes. Never even looked at me, and I was a foreman. The suits loved hiring Mexicans. They were cheaper labor, never joined the union. There were one hundred ninety employees in all, but only two were Negro, and they were both night-shift janitors."

Frank said one of the night-shift janitors, Jackson, was a friend of his. He said he was a good man with a nice wife and two cute little kids.

"He was a hard worker, trustworthy, and wanted to get promoted to candymaker or maybe just get trained to run the nougat machinery."

Frank said he put in a good word for Jackson, even wrote a letter, but the Chicago suits would have none of it.

"Francis, when I retired, those tightwads did not even give me a watch or a six pack of beer. That's why I loved working for your grandmother. The pay was less, but everyone here was happy. A kind word, free cup of coffee, and some donuts go a long way to make for a happy workplace."

Frank took a swig of coffee from the Paul Bunyan mug Grandma Rose gave him after she visited Itasca State Park and Bemidji with us two summers before she died.

"I miss her, Francis, like I know you do. She was good to me. When my wife died, your grandmother donated all the sweets for the funeral luncheon, closed the store, and gave everyone the day off with pay to attend our church. She gave me a nice sympathy card with a fifty-dollar bill in it and had ten Masses said in Sheryl's name, and we are not even Catholic. She was a better boss than any man I ever worked for."

My first Saturday, Frank had me measuring raw peanuts in sixteen-pound portions, then unwrapping two pounds of butter and measuring out three ounces of pure vanilla extract, one half cup of baking soda, and three tablespoons of kosher salt.

After I got through the first two batches, he flipped my paper hat inside out and upside down and said, "You got it down quick, my young candymaker friend. Old Man Frank can now concentrate on the hot batches instead of fussing with ingredients and cleaning my utensils!"

I was no longer nervous about my skills. I handed him a clean paddle. "Thanks, Mr. Zelman!"

He was laughing when he took the paddle and started stirring our next batch, blending the sugar and corn syrup into the water. "Mr. Zelman? Francis, candymakers are on a first-name basis. Even your grandmother went by that candy-kitchen code!"

"OK, if you say so, Mr. Frank."

"Oh well, that is a start, Mr. Francis."

I loved hearing Frank tell stories about Grandma Rose. It was like she was in the kitchen with us. My favorite was the penny-in-the-peanut-brittle tale.

Frank said, "We taped a penny to the small weigh scale as it was off just a tad. The penny came loose, ending up in a box of peanut brittle that some uppity Summit Hill high-society lady purchased and promptly returned. Of course, she asked for the owner."

Frank said that my grandmother listened and then revealed a beautifully wrapped five-pound box of our Royal Crown Assortment and presented it to the woman.

"Francis, she told the old windbag that the penny was part of our St. Paul Winter Carnival promotion and she just won herself the grand prize. You know, like the Winter Carnival medallion that is hidden in the snow each year by the *St. Paul Pioneer Press*.

The 'Lucky Penny' earned the complainer our most expensive box of hand-dipped chocolates, plus a free pound of peanut brittle every Christmas for five years."

"Do you think that the old bag will come in this Christmas so I can see her?" I asked.

"I think not. I heard that the woman's husband got transferred to New York, and we will probably never hear squat from her again."

I hoisted the bucket of raw Spanish peanuts and slowly started adding them to the bubbling-hot mixture while Frank stirred.

"I bet her husband is not that lucky," I said.

With my help that first Saturday, we manufactured and packaged fourteen batches of peanut brittle, almost seven hundred pounds, according to Frank.

"We did not burn a batch, lose a peanut, or catch hell from anyone," he joked at the end of our shift while I sipped on an Orange Crush and he popped the cap off a bottle of beer.

Frank and I made a pact over our pop and beer to try to hit twenty batches next Saturday, a record he said was unlikely, but worth trying for. I'm not sure why he even wanted to try, as he was paid by the hour, not by the batch.

The chocolate dippers got paid on "piece work," so the more pounds they hand-dipped, the more check they took home. I did the math and figured if I premeasured all the ingredients and kept three batches ahead, Frank could crank out twenty if we ate lunch on the fly.

The only problems were the two tables: the main marble pouring slab and the steel transfer table. After ten batches, they were so hot, it took forever to do the cutting, transferring, spreading, and packaging. We had to wait for them to cool so we could break and pack into one-pound boxes lined with wax paper. This slowed things way down, even if we kept all three box fans blowing on the candy and opened the back door to let the cold air in.

Izzy solved this problem for me after I told him about the

record and our moms letting him help me the following Saturday. He looked at me plain as shit and said, "Hey, moron! I have an idea that will save your factory a lot of time and cash. I'll show you next Saturday, but it will cost Frank a couple bucks. When we are finished, your dad will give you and Frank both a huge bonus!"

22

Breaking the Record

DECEMBER 1967

In all labor there is profit, but idle chatter leads only to poverty.

—PROVERBS 14:23

The following Saturday, Dad opened the kitchen half an hour early and left Izzy and me so he could meet his bookie for coffee. Frank was firing up the stoves.

"We are going for that record today, my two candymaker friends, right?"

Izzy sounded confident. "Guaranteed, Mr. Frank, but we need two dollars. I think once we make our record, Francis's father will give you a raise and pay you back the two bucks out of his petty-cash fund."

Frank thrust three dollars into Izzy's hand and teased, "I trust you boys, but if you spend it on whiskey and women, I'll have you both fired!"

Izzy refused to share his idea, motioning for me to go outside and get the store's wheelbarrow out of the shed. He started rolling it to the corner store two blocks east on University Avenue with me jogging alongside.

When we got there, he said, "I'll guard the wheelbarrow. You go inside and get as many blocks of ice as our money can buy."

"Are you crazy, Izzy? Ice?"

"Yes, ice. Trust me!"

Against my better judgment, I bought all the blocks of ice we could fit in the wheelbarrow. I still had fifty cents left. Izzy tried to talk me into two packs of smokes from the vending machine, but I ignored him.

We must have looked silly, two kids in the middle of December, my eyeglasses fogged from heavy breathing, pushing a mountain of ice up the street in a rusty wheelbarrow.

Two smart-asses were driving a Volkswagen slug bug. The passenger rolled down his window at the Rice Street stoplight, cupped both hands around his mouth like it was a megaphone, and yelled, "Hey, dipshits, they don't start building the Winter Carnival Ice Castle until January. You'll have to make a crapload of other trips before then!"

We were both pushing hard and sweating, and now we were being heckled.

Frank was ready to roll when we got back.

"Where are the donuts, boys? And there had better be a loaf of bread and a few pounds of butter for three bucks."

Izzy spoke first. "Mr. Frank, you need to wait until batch number nine, and I will show you how we spent the money."

"OK, Izzy, and if Francis's father is not around when we hit batch number twenty, I will let you both pour out the last batch and teach you how to cut and transfer."

I was now determined to make the record. "You're not messing with us, Mr. Frank? You would really let us try?"

"Our candymaker code of honor," he said. "I'll be chugging my second beer to celebrate—way too risky to have me pour!"

Izzy and I enjoyed inhaling the brittle mixture's aromas. We watched the batches foam to the brim when the butter, vanilla, and soda were added just before the mixture was poured on the huge marble table. Almost every customer who walked in the front door would say the same thing when we were making brittle: "Smells so good in here," they would comment. "What are they making?"

After each batch was poured on the giant, thick marble slab, Frank took his pallet knife and spread the mixture into a six-foot oval, forcing peanuts all the way to the edge.

He waved his knife at us and said, "Francis, your grandmother insisted that every bite must contain a mouthful of peanuts. If a customer wanted hard candy, they could go buy penny butterscotch buttons at the dime store."

When Frank was done spreading, he took his black-handled machete and made precise incisions, cutting four long strips of hot brittle. The cool marble sucked the heat from the molten mixture. Frank had an instinct for the exact moment that the brittle was still pliable but not too hot to burn his forearms, and with two swift moves, he would slide his arms under each strip and transfer it to the steel cooling table across the room, just four strides away. He flipped them upside down, and then I took my greased palms and separated the brittle into thinner portions, while it was still pliable.

At first the heat sensation on my palms was almost unbearable, and I would stretch and then clap my hands to air them out, stretch and air, stretch and air. Frank laughed when I was done spreading and started doing jumping jacks around his kitchen. I waited until he was out of sight to run both of my palms under the cold-water faucet.

Frank's palms were calloused, and his arms were hairless. He called them "peanut-brittle arms." He had some serious burns. The hot butter almond toffee ones were the worst. When the mixture thickened, the kettle erupted like a volcano, occasionally throwing out hot-lava candy balls. He dodged most. They did no harm if they landed on his apron, but his bare arms and face occasionally suffered.

Frank kept a bucket of ice water on a stand next to each

furnace; if no one was available to grab his paddle when the candy attacked, he just dunked his injured arm in the ice water and kept stirring with the other. If the molten candy hit his face, he stirred with his right hand and placed an ice cube on the burn with his left. The key was to be quick with the ice or water to prevent a blister.

Frank summoned us to his side. "OK, boys, you packed up number nine in record time, but both tables, the marble pouring and the steel transfer, are hot as Hades. They need to cool down for quite a while, so I'm going downstairs to take a leak and have a smoke."

As soon as Frank left us to take care of his business, Izzy pushed me out the back door, handing me my winter gloves.

"Francis, my candy slave, go fetch me two blocks of ice from the wheelbarrow!"

I slipped my hands into my lined deer-hide choppers and brought two bricks of ice inside. Izzy motioned for me to toss one on each of the hot tables. As soon as I did, the bricks started melting, and steam rose to the ceiling above, cooling down both tables within minutes. Izzy kept sopping up the melted water with towels and wringing them out in a bucket. Most of the ice melted, and there was just a small square left on the steel table. Izzy handed it to me.

He laughed. "Suck on this, doubtful Thomas!"

I made sure there was no moisture left on either table and then greased them down for batch number ten.

Frank plodded up the stairs to the kitchen.

"Put your hand on the marble, Mr. Frank," Izzy said, tugging him toward the pour table.

Frank looked confused. "Well, I'll be your chuckle uncle Izzy! What did you boys do?"

Izzy was beaming. I'd never seen him so happy. "Well, Mr. Frank, they have this wonderful new invention. It's called ice!"

It was turning out to be a day I would remember for a lifetime.

It even started snowing: not sissy snow either—big snow with wind too. By the afternoon a drift blocked the back door.

Frank and I would be fine in the snow. Dad had chains for our wagon, and he would give Frank a ride home, but Izzy had to call his old man to pick him up early so he could do the paper route before it got even nastier outside. Frank and I would now have to make the record without Izzy's help.

Frank heaped about five pounds of bulk brittle on a huge silver display tray for the main showcase window and motioned for Izzy to bring it out front to one of our salesclerks.

Frank did all our calligraphy signs for the store. It was a hobby that his wife had taught him. He took a placard and wrote in perfect letters:

Special of the Week:
Izzy's Homemade Peanut Brittle
Buy One Pound, Get the Second Pound Half Off

Izzy could not believe it. "I'll be famous, Mr. Frank. My name is on your candy!"

Frank placed a small warm chunk of brittle in Izzy's mouth. "It's not just mine," Frank said. "It's ours. Yours, Francis's, and mine. You will be famous for only a week, though. Then the sign goes back to just plain old peanut brittle. Izzy, you just invented a system we will use for years to come at Rose's Fine Hand-Dipped Chocolates!"

Izzy's old man pulled up to the back door and leaned on his horn. I shoveled the snow from the door and walked Izzy outside, kicking him in the ass when he turned to get into his old man's lemon wagon.

"What is that for?" he asked.

"For being a bigger moron than me," I said.

"What? How so?"

I pointed to the sky and the snow now coming down all

23

Sweet Hopes Fade

THE WEEK BEFORE CHRISTMAS 1967

Now flee from youthful lusts and pursue righteousness, faith, love,
and peace, with those who call on the Lord from a pure heart.
—2 TIMOTHY 2:22

Frank and I would have made our record that Saturday, even without Izzy, had it not been for an unexpected visitor. We were on batch number fifteen, melting ice on hot tables like maniacs. Mom was working the register and the front counter. She scuttled to the kitchen where Frank and I were starting number sixteen.

"Francis, you have a visitor out front. I'm custom packing the family a box of dark chocolate orange peel, ginger, and marzipan. Take a break and give your friend a tour of our factory."

At first, I thought it might be Izzy pulling a prank. Maybe he told his old man he'd forgotten his hat or gloves.

"Guess I got to go for a second," I told Frank.

I almost shit my shorts. Standing behind the roasted-nut case was Susan Flannagan. Her red hair was in ponytails, fresh snowflakes clinging to them, with a small green bow holding each one in place. She was sporting a red-and-green plaid holiday skirt. Her gray woolen jacket was open, exposing a red turtleneck sweater.

111

She was smiling, her teeth all pearly white. She had ditched her braces last school year. Her hazel eyes burned through the lenses of my eyeglasses.

She smiled at me. "Francis, it smells so good in here."

I wanted to run back to Frank and jump into his bubbling kettle: go down into the fire, never to rise again, and pretend this was not happening. Susan hated Izzy with a passion, and guilt by association meant she was here to do damage to me too.

Susan was munching on a free candy cane that my mom had given her.

"Francis, my mum and pop are in the car trying to beat the storm home, but they wanted me to run in and pick up their order first."

She flashed me another smile so big I thought her face would crack.

"Your mother says that you will give me a tour while she fixes up our custom order."

Her lips and smile looked genuine and inviting, but I still could not trust her. She had just bitten the crook off the cane and was now twirling the shaft between her lips, savoring the peppermint and sucking the juice out of it. The red stripes staining her lips made it look like she was wearing lipstick. Susan stepped around the roasted-nut case and boldly grabbed my hand.

"Your mother said I could see the chocolate-dipping room in the basement and watch you and Mr. Zelman make peanut brittle. This peppermint is one hundred times better, much more tingly, than the dime-store ones. Maybe you will show me how you make them? I mean, someday, if you invite me back?"

She let go of my hand when we got to the kitchen.

"The girls at school will be so jealous! I get to tour Francis's candy factory, not once, but maybe even twice!"

The holy angels just crapped all over my day. When I had woken up, my dream had been for Izzy and me to help Frank break his record. Now I had to show Izzy's worst enemy *my* factory.

She was close behind me, her posture all perfect and erect, and I could smell the mint she was breathing down my neck.

"Frank, this is one of my classmates, Susan Flannagan."

Frank had his left hand on his hip. His right was making a figure eight, loosening the sugar-and-water mixture in the large copper kettle for our sixteenth batch. It had not started to boil yet. He was just getting it going.

"Come over here, young lady," Frank said. "Francis and I will make a candymaker out of you. This place could use another good lady candymaker since Francis's grandma passed."

Frank handed the wooden paddle to Susan and then tied a starchy white apron around her. Then he put my paper hat on her head. Her red ponies hung out from the hat, the snowflakes now gone. She was actually pretty good with the paddle, but then she was good at everything. She kept the mixture moving, not letting it settle and scorch.

There I was, watching her while she wore her cane down to a small white nub. Izzy would have a diarrhea attack if he ever found out about this. The formula started to boil, and Frank took over.

"You two kids run downstairs to the chocolate room. The chocolate dippers are off weekends, but you could show Susan how to break the chocolate bricks and fill up the overnight melters. Maybe show her how our dippers temper the chocolate and fill and cool your grandma's antique St. Nick molds. Oh, and be sure to quiz her on how to read the signature designs on each bonbon so she won't have to punch a finger in them to figure out her favorite flavors."

I trudged down the gray wooden stairs. Izzy's archenemy followed.

"Oh my gosh, Francis! I can barely take it all in! There's every variety of chocolate that a girl could want."

She pointed at the Santa figures.

"And the shiny silver Santa Claus molds are beautiful in themselves. Are they ready to be plopped out yet? Will you let me release one, just one, please Francis? Is the chocolate hard now?"

For a brief moment, I saw her intention was pure, and her joy seemed real. She was almost human. She even looked kind of pretty. The same girl who annoyed me, and who my best friend despised more than Satan, was currently displaying real passion and giving me some romantic thoughts.

I handed her one of our larger metal Santa molds. When I did, my hand brushed hers, but I withdrew it quickly to grab another chocolate mold.

"Hard enough?" she asked again.

I was searching for words, stammering a bit. "Ah, ah, well I think so, but the dippers won't care if he is not perfect. Just remove each metal clamp. If they tempered the chocolate just right, he should plop right out and not stick to the metal. Mr. Claus should be sleek and shiny brown with no gray streaks. Even one streak and my grandma taught me that they go back into the overnight melter for a second chance."

Her delicate fingers were slender. Her nails had red holiday polish that her mom must have OK'd since school was out. The nuns said earrings, perfume, and polish for girls her age was just advertising for trouble.

Susan's mom was Lutheran, though. She had just married a Catholic, so she had to promise that her daughter would be baptized Catholic. But I guess if you marry a rich doctor and have a life on easy street, you can talk your husband into letting your daughter wear nail polish and can even make him give up some of his church's beliefs.

Mrs. Flannagan did not like their neighborhood public school, so she sent her only child to Holy Family. Mrs. Flannagan was not one of those evangelical Wisconsin Synod Bible-banger Lutherans; she was Missouri Synod, so I figured that a little bit of red nail polish might be OK with the Lutherans from Missouri.

Izzy claimed that the Flannagans were all hoity-toity and full of themselves, that both parents came from money and their families were mostly all doctors.

Izzy said Dr. Flannagan probably smelled and touched melted skin and witnessed other things that would make most people puke their guts out.

Izzy's old man told Izzy that on the day of the explosion and tragedy at the brewery, Dr. Flannagan worked long into the night and saved nine of his coworkers' lives. Only one man died, and it was weeks later from an infection. Dr. Flannagan even called in his buddy burn guys from the Mayo Clinic in Rochester and helicoptered them to St. Paul on his own dime to help put the men's charred bodies back together.

Susan released the Santa mold perfectly, setting the jolly character on a piece of fresh parchment. Smiling again, she took a step back in admiration. When she did, her skirt brushed my leg, and her coat touched my bare arm. I thought it was an accident, so I leaned back again, but she did it again.

"You can take Santa home if you like. No charge," I said.

"Oh no! He is so perfect and exquisite, Francis. I could never eat him."

She then turned to face me and came close, looking directly into my eyes.

"Francis, I know what Izzy calls me. I'm not sure why he hates me so, but it would make me happy if you called me Susan. That is what I like to be called. I was named after my grandmother."

She moved even closer. I felt her warm minty breath and enjoyed inhaling it. She lowered her voice to a whisper and said, "I'm so sorry about your grandma, Francis. I lost mine two years ago, and I still miss her terribly."

She put one hand on my shoulder and the other on my cheek. Her wool coat was open, and I could see the forms of her breasts through her red turtleneck. She pressed her body into mine so I could feel her through the sweater. I did not turn away.

"The peppermint made my tongue tingle, Francis. Will you kiss me?"

I froze. My feet felt like they were made of cast iron and stuck to the terrazzo floor.

I responded, "What's that supposed to mean?"

Mom's voice saved me.

"Hey, kids, come on upstairs. The order is ready, and Susan's parents are still in the car waiting."

Susan turned away and bounded up the stairs.

"Merry Christmas, Francis!"

I could see her white tights under her holiday skirt. I went into the basement's men's room to calm myself. Susan's tour left me with some feelings that I'd never had before.

Frank winked at me when I finally came upstairs. He was pulling the cap off his end-of-day beer with one hand and holding a fat salami sandwich in the other.

"Everything OK downstairs, Francis?"

I thought he might have spotted a bit of lipstick or red peppermint on my cheek where she had touched me. "Huh?" I said.

"Well, your friend ran upstairs fast, and I noticed she grabbed your hand on the way down. If your palms are sweaty, I hope you followed the directions in the bathroom—wash hands before returning to work, right?"

I laughed, grabbed my brown lunch bag and an Orange Crush from the fridge, and said, "I'm not going to work, Mr. Frank. I'm going to eat."

Our workday was over. The record would have to wait.

24

Starting Over

BEFORE CHRISTMAS EVE 1967

For the wrongdoer will receive recompense for the wrong
he committed, and there is no partiality.
—COLOSSIANS 3:25

I had completed all five weeks at a real job. I loved working with Frank, and being a candymaker seemed like it might be a good career, if I could skip the burn tattoos. I was on top of the world on my last Saturday. At the end of my shift, my dad handed me my first pay envelope and said, "Good work, Francis. Frank speaks highly of you, and I am proud of your work ethic too."

The next day, I bought myself a small combination safe at Woolworth's with two of the twenty dollars I'd earned making brittle. I stashed my canoe money and my journal in the safe and placed it under my bed.

Then, two days before Christmas Eve, I received an unwelcome surprise. Dad came home around eight that night after working late at the factory and beckoned me to the kitchen.

"Francis, come out here. I have a bone to pick with you." Whenever he used that expression, it usually meant I was in trouble.

117

I was barefoot, already wearing my pajamas. The kitchen lino-leum was cold on my feet. He pulled a chair out from our table, motioning for me to sit. Then he stood, hovering over me. He placed a large white envelope in front of me and tapped it twice.

"Open it," he said.

I followed his orders and pulled out a black-and-white photo-graph, along with a five-dollar bill. When I saw the photo, my jaw dropped. I wanted to hide under the table. It was a photograph of me blasting Lucifer with the chemicals from our factory's fire extinguisher.

My plan had been to not say a word until asked, but I sensed I was in for more trouble than I thought I would be for saving Kevin. I just kept looking down at the cash and picture. Dad finally broke the silence.

"Mike from Lund's Hardware just had it developed. Gave it to me at his store this afternoon. Francis, you have some explaining to do. I'll wait until you are finished to punish you for your lies and misdeeds."

I confessed to exactly how things had gone down that night, what I had been thinking and why I responded the way I had. My father was not impressed. I wanted to lash out and scold him for letting Grandma Rose's dog escape. If Kevin hadn't gotten loose, none of this would have happened.

I figured I was in for TV-time takeaway and a grounding, but it was much worse.

"Francis, you are old enough to know right from wrong. Omitting telling me about this was a lie, not to mention an expen-sive one. Now I must have the extinguisher repaired, refilled, and serviced. That will cost the business at least twenty-five dollars."

I stood up to defend my actions.

He yelled, "Sit back down!"

Dad lit a cigarette. Then he sat directly across from me. "I'm not through with you yet," he said. "Where is the money you earned helping Frank?"

"In my room."

"All of it?"

"No, sir." I started fiddling with Mom's plastic tulip center-piece that was on the table between the two of us.

My father shoved it out of the way. It tipped over. A red tulip fell out of the arrangement.

"I used two dollars to buy a safe at Woolworth's, sir," I replied. I turned the vase upright and put the red flower back in.

"Then go get it. Bring all your money to me."

"OK."

"Every last penny, and pronto, son!"

I obeyed and came back with the safe. I set it on the table. My hands were trembling as I tried to open it. I was trying not to cry. My Izzy money meant everything to me. It took me four tries before I got the combination correct. Dad just sat there, flicking his ashes into an empty tuna tin.

"Here," I said, handing him twelve dollars.

"You think this is funny, young man? Where is the rest? There should be eighteen dollars in there."

"Under the Christmas tree, sir."

"What?"

"I used six dollars of it to buy gifts for you, Mom, and Mandy and to get a chew bone for Kevin."

My father did not know how to handle my curveball. He hesitated before replying, "Do you think this is a fair lesson about responsibility, son?"

I wanted to be a smart-ass and respond with sarcasm about his misdeeds: illegal gambling, hiding his nudie pictures, having one too many beers on occasion. But I knew better. I was the kid, he the parent, and before I could think it myself, he said what he always said at times like this.

"You do know this is for your own good, right, Francis?"

"Yes, sir."

"I'll consider twelve dollars your full payment, and you can keep the safe and the five dollars from Mr. Lund."

"What?"

"That's right. He took up a collection with the neighbors. They think you are a hero. Lucifer has not come around since. Good night, Francis."

I tossed and turned before falling asleep. I needed to find another way to raise back my confiscated funds. This was war! Even electrocuting my privates would not stop me from paying for that canoe trip.

25

The Best Present Ever

CHRISTMAS EVE 1967

Thus, sayeth the Lord God of Israel,
"Write the words I have spoken to you in a book."
—JEREMIAH 30:2

Grandma Rose referred to those she liked and trusted as "good people." She was generous and kept the nuns and priests well supplied with free candy. Customers from church and our employees got 50 percent off.

This irritated Mother a lot. Mom worked for free during the holidays and complained that Grandma Rose's giveaways were dangerous practices for any business. It annoyed her when Dad had to wait a few weeks to cash his paychecks. I overheard her threats when Grandma was still alive. She chewed out my father late one night after he came home from bowling.

Mom had helped at the store all day. Then she sat at our kitchen table for two hours, struggling with our bills, while Dad was out having fun bowling and tossing back a beer or two. After his night out, my father walked into a trap, and instead of asking how his team did that night, my mother threw a pile of invoices at him.

"Antonio, if you don't have a talk with that woman, I will. These are all overdue! Just because she is paying for our children's Holy Family tuition and buys them more gifts than she can afford does not mean we stand at the end of the line for your hard-earned paychecks."

Grandma was always generous to both my sister and me. When I made my first Communion, she gave me an Emerson transistor radio. They had just been invented, fit in the palm of your hand, and were expensive and hard to find. Later, for my birthday, I got a brand-new black-and-white Columbia bike with real chrome fenders. I was the first kid at my school and in my neighborhood to own both.

If she had been healthy and alive this Christmas, I probably would have gotten a motorized scooter and Mandy a three-speed bike.

Dad had a hard time at Christmas Eve dinner without her. All of us did. Mom put on her happy face for us kids, but I wanted to cry when Dad also choked up during the blessing. Grandma Patricia reached out and held his hand. I guess that was the first time in my father's life that his mom was not with him on Christmas.

After dinner, we chomped on cookies and exchanged gifts under our lopsided balsam fir. Mandy's job was the tinsel, and she overloaded it.

We had inherited Grandma Patricia's old-fashioned bubble lights when she got a fake tree, but last year a piece of the tinsel worked its way into one of the bulb sockets. The lights popped like firecrackers and smoked up the room, and then all the lights in our house went out. Dad bought a new set of regular bulbs for this Christmas.

Things were going swell until Dad hauled out his large rack of movie picture lamps and his 8 mm camera to film us opening gifts. It slowed down our whole rip-and-tear process because my sister and I had to pause and act for his camera.

We always received practical things from our parents on

Christmas Eve. The fun stuff would be under the tree from Santa the next morning. I opened my new rubber winter snow boots and Mandy got snow pants. We each also scored pajamas. Mine were Minnesota Twins flannels. Mandy ran to her room, changed into hers, and emerged modeling her pink Barbie-doll pj's.

After gifts, Dad drove Grandma Patricia home, and I helped Mandy set out some milk and cookies for Santa. Mom laughed when I set a bottle of beer next to the cookies.

"Mom, do you think Santa prefers his beer in a bottle or a can?"

"I'm not sure, honey, but do you think he can drive his sleigh afterwards?"

I showered, put on my new pj's, and hit the hay. Before I fell asleep, I started working on my business plan to market my new candy moneymaking operation. February would be prime time, with Valentine's Day and all. I would get back that twenty dollars or die trying.

My mother knocked on my door. She opened it, turned on my night-light, and handed me one more gift. I put on my eyeglasses.

"I saved this for you to open last, Francis. She bought it special for you before she passed." Mom kissed me on the cheek. "Merry Christmas, Francis."

She quietly shut the door so I could open my gift in private.

The present was beautifully wrapped in a large box. It was solid and heavy. Under my nightstand light, the stars on the silver wrap were shimmering. There was no bow, but on top was my grandfather's crucifix. Mom must have put it there and taped it down. It was the one Grandma Rose was grasping the day she died. Tied to the bottom of Jesus's feet was a red ribbon with a playing card attached. I flipped the card over. It was the ace of hearts.

I held the box for a while, wondering what was inside. I was careful not to tear the paper as I peeled it from the box. I lifted the top off the large brown carton. On top of the white tissue was a Christmas card with a sketch of Saint Francis on the front. I opened the card and read my Grandma Rose's note, written in her perfect cursive:

Dear Francis,
Merry Christmas.
You are special in more ways than you know.
You, Miranda, & Isadore are all Aces. Never let anyone tell you otherwise.
You are also a great writer. Please continue with that journey.
With All of My Love,
Now and forever,
Grandma Rose

I removed the tissue and lifted the gift from the box. It was an IBM electric typewriter. Only the best offices could afford them. I took time admiring the steel ball at its center and wondering how they could cram the whole alphabet on a steel circle the size of a golf ball. It was a magic ball that formed letters and sentences, that could write stories and even spell cuss words.

I set the typewriter on my desk and placed the crucifix next to it. I would wait until morning to plug it in and read the directions.

I shut off my light. I suddenly felt her peace inside me. My pillow started collecting my tears. It was the first time I'd cried since she left me.

26

Saving Kevin

New Year: January 1968

Like a dog that returns to its vomit. Is a fool who repeats his folly.
—Proverbs 26:11

Over Christmas break, my mission was to pay back Grandma Rose for my best present ever. My goal was to train her dog, now our dog, to poop and pee outside. She had loved that dog as much as she loved me, but at least I was potty-trained.

Dad threatened to put Kevin on the next space capsule to the moon if he kept doing his business in the house.

I started laying newspapers all around our home, figuring the annoying pet might learn to hit his mark most of the time, which he did, but he still went after Dad's things.

Mom was not fond of Kevin, but she made an effort to get along. Mom called him "Little Sheet." Mother never cursed, but I knew what she meant. One Sunday evening, his bowel bomb ended up on Dad's bedroom pillow, and Mother acted quickly.

"Francis, be quiet. Go to the kitchen and sneak me a wet rag with a spot of detergent."

Dad was watching *Gunsmoke* in the living room, so he never found out. However, the following night, our roof almost collapsed and the poor dog nearly died when my father found a turd on his clean bowling shirt.

"Goddamn it, Eleanor! Get that skunk-weasel out of here before I shoot him. He just crapped on my clean bowling shirt."

Mom took a sponge and some Lava soap and scrubbed it clean, while Dad just stood there bare-chested. He continued ranting about the dog. Mom held her ground, but I sensed she was about to commit a crime when she followed her husband, the brick of soap still in her hand, as he stormed out the back door cussing with a big wet spot on his shirt right over his left nipple.

Before Dad could slam his car door and speed away, Mom yelled so loud that the whole neighborhood could hear.

"For your information, Antonio, when you come home, you will both be in the doghouse together!"

Kevin's offering that evening must have been a good-luck turd because my dad rolled a 660 series, the highest at that bowling lane in eleven years. I imagined my father throwing an angry black ball, pretending all those pins were Chihuahuas.

I figured bowling was as good for Dad as bridge club was for Mom. It kept them both sane while they tried to save our factory from debts that could put them out of business. We lost our biggest customer, a department store, the same day Grandma died.

Their Christmas, Valentine's, and Easter orders were half of our wholesale business. The department store switched to a big, nationwide chocolate brand when a new buyer came on board. He probably got bonus payola under the table.

My folks had both been working overtime to keep our factory running when Dad got the phone call from the purchasing guy. Mom told me Dad had slammed down the phone and hollered, "What next?"

The next call had been from me at the nuns' nurses' station. My eyes had been blurry from tears, and a kind young nun had dialed for me, keeping her soft gentle hand on the back of my neck while I tried to explain to Dad that his mother, my grandmother, had just died and that he needed to come over right away.

The only good thing about Kevin was that he stayed out of my room. One time he dropped a mini-cigar on my Minnesota Twins bedspread. I was home alone, so I picked him up like a rat by the scruff of his neck and put him in our freezer next to the ham. It was only three seconds, but he whimpered like a baby. When I let him out, he started licking me, all grateful, like we were best friends. I felt ashamed. If Grandma Rose had seen me, it would have killed her a second time.

27

Elections

JANUARY 1967

Remind them to be subject to rulers and authorities, to be obedient,
to be ready for every good deed.

—TITUS 3:1

In seventh grade Holy Family held our student council election
to determine who would be the president of the whole school the
following year, in eighth grade, our last before graduating. Only
seventh graders got to vote.

Izzy and Travis encouraged me to run but I did not think I
was popular enough to win. No other boy stepped up to challenge
Susan Flannagan, so it looked like she would make Holy Family
history and become our first-ever girl president.

Izzy ignored my wishes and rounded up all the boys' signa-
tures on a petition with my name, so Sister said I had to do it,
even though I said no.

She pinned me down after I served morning Mass.

"Francis, many of your classmates think you would be a good
leader and want you to run for president."

"But, Sister, we already have a candidate. Why me?"

"Francis, having an election without an opponent is not

democratic. Just think for a minute. Nixon would have been our leader if Senator Kennedy had not stepped up."

Sister kept pushing and made me run, but I'm sure she wished she could take it back once I made Izzy my campaign manager.

Izzy had a plan for us, not only to run the school, but for how I could eventually be mayor of St. Paul because I would own our family's candy factory.

"Hell's bells, a candy factory! That's bigger than that Italian Parino family owning all the liquor joints in St. Paul."

Izzy insisted that, as a mayoral candidate, I would earn 100 percent of the Irish-Catholic votes: the Catholic Italians on the East Side, and the German Catholics on the West Side. He was sure the French Canadians and Poles in Frogtown would go our way, too, but he said we would lose most of the Lutherans and Scandinavians in Swede Hollow, as well as the Jewish families up in Highland Park.

"The Catholic Mexicans from La Familia parish on the river flats would go for us, but you might need to learn a little Spanish to lock them down," Izzy said. "I looked it up in the *Britannica*, Francis. St. Paul has more Catholic churches and schools than any city in America, except maybe Philadelphia or Boston. We get the Catholics and bribe everyone with free candy, we get the power."

Our school was mostly white kids and a handful of Mexicans. Clinton, our only Negro student, was a good friend of mine and Izzy's. We also had a Korean girl in our grade, Geena Rae. The rumor was that she and her parents managed to cross the border, escaping to Seoul from North Korea, but Geena Rae's grandparents were murdered when the North Korean government found out.

One mean girl, Sophie, often gave Geena Rae a hard time and razzed her on the playground behind Sister's back.

I think she bullied Geena just because she was from a different country and brought some odd-but-interesting Korean foods to lunch. Sophie never let Sister see or hear her remarks.

Sophie taunted Geena. "When are your North Korea comrades going to bring me some of that poison kimchee, Geena?"

Izzy heard this and calmly approached Sophie, his nose to hers. I thought he was going to punch a girl, but he brought her to silence with his words instead.

"Sophie, Geena Rae made the honor roll and the girls' basketball team. She won our geography stand-down quiz. I'll bet you this here Snickers bar that you can't find either Korea on a map. You probably think they are in North and South Dakota."

Izzy started drafting our platform and ripping Susan's.

"Her plan is all full of goodie-two-shoes bull-crap that sucks up to the nuns and priests and does nothing for us," he complained.

She wanted to add a new mission drive for the March of Dimes.

Izzy said, "Suck-Up stole that idea from her old school in Texas."

She wanted every student to design a handmade float out of a shoebox, and then she would arrange them on lunch tables in the gym. The whole school would parade around to "Ave Maria," dropping dimes in a jar next to their favorite float.

Izzy was peeved. "Like sticking ten cents in a shoebox with Barbie and Ken making out on top is going to wipe out birth defects," he grumbled.

I threw out most of Izzy's ideas, like candy-and-cupcake breaks every afternoon. We finally agreed together on my campaign platform:

1. Allow seventh and eighth graders to play King of the Hill on the big winter snow pile again. (It was banned when Travis busted his wrist the previous December.)

2. Have soda-pop Fridays once per month, where we could bring our own pop to school and not be forced to drink from those waxy-tasting red-and-white milk cartons. (Susan had an uncle in Wisconsin who was a dairy

farmer. That's why Izzy insisted this campaign promise was nonnegotiable.)

3. Charge a one-time tuition athletic fee of forty cents per student to replace the faded, tattered boys' basketball and football uniforms that had been handed down since I started kindergarten. For some reason, many jerseys were missing the giant *H* on the word *Holy*. Our opponents razzed us that the word *oly* was short for *Old Ladies*.

4. Have a Grandparents Day where we would give grandparents a tour of our classroom and then have cake and coffee for them in the cafeteria.

5. Add a top-seller drawing for our school's annual candy bar fundraiser. Izzy said if we got Joe's General or Woolworth's to donate a bike and then held a drawing for everyone that sold two boxes of candy bars, we could triple our field trip funds. That was a good idea.

Putting the candy bar fundraiser in our platform last year gave me my great moneymaking idea for this winter and spring. I had not forgotten how my dad stole my hard-earned wages—money that was meant for my canoe trip with Izzy. I was going to do my own damn fundraiser!

I'd "borrow" candy from our factory, small amounts at a time so it would not be missed, and sell it at school, at Boy Scouts meetings, and in the neighborhood, offering a food service like Bella Pizzeria, which delivers directly to its customers. Except I would not charge for my delivery nor encourage a tip. I would pay the candy factory back next year when I had a real job. I'd add small amounts, under a dollar, every week to the store's petty cash. Dad never kept accurate books on the secret cigar-box slush fund he used to buy gambling tickets each week.

It would not really be stealing, just borrowing, or taking out a loan, like the business did every September at our bank to help fund manufacturing supplies before the money from our holiday sales started pouring in. I would give myself a short-term loan.

I figured then that if all the boys voted for me and I voted for myself, I would win by two votes. But I wanted to run a fair and clean campaign, even though Izzy despised Susan.

However, a small problem arose when Izzy decided to do some electioneering for me in the boys' and girls' lavatories without my knowledge. He designed small note-card signs for both bathrooms. The first ones were OK. He put those above the hand-washing basins. They just read, *Wash Your Hands and Make a Clean Vote for Francis Paulson!*

However, he then added others, placing them above the boys' urinals and in the girls' bathroom stalls. Those read, *Remember to P. P. twice for: President Paulson. Francis is #1. Susan is a #2.*

The next morning, Sister asked me if I knew about my new ads. I told the truth that I did not. She then called Izzy to her desk. He looked all surprised and lied like a rug.

"Sister, we run a clean campaign. I bet this is Susan trying to get Francis in trouble to steal our election."

Sister had no proof, but her only option was to fix the election. She did, and I lost by one vote. Susan Flannagan was going to be Holy Family's first lady student council president.

Mom had a cake waiting for me when I got home. It was sitting in the middle of our kitchen table. The cake topper was a five-inch tall statue of President Lincoln. Below on the white butter frosting's surface, Mom wrote in blue-and-red frosting: *Congratulations, President Paulson!*

I was smiling when I saw her creation. "Francis, I'm so proud of you," she said, and she meant it.

"But Mom, I lost by one vote."

"No matter." She hugged me. "It's not whether . . ."

I interrupted her. "I won or lost, but how I played the game . . ."

She smiled. "That's right, Francis."

Then she finished preparing my favorite meal, a rare treat as it was a lot of work. I loved Mom for what she did, and especially for the sweet-and-sour pork with fried rice. She even bought fortune cookies at a real Chinese restaurant.

Mine read, *Your business will meet with unexpected success.*

That evening, I started working on my business plan and putting my thoughts in my journal, and I kept at it into eighth grade. They say if you write things down and define your goals, there is a much greater chance they will become reality.

28

Spelldown

VALENTINE'S DAY 1968

My beloved is mine, and I am his;
He pastures his flock among the lilies.
—SONG OF SOLOMON 2:16

My River Trip Business Plan: Phase One, Valentine's Day Market:
    Goal: To earn twenty to twenty-four dollars in profits by the
Fourth of July.

1. Tag along with my folks to the candy factory as often as possible without arousing suspicion.
2. Pilfer and package treats in small units that can be hidden easily.
3. Only take confections kids my age would buy or want to give for Valentine's Day gifts.
4. Price low so they are a good deal.

My preferred candy list was red licorice vines, small pouches of conversation hearts, red sour gummy hearts, Rose's red-foil-wrapped sweet cream caramels, and red-foil-wrapped bite-size solid milk-chocolate hearts.

These would all be easy to conceal and slip to classmates. Word would get around. Want Valentine's Day treats? See Francis Paulson. I would give a bite-size Crunch bar as a free bonus for every sale over twenty-five cents. I would buy those from Woolworth's with cash I still had on hand.

Sister Mary Kenneth's St. Valentine's Day Spelldown was to be all celebration, complete with treats, card exchanges, and games until the go-home bell, but Izzy got kicked out before the afternoon party even started.

I had already earned two dollars and fifty cents since word got out about my business. I was smart enough to keep most of my transactions out of the school building during the day, making sales on the playground before and after school.

The exception was Mass. The sacristy was secure; only men and boys could go there, so every altar boy had access. I was serving only one daily Mass per week now, and I was swamped. I sold out the first day of February, so I started taking orders ahead and delivering them the following week. My customers came to me right after church as soon as Father left for the rectory.

The most popular treat for my fellow altar attendants were the red-hot round cinnamon jawbreakers. Travis said they were holy because they went to church with me. He called them Jesus Balls.

Travis said that when he served, he sucked on one after Communion to cover up his breath because he drank whatever was left in Father's mostly empty wine carafes before taking them out to the trash.

About a week before the event, Sister lectured us about our Valentine's Day cards and the upcoming spelldown.

"Boys and girls, if you are exchanging cards, you must give one to every student."

Before the morning bell, Izzy told me, "No cards from me next week. I'd eat manure before I'd give that tattletale, goodie-two-shoes Suck-Up Sue a valentine."

I learned later that he did give her a valentine. He swiped her fancy fake rhinestone sunglasses and glued several small chalky-tasting conversation hearts on both temple extensions. It was the same bad candy the girls would leave in our desks if they were sweet on one of us boys.

Izzy wrote his own sayings on each of the hearts: Dog Face, Teacher's Pet, Get Lost, and Small Boobs. He then snuck the glasses into her lunch box. He also opened her *Flying Nun* lunch thermos and emptied a small glass jar of frozen fish eyeballs into it for good measure.

After exchanging cards and having treats, we had free time to paint and play Battleship or checkers. Susan followed me when I got my paintbrush and tried handing me a small gift wrapped in tissue. It was about the size of a plum, and she'd tied it with a red ribbon. She touched my hand for way too long until she finally let the gift drop.

"Happy Valentine's Day, Francis."

I jammed the package into my corduroy pants pocket next to my hankie and unspent milk money. Many students, including me, got around Sister's "everyone gets a valentine" rule by giving a bigger card or adding a bonus treat for best friends or for anyone we were sweet on. I put milk-chocolate hearts wrapped in red foil from our candy store in my cards for all the guys who had voted for me during our student council election the year before. My cards were all the same. They showed Charlie Brown with his catcher's mitt missing a pitch and read, *I Hope You Have a Ball This Valentine's Day*. I taped the foil hearts into Charlie's glove.

Holy Family's St. Valentine's Day Spelldown was an annual big deal. Father Matt came in the week before to publicize it and gave us all a Tootsie Pop along with the rules.

"Young men and ladies, there will be four prizes, and the last student standing will earn a twenty-dollar tuition gift certificate for his or her family."

He hoisted a large wood-framed brass trophy of sorts, like it was his wine chalice at our daily Mass.

"The top speller will also get their name engraved on this plaque, which has been in our school's entryway above the statue of the Holy Family since we started the St. Valentine's Day Spell-down in 1954."

Izzy was an excellent writer and a master speller. They were the only two subjects he cared about. My best friend was set to win the final showdown with his archenemy Suck-Up Sue. All of us boys were rooting for him.

Sister had encouraged us to study ahead.

"Students, every word this year will be a proper noun, and if you don't know what that is by now, I will see you here, in my class, again next year."

Suck-Up Sue raised her hand. Izzy caught my eye, pointed to the dirty black spot on Suck-Up's forehead, and then put his finger down his throat, pretending to gag.

The first day of Lent, Ash Wednesday, had been the week prior. We all received ashes on our foreheads to remind us we would all be dust when we croaked. Susan still had not washed hers off.

Sister acknowledged the raised hand.

"Yes, Susan, do you have a question?"

"Sister, can you please give us a better clue as to what type of words will be at the spelldown so we can all study really, really hard?"

"The words will include some of our fifty states and state capitals, as well as biblical proper nouns. All of those will come from the book of Genesis. You will all learn about geography and the Bible while you practice your spelling."

When Sister turned her back, Izzy fired a giant rubber band at Susan, but thankfully it missed, hitting me instead.

I took fourth place that afternoon when I froze and spelled Delaware incorrectly: *D-E-L-A-W-E-A-R*. Like I really needed a jar filled with M&M's when my family owned a candy factory. Susan was next and got an underhand softball from Sister Mary Kenneth: *Adam*.

Izzy was on deck. Sister pointed toward him.

"Isadore, your word is *Massachusetts*."

A few of the boys rooting for Izzy groaned; the word would be a tricky one. Izzy stood tall, projecting his voice so all could hear clearly. "Capital *M*," he announced.

Building up the drama, he paused for a moment and frowned like he was focusing but worried. He repeated himself.

"Capital *M*."

Sister interrupted. "Yes, Isadore, you said that already. So far, so good."

Izzy started in a third time. "Capital *M* . . . *A-S-S*."

Sister did not pick up on his separating the *M* from the *A-S-S*. A few boys got it and started chuckling. Sister encouraged him again.

"That's OK, Isadore, take your time. Sound the rest out in your head before you speak."

Izzy wrinkled his forehead again, pushing the drama about as far as he could. When he side-glanced at me, I knew exactly where he was going, and it would not be pretty. He had tested the word on me when we practiced, and I had laughed so hard I'd almost peed my blue jeans.

This time, I shook my head no at him, praying he would not seize the moment for a few giggles and give up his tuition award and the Hula-Hoop grand prize. A wide grin formed across his face, and he finished his word slowly: "*O-F-T-W-O-S-H-I-T-S. Mass of two shits!*"

Sister's face flamed red, and she screamed, "Isadore!" Then she whacked him on his rear with her pointer and dragged him out of our classroom by his ear.

Izzy's old man beat him bad that time. He used a sawed-off hockey goalie stick and his fists. Izzy's right eye was bruised, his cheek swollen. Izzy hid his face from my mom when he came over that night. Mandy and I kept him occupied playing Monopoly and made him keep ice on his jaw.

Izzy's mom had to know what had happened. His old man was off from the brewery that weekend, so his mom let Izzy sleep over both nights. I hoped she would protect him by asking our priest to put a scare in Izzy's drunken old man.

That night, Izzy told me that his old man kept our priest supplied with free cases of beer. They were the bottles with crooked labels or too many scratches.

"Once a month, my old man has Fridays off, so he hangs out at the rectory playing poker with Father and Cigar Ron. They drink whiskey and beer until two some nights. I guess you can't get much closer to God than getting drunk with your priest."

Before bed, I put on my pajamas and was about to throw my uniform trousers down the basement laundry chute when I remembered Susan's tissue-wrapped Valentine's Day gift in the pocket. I unwrapped it. There were seven conversation hearts and a note that read, *One for each day of the week, Francis.*

Each heart read, *Kiss Me.*

29

Boys to Men

St. Patrick's Day 1968

How can a young man keep his way pure?
By keeping it according to Your word.
—Psalm 119:9

My River Trip Business Plan: Phase Two, St. Patrick's Day Sales:
Stock up on foil-wrapped chocolate shamrocks and all green-wrapped hard candy: sour apple suckers, key-lime-pie stick candy, gummy shamrocks, spearmint balls, green Lik-M-Aid candy, and green rock candy.

The rock candy came on swizzles. They were made for adults to swirl in fancy cocktails. Some sales guy had talked Rich Grandma into buying two cases of swizzle sticks before she died, and when she opened them, they were not assorted colors, but all green.

The swizzles were dogs. They did not sell, except for a few dozen before St. Patrick's Day. I guess our customers just drank beer or cheap wine, not fine cocktails. The sticks were made of crystalized rock sugar and would never go bad, but they took up valuable space on our limited storage shelves. Mom did not even put them in the display case for St. Patrick's Day.

I figured March would produce respectable sales, but not as good as February. I would not even have to pay for the rock candy swizzlers, as they were headed to the dumpster. They retailed for a quarter each, but I sold them four for a quarter. I refused to sell one at a time. The first week in March, I sold only swizzles, and they went like crazy. I had banked a little over three dollars. Then Sister, our priest, and the March of Dimes tried to put me out of business.

Father and the nuns announced a special all-school assembly. When we filed into the gym, we were each handed a small cardboard March of Dimes bank. Father showed us some slides of children with birth defects and talked about how they needed our help.

Then he asked every Holy Family student to make a small sacrifice during the Lenten season. He demanded that we give up sweets for the deformed and crippled children and for Jesus. The money we would have spent on candy, donuts, and ice cream was to be put in the cardboard bank to help those children less fortunate than ourselves.

Then he ended with everyone praying the Our Father. Right before dismissing us, Father hit us with his most powerful message. He pointed to the crucifix on the gymnasium wall.

"Boys and girls, please remember God loved you so much that he gave up his only son on that cross so you can earn eternal life. A sacrifice far greater than abstaining from sweets for a few weeks."

On the way back to class, Izzy gave me a quarter for four more of my green rock swizzles.

"I'll still buy your candy, Francis. I'll quit enjoying sweets for Lent the same Lent that Father quits drinking liquor."

Holy Family's Boys to Men Purity Party took place with our dads right after the St. Patrick's Day evening Mass. The men went to the basement cafeteria for two hours where they played bingo for huge chunks of corned beef that had been donated by Travis's dad's butcher shop near the stockyards. There were six-packs of Hamm's Beer that Izzy's old man had stolen from his job. While the dads ate and drank, we younger men were ushered into the school's chapel.

The girls went with the G-Man to the library for their chastity conference while their mothers went home to take care of their other kids or stayed for catechism and Bible study. The ordeal was mandatory for all eighth graders—if we planned to graduate.

It was our male rite of passage to make us aware of carnal sins should we abuse our minds and bodies when it came to girls. It was a one-night, two-hour course. During the first twenty minutes, we watched young Father Joe stuttering his way through his outline on self-abuse.

I already had touched myself; the first time was by accident, the second on purpose. I did not know there was a proper name for it. The dictionary said *masturbation*, but Izzy called it "stroking the snake." Father Joe called it "self-abuse," and it was a whopper of a sin. In fact, even thinking about it was a sin. Father said that Matthew 18:9 said, "If your eye causes you to stumble, gouge it out . . ."

I wondered how many boys at Holy Family would be walking around without eyeballs and missing their three-piece units if they followed Apostle Matt's advice. I would be one of them.

Our head priest, Father O'Malley, gave the lousy job of teaching us to his young assistant, Father Joe, the one who had droned on about my dead sister eating potato soup. Father Joe was so young he still had acne. Our seminar also came with a mimeographed handout complete with sketches of spermatozoa, their wagging tails diving for little round eggs, accompanied by scripture quotes that we could take home lest we forget the lessons learned that day.

After his stuttering talk on how not to self-abuse (saying the Rosary and playing sports were just two ways), Father Joe started the movie *As Boys Grow*. Izzy leaned into my ear and, pointing to my crotch, said, "Get it, Francis? How our boys grow?"

To make things even worse, the sex lesson was in our Our Lady's Chapel. Halfway through the movie, the film got stuck in the projector's hot bulb, right as the basketball coach was explaining what a wet dream was to his team in the locker room.

The film bubbled, sizzled, then smoked, stinking up the room. The projector bulb burned a hole right through a kid actor's jockstrap, stopping the movie. Izzy looked at me, then at the fire alarm and extinguisher. He jumped out of his chair, but I grabbed his shirt and pulled him back.

When Father turned the lights back on, I bit my lip and kept focused on Mary's glued finger to keep myself from giggling and getting kicked out. Father then turned his back to pull out the projector plug. When he did, Izzy started applauding, and everyone joined in. Father calmly walked back to his lectern and went on teaching like nothing had happened. I liked him for that. Way cool.

Izzy kept dogging me during the whole class, trying to get a reaction from me. He took his pens and colored pencils and gave his squirming sperm critters faces with smiles and eyeballs as they swam up the semen river toward a lonely ovum. He passed his sketch to me to see if he could get a rise out of me.

One of his little spermatozoa creatures had a cartoon bubble with my name above it. My sperm guy was swimming toward an egg that Izzy decorated with big lips, eyelashes, a chapel veil, and red lipstick. He labeled the egg *Suck-Up Egg*.

Thank God my real father spared me his "self-pleasuring talk" and that I got it all from our priest. However, a few weeks before Izzy and I were dropped off at the Boys to Men event, Mom attempted to tackle the subject about responsible boy-girl relationships.

It was my fault. I had brought on the awkward conversation. I had found my father's high school yearbook in a cedar chest in the basement when I was trying to find where Mandy had hidden the farmer matches and lighter fluid that had gone missing from our garage.

I paged through the yearbook and found a photo with Dad in it. The picture was of him with the high school bowling team. He was the captain and was holding the trophy. His face was serious, his black hair slicked back with way too much Brylcreem. Compared to the other boys on the team, most girls would have given Dad high marks from only the neck up. He was not fat but husky and had flat feet. My father said that was why he got turned down when he tried to enlist in the army. Most of his classmates were graduating early so they could fight Hitler or get back at Japan for Pearl Harbor.

The name under his photo puzzled me. It said Antonio Polanski. I just figured the moron in charge of the yearbook had screwed up since that had been Grandma Rose's maiden name before she married Gramps.

Mom was in the kitchen shucking corn. "What are you reading or writing now, Francis?"

When she saw the yearbook, she looked at me like I was holding one of her husband's issues of *Playboy*.

"Why is Dad's name wrong in his yearbook, Mom?"

I knew in a second that this was a question I should not have asked. Mom's jaw went slack. She took me by my wrist, leading me to the couch in the living room. Sitting next to me, she put her trembling hand on my knee.

"You know, Francis, being responsible with your body is what the Lord wants from you and all boys. When a young man is not responsible with his body, people are harmed."

I was confused. "What?"

"Your father got hurt badly as a young man. Being called a bastard is something you never would wish on your worst enemy."

I tried to take it in. First off, I did not have a worst enemy that I knew of. I had Ronny Downs who'd beaten me up and busted my eyeglasses because I made the basketball squad and he got cut, but I did not know what a bastard was. Most kids at Holy Family never swore, except for Izzy. I learned most words from him, but he never said the word *bastard*.

I only learned about the big bad word, *fuck*, when Izzy heard it from Jack. When I asked Izzy what it meant, he looked at me like I still believed in the Easter Bunny.

"You know," Izzy said. "It's when your mom and dad do it."

Then he made a fist with his left hand and took his right middle finger and plunged it back and forth fast into the opening in his fist.

I continued listening to Mom. I nodded like I knew what she was talking about so I could get rid of her. She stopped talking and started fidgeting, twisting her dish towel into a knot. She seemed uncomfortable with going any further with our chat, so I figured it was time to leave.

"It's OK, Mom. Dad looks handsome in the photo. Who cares if they messed up his name. Izzy is waiting for me at Cherokee Park. I'll be back in an hour for supper."

At the park, we jumped back on our bikes and rode to the library, where we looked up *bastard* in the dictionary.

BASTARD; NOUN:
A person who is illegitimate.
Born of parents who are not married to each other.
Adjective: Bastardly.

Supper that night was overboiled corn, burnt liver, bacon, and onions. My father never had a clue that I knew he was a bastard. He just kept gnawing away at his tough, overcooked liver.

30

Defending Susan

Do not desire her beauty in your heart,
Nor let her capture you with her eyelids..
—PROVERBS 6:25

Mandy had taken a real liking to Susan ever since they were paired up in school as buddies. Susan had treated Mandy like a princess the day they were burning matches, and she'd been nice to her ever since. This made Izzy insecure about Susan's motives and my improving relationship with her. He was less talkative around me. Sometimes he ignored my questions and attempts at conversations. Then, on a Monday after school, he let me have it, Izzy-style, while we walked to Joe's General. He threw his half-smoked cigarette butt in the street, went after it, and then almost got hit by a motorcycle while he was slamming his foot on the smoldering remains as if it were my head.

"Paulson, I can't believe you turned into a total jackalope piss-sucking ignoramus."

My first clue that he was a lunatic was my name. Izzy never called me Paulson: Francis, moron, jackass, dickwad, numb nuts, but never Paulson.

He continued ranting. "Suck-Up will destroy you and ruin Mandy, too. You want the Worm to turn into a big-ass tattletale, a nun's little bitch, a shrew like Suck-Up?"

I tried to ignore him, recalling Susan's joy at the factory when she opened the Santa mold and then me getting excited when she tried to kiss me. Then I thought about those conversation hearts she pressed into my palm on Valentine's Day. I decided to draw the line and defend my new friend, Susan Flannagan.

"Shut up, Izzy! Susan is not bad! Besides, Mandy needs a girl to teach her girl stuff. You and I can't do it, and my mom is falling apart with the business going to pot and her trying to pray everything away. Cut Susan some slack and give her a break."

"Oh, now you call that witch Susan? What did she do for you that you dropped the *Suck-Up?*"

"Izzy, right now, I want to add *F-up* to your name. Leave her alone. I mean it."

"No! You'll see, I'm right. She'll destroy you. She can't be trusted!"

I was getting steamed. "OK, genius. Tell me. In what way? How so?"

"Paulson, take off your halo and read my book, you goodie-two-shoed altar boy. Isadore Principle number thirty-six: Once a Suck-Up, always a Suck-Up—it's in the Bible."

"I'm sure it is. You probably crossed off a passage and wrote your own."

"I shit you not, Sherlock. The book of Isaiah talks about hypocrites. Hypocrites with small teats!"

I wanted to jump on him and smother his mouth in the dirt, but I responded with my words instead.

"At least she doesn't have a small brain like you do. This I've got to hear before I beat the snot out of you to pull you out of your trance."

Izzy lit another smoke and said, "Well, I made up the teat part, but look it up. It says, 'I'm holier than thou. Do not come near me. You are smoke in my nostrils.'"

He then inhaled and blew the smoke out of his nose and into my face.

I ignored the smoke. "Izzy, Susan treats you like a smelly wet turd because you're pranking her all the time. She refuses to let her guard down and maybe let you see that she has feelings."

"Quit defending her, Paulson! She's using the Worm to get us to hate each other, and after that she wants you to dump me and then she'll get into your pants. Then once you're smitten and you pop a big one, try to goose her. She will drop you like a hot potato."

I took two steps back so I would not sock him in his gut. "Izzy, what are you really smoking that is making you so nuts?"

He stepped toward me again. "Francis, you're an ignoramus! You're so blind you can't see her clues! I watch people. Suck-Up is always eyeing you. Stands in front of you in the lunch line, wiggling her bony ass. Probably would stand behind you at the urinal if she could. Even hold your hairless Mr. Happy and shake the last two drops down your trousers so you don't strain your own wrist."

Izzy faked a karate kick to my nuggets with his right foot and knocked my new straw fedora off with his hand. "She even laughs at your stupid jokes, and you are not funny. My jokes are funny, and I get called immature."

I pulled my fists out of my pockets and released them. Maybe Izzy was right. "Really? You think she likes me that much?"

"Yeah, she is batshit crazy for you and not to be trusted."

I tried defending Susan's honor one more time. "All I'm saying is that Mandy worships her, and maybe it was hard for Susan, moving to St. Paul from Texas. Then her parents forced her to go to a Catholic school with lunatics like you."

Susan really was one of the prettier girls in our class. Tammy got most of the boys' attention because she was Italian and had long dark hair and big boobs like Sophia Loren. Tammy was a cheerleader and always got yelled at by the nuns for rolling up her skirt so it would go above her knees. But she was dumber than dirt. Susan was smart and naturally pretty, even though her breasts were half the size of Tammy's.

I would not tell Izzy, but if it was true, I was warming up to the idea of having my first romance with a real girl—not a picture of one with a staple through her belly like in one of Dad's magazines.

I tried to reassure my friend. "Izzy, nobody will ever mess up our friendship, and what if Susan is really after you, not me?"

"No way! She is always getting me into trouble. If she knew how to use handcuffs, she would take me to prison, send me to the electric chair."

I laughed and told Izzy about my father's dating advice.

"Izzy, my dad once told me after a beer or two that sometimes girls do the opposite when they are sweet on a guy, that even my mom was rude to him, gave him the cold shoulder before they hooked up and started dating."

Lowering my voice, I mimicked Dad.

"Francis, when you're old enough to start dating, be careful. Some girls are just looking for a ring on their finger and will do anything to get their M.R.S. degree. 'Women love the chase, being pursued, enticing guys, sometimes even trapping them into marriage, like a fur trapper or hunter would with their wild prey.'"

Izzy interrupted me before I could finish my dad's lecture.

"Yeah, then your life will never be the same again. Do you suppose that's why my old man and your dad bowl, gamble, and drink? So they can remember the good times when they were just guys hanging out with other guys, no worries?"

Izzy pondered his own question for a few moments and then said, "I don't know about your father—he seems normal even though you are a geek—but my old man did some of those things before. When Jack died, though, he became one big fat gambling drunken jackass."

Izzy finished his cigarette, ground it out, and reached into his pants pocket, pulling out a half-dollar. He flipped it to me.

"If Suck-Up really wants in either of our pants, we are stopping at Woolworth's after Joe's, and I'm treating us both to a pair of steel underwear."

I laughed. "OK," I said. "Just don't wear them on a really hot day."

31

Keeping Secrets and Telling Lies

SPRING 1968

Please listen and answer for me,
for I am overwhelmed by my troubles.

—PSALM 55:2

The bathroom fire at Grandma Rose's wake had been gossip with some of the Rosary Society old hags, but I believed Mandy. Her hurt expression when I asked her about it convinced me she was innocent.

The haircut fire was just a goofy little girl screwing up. Dad had matches and lighters lying around for his smokes. I, too, was curious and played with them at her age.

But the bedroom fire that happened the same evening as the Boys to Men night—that put my sister in real danger. She could have ended up like Shannon. I stayed awake that night wondering if I should tell my parents. They had a lot on their minds. Dad was trying to settle Grandma's estate. He lost our biggest customer and was trying to pay down the factory debts. I heard Mom and him talking about being behind on our house payments too.

Mom got frustrated when I asked her for a new pair of tennis shoes. I was outgrowing my only pair. She told me maybe next month because we owed the government back taxes for our business and had to pay those first. I rarely heard my mom say a bad word about anyone, but she complained about how Grandma did the books and was not good about paying things on time. I guess that was one of the reasons we were in trouble now.

"Your grandmother, God rest her soul, charged all the gifts she could not afford, including your typewriter, to three different downtown department stores, and they all keep calling our house, along with the IRS and every other Tom, Dick, and Harry bill collector."

Dad laid down phone and mail laws for both of us. He told Mom he was the only one who should open our mail. She was also not to answer our phone since it would be the bank or other bill collectors who would upset her.

Mom figured out a secret phone code to give Poor Grandma, the bridge club, and church ladies so they could still call her. Poor Grandma was to let our phone ring once and then hang up so Mom could call her back. All others had their own codes, and they used up to six rings. More than six, I could pick up. One time I knew it was a bill collector, so I let it ring nineteen times just to annoy them. They never gave up. Izzy rarely called me—he would just show up in person—but in case of an emergency, I gave him the seventh ring.

Dad never answered at home. Everyone contacted him on the company phone since that's where he was spending most of his time. Someone always picked up at the store since that was how we took orders.

Cigar Ron was the only guy who used to call Dad at home, but he just started showing up in person. He never used the front door. He would sneak in by way of our back porch and give his signature rat-a-tat-tat knock. Izzy said that Jack once told him that the FBI was tapping Cigar Ron's phone to get evidence, but mainly they just wanted to bust the higher-ups.

My father instructed me on how to take the collection calls

and said that if anyone showed up in person, I should shut the door in their face and tell them I was not allowed to talk with strangers.

"Francis, when you pick up the handset, just say your mother and father are not in and ask for their callback number."

"So even if you are here, I should lie?"

"Francis, it's not lying if you are trying to help our family until I get it all figured out."

To make sure I did not freeze when a bill collector called, my father made me a cheat sheet and taped it to the wall by the phone:

1. *I'm sorry. They have the flu and are resting. I'll have them call when they wake up.*

2. *My parents had to leave for a funeral. What is your number?*

3. *They will be back next week. Who should I say is calling?*

4. *They are volunteering at our church. I'll have them call you tomorrow.*

Most days or nights I just answered a couple of calls. My record was eight on one Saturday. I guess bill collectors think most people are home on Saturdays. The last call that day rang fourteen times before I picked it up during a commercial, just to get rid of it so I could finish watching *The Beverly Hillbillies*. It was for Dad about an unpaid insurance policy for the factory. I just kept telling the guy "Yes, sir" and never wrote anything down, including his name and number. I returned to my show, wondering what it would be like to be the Beverly Hillbillies, filthy rich with no worries.

That March evening, when Dad and I got back from the Boys to Men class, Mom put Mandy to bed and told me to "hold down the fort" until they got back from their traditional St. Patrick's Day dinner date at Cliff Coatney's Irish Pub. They went for a pint of green beer and all-you-can-eat fish-and-chips.

My father had started buying more gambling tickets than

ever, selling most of them on the side for Cigar Ron. He got commission for every ticket sold. His customers were from our church or his bowling team. Some were store employees and salesmen. Dad's clients were small-time gamblers who usually spent no more than five or maybe ten dollars on the Super Bowl or the World Series. He had customers waiting at Cliff's Pub that night too.

I was in my bedroom doing homework, smiling and thinking about Izzy's cartoons and young Father Joe's sex lessons. I had my radio turned up really loud. I remember the song that was playing when I first smelled the smoke was "Ring of Fire" by Johnny Cash.

I had set aside my algebra book, put on my cowboy hat, and was pretending that my Elvis plastic guitar was Johnny's guitar as I yelled lyrics into my number-two-pencil microphone. I then smelled the smoke, even though my door was shut.

At first, I thought Dad had left a cigar or pipe smoldering in his ashtray, so I headed to the kitchen to snuff it out, but the smoke was coming from under Mandy's bedroom door. I heard her whimpers as she pounded on the door, unable to open it.

The door swelled up whenever it was damp out, and it was stuck and much harder to open from inside the room than from the hallway.

I threw myself against it to pop it open. She jumped into my arms, crying. I tossed her aside, tore off my Minnesota Twins sweatshirt, and smothered the flames, putting out the sparkler and construction paper that Mandy had lit inside Mom's metal scrub bucket.

I turned back to Mandy. Her tears had stopped, and she yelled at me like it was my fault.

"I was stuck! Don't let me be stuck in there!"

I carried her to my bed, kissed her forehead, and shut the door. Going back to her room, I opened the windows, allowing the cool March breeze to air it out.

A couple of hours later, I heard my folks pull up the driveway.

They both seemed relaxed and happy. I figured a few green beers can do that for an adult.

Mandy was sound asleep. I hustled her back to her own bed and closed her windows and door. My folks did not pick up on the odor as my father's cigars and cigarettes always made our whole home reek.

I talked with Mandy about the danger of playing with fire the following day. She cried and seemed remorseful. I finally got through to her and did not need to involve my folks since they had other things to deal with. I handled this one. That was the least I could do for our family.

32

Gamblers and Guns

APRIL FOOL'S DAY 1968

Abstain from every form of evil.
—1 THESSALONIANS 5:22

I never considered our home a "shit box," but that is what Cigar Ron called it. Dad was rolling a bad game. The candy store team was in the running for some end-of-season league money, so I asked to go with him and watch. After our candy team collapsed during the second game, Dad snuffed out his cigarette, popped open another beer, and gave me a handful of nickels. "Francis, you are not bringing us luck. Why don't you go get yourself an Orange Crush and some M&M's and play some pinball?"

I slid into the kid booth near the bar and wrote a poem for Sister's English assignment, a contest of sorts collecting the students' best prose, art, and poetry that she then published each May and sold for a dollar to all parishioners after Mass during the Feast of the Ascension, a holy day of obligation. Last year it raised over four hundred dollars for our library.

Susan designed the cover art. She was very good. I liked it. It was modern art, real hip, like the crazy patterns on the TV show *Laugh-In*. In the middle, it said *Sock It to Our Authors* in paisley designs. She carefully hid sketches of things she found at our school in an array of patterns, like a desk, clock, fire alarm, Sister's handbells, and even our school's mouser cat, Sampson. Izzy said she probably stole the art from her old Texas school.

I was surprised to be included later since my poem had taken me only a minute to create at a bar and I put little effort into it. Everyone laughed when Sister later read it, so I think she felt she had to publish it.

Storm
By Francis Paulson

The Thunder Roared
The Lightning Flashed
A Tree Fell
A Frog Got Smashed

Mom was working late at the factory while the bowling team tried to bring home some money. Mandy was sleeping there under the packing table in a bunk Mom had made up for her for when she and Dad worked late filling last-minute rush orders. I did not want to hang out at the factory, so I convinced Mom to let me go to the bowling alley with Dad. Usually, that was forbidden on a school night.

Rose's Fine Chocolates was printed on the back of the bowlers' shirts because the factory had sponsored the team for years, but Dad refused Mom's suggestions to give up the team, an unnecessary extra expense for our business. She claimed that only one bowler from the whole league ever came into the store, and he never spent over two dollars.

I noticed Cigar Ron was at the bar drinking a boilermaker, and it clearly was not his first. He was flirting with Ginny, the bartender. Ol' Ronnie did not say hi or even notice I was there.

Ginny was the bowling alley's only bartender and waitress.

She had large boobs. She was nice to everyone, even me. She refused to charge me for the M&M's and the Orange Crush I'd ordered. She said it was on her.

She blew me a kiss and teased, "I wanted them little chocolate pills for myself, handsome Francis, but it will ruin my girlish figure, so you get to eat them tonight, honey."

All the bowlers loved Ginny, but their girlfriends and wives did not. She was divorced and worked at two different bars on the West Side of St. Paul to pay her bills and support her daughter who had polio. Ginny had big beehive hair. She was blond and really pretty, like a Barbie but with bigger breasts, shorter skirts, and tighter pants. Izzy said that was how Ginny got big tips, but Izzy always said big "teats" instead of tips and then laughed his ass off.

Anyway, I liked Ginny a lot. She was nice to me, and my dad loved my mom, so he never flirted. He would tip her just a dime, not a dollar like Cigar Ron would. Izzy said Cigar Ron gave Ginny fifty dollars as a tip before Christmas one year.

Izzy said, "I bet Gamblin' Ronnie got to caress her ba-zoombas for that!"

I told Izzy it was probably hush money so Ginny did not squeal to the cops that Cigar Ron was running illegal books at her bar.

Cigar Ron was slouched at the bar, puffing away on a dark cigar and bragging to his suspicious-looking boss while they both downed beers with shots of whiskey dropped in them. I listened, wondering why the more people drank, like at Grandma Rose's funeral, the louder they talked.

Cigar Ron bragged, "Last year I cleared over one thousand bucks selling tickets to all those Catholics from Holy Family who built those 1950s shit-boxes after the war. Hell, the Mexican folks on the river flats don't even spend that kind of money gambling."

His boss was short and greasy and looked like a weasel, like the scumbags in *The Dick Tracy Show* cartoons. Cigar Ron's boss took a long swill out of his mug, gargled, swallowed, and spoke loudly enough that I could hear.

"Holy high-roller fuck, Ron. If you figure out how to do a soccer book, you'll get all those gambling Mexicans making you even more pesos. I got a cousin who knocked up a girl in Juarez. She had a hot bod and was a great cook, so he married her. They raise the kid in El Paso. Maybe I'll have him teach you how to make a soccer book and make you and me St. Paul's goddamn peso millionaires."

The drunk talk and nasty remarks bothered me more than the shit-box comments. I thought it was odd, since I saw Cigar Ron's house once when Dad took me to collect the twenty-five dollars he'd won on a Vikings gaming board. Cigar Ron's house was like ours, except it was a stucco two-story instead of a rambler. I guessed stucco makes your home a mansion, not a shit-box.

Whenever the Rose's Fine Chocolates team finished bowling, the men would always sit at the bar, and the low scorer bought the first round. Dad said I could not sit at the bar since I was a kid, so he always gave me a few nickels to play the pinball machine. Kids were not supposed to play the machine, but Ginny liked me, so she let me play. It was the only bad thing I did that Izzy went ape over.

"Damn your goodie-two-shoes altar-boy toothpick dick, Francis! You get to play pinball and sneak peeks at Ginny's curvy body. You are one lucky holy boy!"

The machine was called Help Me, Rhonda, and it had lots of women who looked like Eve with fig leaves and trees covering parts of their bodies below their necks and above their knees. They all had big hair and busts. Izzy insisted, once, that Rhonda was a go-go dancer. I punched him, telling him it was just a cartoon.

If the player drove the steel ball past Rhonda, it set off quite a display of flashing lights, wolf whistles, and noise. If those bells and lights went wild, you got a free play and a free beer from

Ginny. The whole bar full of guys would yell "Score!" and applaud.

I beat the game only once. Ginny slipped me an Orange Crush and gave me a hug. I told Izzy I then got a sneak peek down her blouse and saw her black brassiere.

I lied. My eyes were actually closed, but Ginny sure did smell good.

Izzy went crazy. "No way! I pray all day that Ginny will adopt me now that Grandma Rose is gone!"

Izzy's old man got kicked off his brewery's bowling team last season, but he still hung around the alleys. Usually, before his team got to the last game he was so full of beer that all he rolled were gutter balls. Ginny always called him a cab, or she and the dishwasher would drive the old man and his car home after closing.

I went to use the men's room. I had to poop, so I used the last stall and latched the door. I had just sat down when I heard two familiar voices enter the room. One was Cigar Ron's boss. The other was Izzy's old man. Izzy's old man asked the boss, "You got my present on you? If so, I got cash."

Cigar Ron's boss said, "Do I look like a motherfucker that don't keep his word? What the fuck you going to use the pistol for anyway?"

Izzy's old man whispered, "I'm not saying you are not a man of your word. I just want it for protection before they all come up here from Minneapolis and start messing with our city."

"OK. Here it is. But leave it in the bag. It's hot, and I gave you one helluva deal. It will blow a hole the size of a golf ball through the head of anyone that messes with you."

Izzy's old man closed the deal.

"Go ahead. Count it. It's all there. I added an extra five bucks as a tip, you know, to show my appreciation."

Cigar Ron's boss liked the tip. "Thanks! You and the missus have a happy Easter."

I remembered that night for Cigar Ron's shit-box comment,

the transaction with the gun, and the surprise waiting for me when I got home. Izzy had left it on the porch with a note that the package was for me. It was in a large box. Inside of the box was a garbage bag wrapped inside of a larger garbage bag. I opened the last bag. There was a note on the bag. It said, *I want you to have this. Your Best Friend Forever.*

It was Izzy's award-winning Christmas art project, the beer-can wind chimes that we all applauded. The ones he'd made for his old man.

33

The Champ

And one of his signs is the creation of the heavens and the earth,
and the diversity of your languages and colors.
Surely in this are signs for those of sound knowledge.
—QURAN, AR-RUM 30:22

It counted for a third of our grade. Sister made us submit two names of important people, dead or alive, that impacted our country, church, or the world in a positive way. She would assign one of these to each of us, and we were to deliver a fifteen-minute speech in front of the class. She created the two-people rule because last year the boys all chose baseball players like Willie Mays, Sandy Koufax, Carl Yastrzemski, and the Minnesota Twins homerun slugger Harmon Killebrew. Only one name got through Sister's censorship. That was Yastrzemski. He was Polish and a devout Roman Catholic.

Izzy was beaming when Sister tossed out Susan's Helen Keller submission. Sister patted her pet student's shoulder.

"Susan, Miss Keller accomplished great things for those not blessed with sight or hearing, but she worshipped a false religion from the writings of Emanuel Swedenborg."

Sister claimed Swedenborg's faith was a corrupt interpretation as it encouraged universal brotherhood of mankind. "Class, our one and true Roman Catholic Church considers Helen's church a 'sect' and a 'cult.'"

Susan recovered from her slap-down, and on her speech day, she delivered all the boring information about our recently dead pope, John XXIII. Izzy made sure she saw him faking yawns during her performance.

I submitted three names, astronauts Grissom, White, and Chaffee, and I knew I could handle all in fifteen minutes. I loved following NASA's Apollo rush to beat the Russian commies and be the first to land a man on the moon, so I asked for my speech to be on the three Apollo 1 astronauts who died during the launch-pad fire on January 27, 1967.

Sister smiled. "Nice work, Francis. If you can handle all three, I'm sure your classmates will learn something, and I will give you extra credit."

Then Sister had us all bow our heads and say an Our Father, Hail Mary, and Glory Be for the souls of the astronauts and their families. She did not tear up, like with Kennedy, but I thought it was a very kind thing to do. It made me proud to go to Catholic school.

Izzy did not have it so easy with his selections. His brother, Jack, was a big influence on Izzy, and Izzy was against the war in Vietnam. Jack also said Martin Luther King Jr. was a true leader, and Jack even hitchhiked to Chicago and marched with Dr. King to help gain equality for Negroes, especially those living in Mississippi, Alabama, Tennessee, and Kentucky, where the KKK still functioned. I'd heard life was worse there than it was in North Minneapolis or the Rondo neighborhood in St. Paul.

Izzy's choices were Martin Luther King Jr. or Cassius Clay, the heavyweight champion of the world who knocked out Sonny Liston in 1964. Sonny was the previous champ, and Cassius was the unknown, and unproven, underdog.

Shortly after that, Mr. Clay converted from Baptist to Islam. Then he changed his name to Muhammad Ali. Later, he was stripped of his boxing title for refusing to be drafted into the army, and the FBI arrested him.

That was an easy one for Sister. She said, "Isadore, although not Catholic, Mr. King is a good Christian and leader who also believes in our Lord's resurrection. Mr. Clay's new beliefs in the Nation of Islam are not what we need to learn more about. The class will love learning more about Dr. King."

That was all the motivation my friend needed. Izzy said "OK" and then started working on his research and speech about Muhammad Ali. When I told him that Sister Mary Kenneth might fail him, Izzy said, "Yeah, Nun Kennedy will flunk me, but unlike the Champ, I won't go to jail for standing up for my beliefs."

I never saw Izzy put so much effort into a project. He even enlisted the help of our friend Clinton. Clinton did his speech on Rosa Parks, who defied Alabama laws in 1955 by not giving up her seat on a bus to a white man.

Holy Family had a few Mexican students, one in the first grade and one in our class, but most of the Mexican families went to the Catholic church and adjoining school on the lower West Side, near downtown.

Clinton was our school's first and only Black Catholic student. His mom moved him out of public school in Chicago when he was in the second grade. Since then, he'd lived with his grandmother near St. Paul's Rondo neighborhood. Clinton's mom wanted her only child to get a great education, and that was hard to find in some of Chicago's public schools, especially those in poorer, rougher neighborhoods.

Clinton's grandma was Catholic, worked at the Cathedral of St. Paul in the chancery office, got a nice tuition discount, and was able to pay for all of Clinton's tuition. She even rode with him across town on the city bus to and from school every day until he was in fourth grade and could do it on his own.

Izzy asked Clinton to help him with his research and speech. Clinton was smart when it came to school, and he also had great people skills. Everyone liked him. He made friends out of enemies. He was tall and skinny with big hair. He had asthma, but as our star center, he still helped take our basketball team to the Twin Cities Catholic schools' championship game against the rich kids at Trinity School last year.

I was just a bench scrub. I got to warm up but did not play. I saw it all come down in the locker room after we beat the rich Catholics from Summit Hill. Clinton scored our winning point with a free throw as time ran out.

We shared the locker room with the Trinity athletes. One of their players, a forward who fouled out, shoulder-butted Clinton in the locker room, knocking him off balance. Clinton fell hard on the wet concrete floor.

The kid called Clinton a derogatory word, mumbling it, and said that Clinton got lucky.

The whole locker room was watching. Clinton got up, stood tall on the bench, took off his jersey, flexed his bony muscles, and said, "It might have been a lucky shot, but I am only one member of our team, and we won it together. My name is Clinton, and ice cream at King's Soda Fountain is on us for those on your team who want to join us. Thanks for a great game, Crusaders!"

One of the Crusaders punched his teammate in the gut, and most of their team showed up at the drugstore and passed a hat to cover our whole bill.

One Saturday, Izzy and I rode across town to Clinton's neighborhood to meet his grandma and have Clinton help Izzy with his project. Some neighborhood kids surrounded us and started messing with Jack's three-speed Schwinn bike, the one Izzy adored and always rode after Jack passed.

One of the kids grabbed the bike and taunted Izzy. "Nice bike. You lost?"

The ringleader grabbed at Izzy's bike handlebars like he was going to jump it. "You don't belong here," he said. The kid was holding a water gun, which he seemed to realize at the same time we did. "We got real guns too."

The kid looked at me next and said, "Your bike is crap. Scram!"

He spit at me, and it hit my glasses. I almost crapped my pants, but I stood by my friend.

Izzy said, "Leave us alone. We are just here to visit our friend Clinton Martin."

One short, fat, quiet kid said, "Hey, Ashton, leave them alone. If they are friends of Clint's, they are solid."

I will never forget Izzy's speech the day we gave our presentations. He slammed it out of the park, and our whole class knew it. Even Susan said, "Nice job, Isadore."

Sister called Izzy to the podium. "Class, Isadore will now give his speech on Dr. Martin Luther King."

Izzy walked to the front of the room, flashed me a smile, and said, "Everyone knows Dr. King is an important American, but my talk is about another brave American, the former heavyweight boxing champion of the world now known as Muhammad Ali."

That was Clinton's cue to come out of the cloakroom as Izzy's sidekick. Clinton had on a white terry-cloth robe and a boxing belt around his waist that Izzy had fashioned out of aluminum foil and a beer can. Izzy had given Clinton Jack's old boxing gloves, and Clinton waved them over his head as he ran to the podium and stood next to Izzy. Then, Izzy rang one of those hotel button bells, like a real boxing round was going to start. On the back of Clinton's robe, Izzy had spelled out *Muhammad Ali* with black electrical tape.

The class was glued and engaged. Sister had no choice but to let the fight proceed. Izzy and Clinton tag-teamed the whole speech and scored their own knockout in three rounds, right on fifteen minutes.

Izzy started out unsure, slow but steady. "My famous

American is the former Cassius Clay and the rightful Heavy-weight Champion of the World."

Clinton grinned, pumping the air above his head with his gloves. Everyone cheered and laughed, just like at a real fight. Izzy continued, "Any one of us at Holy Family can go to Joe's lunch counter and have a soda in St. Paul, but Mr. Clay was kicked out of his hometown lunch counter for the color of his skin."

Clinton was a good actor. He went limp, dropping his arms and gloves at his side, hanging his head at Izzy's remarks. The class was silent.

Izzy set up the fighter's background. Cassius was born to a Baptist dad who bore a slaveowner's name. His dad, a house painter, was a good, hardworking Christian man.

Izzy said that after young Cassius's bike got stolen when he was twelve, he sought revenge, but a local cop took him under his wing and got him into boxing in his Kentucky neighborhood. Clinton nodded his head like everything Izzy was saying was gospel truth.

Young Cassius was a great boxer. He never gave up, and he went to the Olympics where he won the USA a gold medal. Shortly after that, he was thrown out of a whites-only restaurant, so he tossed his gold medal into the Ohio River.

Mr. Clay then went pro, knocking out Sonny Liston in 1964. After the victory, he switched from Christianity to Islam and wanted to be called by his new name, Muhammad Ali. He gave up his Christianity for Malcom X and the Nation of Islam. He also refused to register for the draft or fight the white man's war in Vietnam. Sister pushed up her wire-rimmed spectacles and looked at the crucifix, then at her watch.

Clinton reached into his robe and took a pretend medal, a piece of round cardboard Izzy had wrapped in gold foil, and threw it into a metal mop bucket that said Ohio River on it.

Clinton was not acting now. He quit hamming it up and just spoke soft and slow, reading from his notes the exact words the

Champ himself had spoken. The class was still hushed, all eyes focused on Clinton. Clinton started to speak from his note card. I'm sure Sister almost started wetting her underthings.

"Cassius Clay is a slave name. I didn't choose it. Don't want it. I'm Muhammad Ali. It is a free name and means 'beloved of God,' and I insist people use it when talking to me."

Everyone's eyes were glued to Clinton and Izzy. Izzy put on a shirt and some earmuffs over his ears like they were an announcer's headphones. The back of his shirt said *Howard Cosell.* Izzy mimicked the announcer's voice pretty well and started asking Clinton his sports-reporter's questions.

"Muhammad, why are you allowing them to strip you of your title?"

Clinton responded exactly as Ali did. "Howard, to you and your fans, I'm not going ten thousand miles to murder the brown people of Vietnam simply to continue the domination of the white slave masters of darker people the world over. I have been warned that this will cost me my world title and millions of dollars. I've got nothing against no Viet Cong. No Vietnamese ever called me *nigger!*"

Clinton took off his robe, throwing it on the floor next to the mop bucket. The whole class started clapping. Clinton and Izzy linked arms and left the room, followed by Sister's glare and her pointer, which was showing them the door to the hallway and motioning for them to go to the G-Man's office.

When Izzy and Clinton got to the office, it was locked, so they hid out in the boys' locker room for a few minutes and then came back to class. The G-Man, Sister Mary Kenneth, and our young Father Joe were at the front of the room. There was a black-and-white photo of Dr. King on Sister's desk. Everyone was kneeling. Sister motioned for Izzy and Clinton to take their Rosaries out of their pockets and hit the floor on their knees.

The news just reached us—Dr. King had been shot in Memphis while helping lead a sanitation workers strike.

34

Freak Show

No man who has any defect may come near: no man who is blind,
lame, disfigured or deformed.
—LEVITICUS 21:18

My eyes were irritated by the smoky haze, but the early-summer scent of burning grass was pleasant. I was on our backyard tire swing completely lost in a daydream about the state fair at the end of August. I was fantasizing about holding Susan's hands and kissing her inside the Old Mill river ride.

Last summer, I begged Mom to let me go with Izzy to the freak show on the Minnesota State Fair's Midway.

She scolded me. "Good Catholic boys don't go into those tents, Francis."

Izzy and I did it anyway, and we let my sister tag along to see Dragon Man, the Breather of Fire. Izzy made Mandy pinky-swear not to squeal and bribed her by promising to buy her a poster of Dragon Man blowing balls of fire from his mouth and nostrils. It was the same picture that was on the life-size banner outside of Dragon Man's tent. Izzy bragged he would get Dragon Man's autograph for her too.

Izzy coached me about manipulating my mom and on how to twist the truth to get what I wanted.

"Hell, Francis, just tell her the truth. She will laugh and not believe you, just like my ma. If you memorized my book, you would know it is Isadore Principle number thirty-three: Tell old codgers the truth, and most of the time they will never believe you."

"I like your mom, Izzy, but your mother is naive to believe you and put up with your old man's abuse," I said. "Probably happened after your birth. You said you came out ass backward."

"It's called breech, numb nuts! Jack said it took me four days to pop out and that I damn near killed her."

"So, you're a son of a breech?"

"Ha, ha, moron. You're a regular Groucho Marx. So funny, I forgot to laugh! I just told my ma that you and I were going to drop the Worm off at the freak show while you took me into Club Libido, the nudie tent. She laughed and said, 'Have fun, honey.'"

"Izzy, you're a bullshit artist."

"Tell the truth, Saint Francis. It works almost every time."

Izzy told me he dreamed of sneaking into Club Libido, the tent with half-naked dancing girls. He said his old man used to pop a few pints at the beer garden and then get rid of Izzy and Jack by giving them a few bucks for Pronto Pups, malts, and the roller coaster. When they were out of sight, his old man slipped into the girlie show.

All I wanted was to meet Fat Albert, the Fattest Man in the World. I had read about him in the *Guinness World Records* book.

Our promise of Dragon Man had Mandy more excited than she was each Fourth of July. She jumped around like a bottle rocket on the bus ride to the fairgrounds and kept pestering us with questions about Dragon Man.

"How come Dragon Man does not burn his tongue off?" she asked.

"Cause he's sucking on ice cubes. He can't taste the kerosene or feel the fire," Izzy said.

Mandy stomped her feet. "How does he walk on the burning red-hot coals?"

Izzy laughed at her antics. "He does voodoo magic and hypnotizes himself. They say he yells out 'Cool moss' while jumping around like a kangaroo."

"Izzy, what is hypnotize?"

"Well, Miss Worm, it's like when you're sleeping, dreaming—you have unknown Superwoman-like powers."

"Could I spit fire?" she asked.

Izzy took her sun visor and pulled it over her head, covering her face. "If you do, I'll have to wash your mouth out with toilet water to put it out."

Mandy insisted she wanted to join the carnies and work at the fair when she was older. She was so happy that day and kept waving at cars out the bus window. She then turned to me for her next question, looking for a serious answer.

"Francis, it would be fun living with the carnies, the state fair people. Can I do that when I grow up?"

I pulled out a bag of M&M's, letting her grab a fistful.

"Mandy Paulson, you can do or be anything you want, and I know you will."

Izzy corrected me. "Wrong again, big brother. She can't be pope. Only you or I could be pope. Girls don't have the right equipment. But she could be the freak show's Worm Lady and get to eat all the free candy, ice cream, and pop on the Midway."

Mandy's tongue was gross when she started talking; her mouth was still full of M&M's.

"And could the Worm Lady help out Dragon Man by throwing water on his audience if they caught fire?"

That inspired Izzy to rise from his seat and, standing on it, he addressed the packed bus full of passengers going to the fair. He pretended he was a freak show carnival barker. He pointed at Mandy, who was now kneeling, and spoke loudly: "Ladies and germs. You are all state fair bus friends, so I will let you into my freak show on a children's ticket. Two for a nickel, one for a dime."

He boosted Mandy from between us and made her stand in the aisle.

"You will meet this amazing woman, Mandy, the Amazing

Worm Lady. She walks, she talks, she crawls on her belly. She eats dirt and has scales! She has not taken a bath in months! Everyone gets in on a children's ticket!"

Izzy sat down. Most passengers were laughing. A few applauded. One guy gave Mandy a dime. My sweet little sister was enjoying all the attention.

Last year was my best fair ever, Mandy's too. Maybe kissing Susan would have topped it. Izzy was disappointed he did not get to peek at the Club Libido ladies' brassieres and short skirts that afternoon, but he loved it when we got to hang out with Fat Albert.

Fat Albert was originally from South Africa, and he sat on a special platform, a giant chair that the other carnies had made for him. He seemed happy, had a nice laugh, and claimed we were his favorite customers all season from all his traveling carnivals.

"Why is that, Mr. Albert?" Izzy asked.

"You can call me Al—that is what my real friends do. You men treat me with respect, like a real guy. You ask me about my favorite baseball team, not how many loaves of bread or pounds of chocolate I eat each day."

Al said that he got paid to take a lot of abuse, and if he mouthed off he would get fired. He said that by being a freak, he saw the best and worst of people, like the smart-aleck teenage boys who asked how he could find his penis with all his belly rolls, and the junior high girls who wrote and performed their poem in front of him one morning.

"Albert, Albert two by four, he can't fit through the bathroom door. So, he did it on the floor, licked it up, and did some more!"

"What did you do to them?" Izzy asked.

"I did what any parent should do if they had she-devils like that. I scared the crap out of them."

"How so, Mr. Albert?" Izzy asked.

"I made sure the boss was not around. Then I took them out back and showed them the outhouse the crew made for me. I said it was deep enough that when I tossed them down there, it would be like quicksand—nobody would ever find them. They started crying and ran away."

"No shit," Izzy said.

Al started laughing, spitting out part of the taco we had bought for him.

"Yes shit! I was bullshitting them. I use a real toilet. I just crouch and hover and don't put my full-ass weight on the seat. They just built the outdoor toilet as a prop for my show."

We left, but not before Al handed us a bunch of free passes to give to our friends to see his show and other Midway shows, and he made us promise to come back next year to talk about whether his World Series prediction had come true. He said Carl Yastrzemski and the Boston Red Sox would beat the St. Louis Cardinals in seven games.

The Dragon Man show was the most expensive on the Midway and well worth the fifty cents. Izzy and I lied about our age to get in on a children's ticket.

It was my finest moment as a big brother when I pointed to Mandy, hoping Dragon Man might include her in the show. He called my little sister to come up on the stage and then put a real fireman's hat on her head.

"What's your name, pretty girl?"

"Mandy Paulson."

"Now, Pretty Mandy Paulson, I'm going to ask you a few questions, and if you answer them correctly, I will give you my autographed Dragon Man poster for your room. Deal?"

Mandy nodded her head. "Deal, Mr. Dragon Man."

"OK, first question. Would you like some free candy? You do like candy?"

"Yes, Mr. Dragon Man."

"Oh, that's too bad. I'm all out of cinnamon fireballs." The crowd laughed, but my sister was too excited to understand that the joke was on her. "Let's try this one next, Miss Pretty

Girl Mandy."

Dragon Man handed her a foot-long giant match prop. "Have you ever played with fire?"

Mandy lied. "No, Mr. Dragon Man."

"So, you have never, ever played with fire, Miss Mandy?"

"No, sir."

"Have you ever had a birthday cake?"

"Yes, sir."

"Were there candles on your cake?"

"Yes."

"Did you blow out those candles, Miss Mandy?"

"Yes, sir."

"Did you blow out all of the candles, or maybe leave one burning?"

Mandy answered his question straight as an arrow. "Last year, I could not blow them all out. Two kept burning."

"Ah! So, you have played with fire! Miss Mandy, the saying goes that you have one boyfriend for every flame left burning . . . You are way too young for a boyfriend and especially for two of them!" The crowd roared with laughter. Dragon Man danced around Mandy while juggling flaming torches.

Next, Dragon Man gave Mandy a tiny squirt gun. He told her to sit in the front row between her two big boyfriends and squirt it at him every time he said the word *fire*. Dragon Man asked the onlookers to give Mandy a "fiery round of applause."

As Mandy walked off the stage, he spat a cloud of mist over her head. It burst into a long stream of flames. Mandy was startled. She turned around to squirt some water at him.

"Too late, Miss Mandy. You're fired!"

The crowd loved it, and they loved Mandy. I was so happy. Izzy was too. Mandy would never forget that August day with Dragon Man. My sister would have stayed all night to see the Dragon Man's show again and again, but I had promised Mom we would all be back before dark.

On the way home, my sister fell asleep on the bus clutching her squirt gun, poster, and Dragon Man's autographed card.

Suddenly, Izzy and his bike attacked me out of nowhere, shaking me awake from my freak-show daydream. Then all hell broke loose.

35

Popular Park Torched

JUNE 5 AND 6, 1968

Now Mount Sinai was all in smoke because the Lord descended
upon it in fire; and its smoke ascended like the smoke of a furnace,
and the whole mountain quaked violently.

—EXODUS 19:18

When Izzy and his bike crashed into me, it knocked me off the tire swing and out of my daydream trance about last summer's fair.

He was panting. I was lying flat on the ground, looking up at him. Then in a coarse, rasping, wheezing voice he forced out, "Fire, fire! The park is on fire!"

It was the last day of school. Mom had called Sister so the nun could inform me that my mother would be meeting at the church with the Rosary Society and Mandy was staying overnight at her friend's house. That meant I did not have to babysit. Dad and Cigar Ron were running about town paying off winning tickets, so fortunately, it was just Izzy and me at home as I tried to figure out what was happening.

"Holy fuck, Francis! I'm in deep sewage!"

I had never seen my friend so alarmed and fearful.

"Izzy, your old man will kill you," I said. "You smell like a thousand cigars. What happened?"

"Francis, I messed up big time. If they catch me, I'm going to jail. I need to hide in your basement and change into your clothes. Do you still have your old school uniform from last year?"

The bottoms of his blue uniform corduroys were charred, and there were cigarette burns on his shirt. I knew I was all in. I needed to help him. My best friend was way out of sorts.

"Francis, I think someone might have seen my uniform as I biked from the fire. They might know to go to Holy Family and look me up!"

I pointed to the sky over the Mississippi River near Cherokee Park.

"Do you mean *that* fire?"

I brought him inside so the neighbors would not see or hear his frenzied meltdown. Izzy stripped, threw his charred clothes in a brown grocery bag, and jumped in our shower. He forgot to close the curtain. Water started seeping onto our linoleum bathroom floor. I shut it, sopped up the floor flood, and asked him to calm down until he was finished.

"Use my robe when you get out. It is on the door hook."

Izzy plopped on the hallway floor outside the bath. I sat across from him, noticing his feet were bright red and blistered as though badly sunburned. He confessed that he had accidentally started a grass fire at Cherokee Park with a magnifying glass.

"I was bored. Just screwing around on my way home from school. It took a long time to get the dry leaf going. The sun pierced through the lens with a small dot of focused heat. I kept a tiny hot blue bead on the leaf that I had placed on top of a crumpled tissue and a pile of brown grass. It burned a hole through the leaf and tissue, then it sparked up and caught on to more dead grass."

Izzy said the burning leaves and grass smelled good, so he added more and got his lips close, blowing until the smaller flames took off, catching the surrounding grass and debris. Soon it grew to the size of a basketball.

I could not believe what I was hearing. "What were you thinking, Izzy?"

"The only thing I thought was to piss it out, but I could not get my stream going. Then the wind kicked up, and I was stomping around in the flames like a fucking moron. My uniform cuffs caught fire. I tried to beat it out with my Twins hat but lost it to the fire. I jumped on my bike and pedaled to Joe's General and then to you."

Izzy said the fire had its own mind and started creeping up the hill toward the outhouses and picnic shelter at Cherokee Park. He prayed to Saint Jude that it would not make it to Mr. Zainey's house and, if it did, that the wheelchaired old man would make it to safety.

"Francis, my throat was raw from the smoke, so I chugged two sodas at Joe's. I was shaking like crazy. Joe had some dumb high school chick working, and she had no clue I was totally messed up."

Izzy said he heard the fire trucks as they raced to the park, their lights flashing and sirens blaring.

"My God, I am such a moron, Francis. I promised God a whole bunch of shit if he made it right so no one died and I don't get caught."

Izzy was right. It was a big fire. Late that night we could still smell the odor of burnt grass, leaves, trees, and the wooden outhouses and large picnic shelter, which were all devoured by the inferno.

Mom told me that everyone at the Rosary Society was talking about it. They prayed a Rosary for lives of the property owners. Dad said that he and Cigar Ron stopped driving to gawk at the sky, before they knew what was going on.

The next day, June 6, the *St. Paul Pioneer Press* published a special edition newspaper with a large front-page headline: *Death of Hope: Bobby Kennedy Shot.*

The senator from Massachusetts had just won the California Democratic primary and a huge chunk of delegates. The young senator was shot up close with a handgun, not far away with a powerful scope and rifle like his big brother, President Kennedy.

Later, I learned that the killer, Sirhan Sirhan, decided to gun Bobby Kennedy down on the first anniversary of the start of the Arab-Israeli Six-Day War. They said he hated the Kennedys for their support of Israel. His family had immigrated to America from Jordan when he was a teenager. He refused to become a US citizen.

They scheduled his trial in California, and if convicted, he could get electrocuted since they have capital punishment there.

The Cherokee Park fire would have made the front page, but the senator got that spot, as he should have. Still, the metro section gave the fire as many photos and columns as the front page gave the assassination: *Arsonist Escapes, Popular St. Paul Park Torched.*

The writer said that the City of St. Paul had to call in extra fire trucks from South St. Paul and West St. Paul because their stations could not handle it alone.

The Worm surprised me, showing up right after Izzy had cleaned up and left. She was barefoot. Her feet were dirty, and her hair was all messed up.

"Mandy, I thought Mom said you were staying overnight at Heather's? Where did you get that Pebbles Flintstone sweatshirt and those jean shorts?"

"I changed my mind, Francis. I wanted to be here with you, watch TV, and eat pizza together on our last day of school, so Heather's dad dropped me off at Joe's to get my end-of-the-school-year free soda pop and chips. Then I skipped home. Izzy gave me the clothes from his cousin Crystal. Her mom was going to give them to the Goodwill."

"Mandy, didn't you see the blaze or hear the sirens rushing to the fire?" I asked.

Mandy opened the back-porch screen door, dropped her book bag on the steps, and said, "What fire?"

36

Dr. Flannagan

SCHOOL CARNIVAL, JUNE 1968

So, whoever knows the right thing to do and fails to do it,
for him it is a sin.
—JAMES 4:17

Sister handed me Holy Family's carnival candy money to give to my father, but I planned to put it in my safe instead. If I added it up correctly, I now had more canoe funds than if I'd been allowed to keep my peanut-brittle wages. However, the outfitter fees had increased, and I had my eye on a ring at Woolworth's that I wanted to give to Susan for her birthday in July. It looked like sterling silver, and it had a fake ruby in it. Ruby was her birthstone. I still had until July to raise the rest of my money for the canoe trip.

Placing the last bill in my palm, Sister said, "Francis, you and Isadore did a wonderful job on the carnival games."

I tightened my fist around the cash. Sister patted my shoulder. "That's nineteen dollars for your father, and tell him your baskets were fantastic!"

Every year, Holy Family School celebrated the end of school with a carnival where we got to eat hot dogs off the grill, snack on popcorn, and play games. After carnival expenses, any money the school earned was supposed to be donated to the March of Dimes, though I also figured out a way to get a cut for myself this year.

Our assignment was completed. Izzy and I had come up with three games that didn't cost a lot of money and that all ages could play.

I got Dad involved, and because he made money off the big all-school candy-bar fundraiser, he donated all the candy for our carnival. Only I did not tell Sister that. I charged her half, keeping the rest.

The tug-of-war and gunnysack-race winners just got a piece of penny hard candy. My windfall came from ripping off a cake walk idea from Grandma Patricia's church festival. Izzy and I called it the May Basket Walk. Dad donated empty unsold Easter baskets and allowed us to choose thirty dollars' worth of treats and prizes to fill them with.

It took us four hours to gather the treats and toys that we knew our classmates would love. Duncan yo-yos were a hot commodity, and Dad had bought too many for our store's Easter baskets. Our candy factory packer filled the baskets with candy that included a plush bunny holding a yo-yo as the basket's centerpiece. Dad charged me only a quarter for each leftover yo-yo. Izzy and I spent the next Saturday at school creating twenty-six baskets, each featuring a Duncan yo-yo.

The math worked out perfectly. We arranged fifteen squares into a large circle in the gym. That would accommodate fifteen walkers at a time. A dime to play meant one and a half bucks every game. Twenty-six games equaled thirty-nine dollars collected.

The May Basket Walk was the most popular event. Students stood in line for over twenty minutes hoping they'd land on the winning square when the music stopped. Sister paid me nineteen dollars to cover what she thought she owed for the candy, and we raised twenty dollars for the March of Dimes.

I jammed Sister's money into my pocket. Izzy left for home,

but I stayed to help Susan clean up. She oversaw that committee and had begged me to help. We were both working on cleaning the glass on the inside of the popcorn machine when she found a few popped kernels and put them to my lips. I stuck out my tongue, accepted them, and started chewing. Then she dropped her bomb.

"Francis, I have something important to talk about, and it can't wait. Please walk me home. I'd like for you to meet my father."

I needed to get home and bank my money, and this did not sound good.

"Why your father, Susan? Please don't blame me for what Izzy did to you at the carnival today. I'm not him."

"Trust me, Francis. This is not about Izzy. It is about your family."

"Me? My family? Your dad already did his part for my family when he helped Shannon."

Susan dropped her eyes, hurt by my suspicions. "Please trust me, Francis. Neither I nor my father will harm you or Izzy."

"OK. But I need to call my mom first to let her know I'll be late. Can I borrow a dime to use the pay phone in the cafeteria? I don't want our principal listening in if I use her phone."

I had to call and hang up and then call again, using the code, to get my mom to answer. The second time I called, she picked up on the second ring. "Hi, Mom. Susan Flannagan doesn't have a ride home, so I'm walking with her. Sorry for the late notice, but I won't be home for supper."

I sensed Mom was uncomfortable with the idea.

"Will her parents be home?"

"Yes. Dr. Flannagan will be. I don't know about her mother."

"Are you sweet on her?"

"Sweet on Susan's mother?" I shot back. Susan was smiling. She'd heard my comment.

"No, wise guy. Sweet on her. Susan?"

I lied. "No! Don't be silly. Just getting her home safely."

"Her friends can't walk her?"

I lied again. "No one else is here anymore. She was on the cleanup committee, and I stayed to help. Dr. Flannagan is busy so he can't pick her up, but he knows I'm bringing her home. He expects us."

Mom got way out of sorts when I mentioned the doctor a second time.

"Ah, ah, well, OK, I guess. Call. I mean, if it . . . gets too late . . . call. If you need a ride, after dark, that is."

Mom had never mentioned Dr. Flannagan or Shannon again since locking herself in the bathroom that awful day my father lectured me on how to "man up" and stay strong.

The lawn in front of the Holy Family statue was already green, and it was a perfect late-spring afternoon.

"May I carry your books, Susan?"

She removed her powder-green jacket and handed it to me. Susan was not wearing tights under her plaid uniform skirt. I stole a peek at her bare legs and the freckles on both her knees.

"You are so sweet, Francis. I'll handle my books, but I'm getting warm. Maybe you can haul my coat?"

She bent down and slipped off her uniform shoes and white bobby socks, tucked both socks into one shoe, and handed them to me to haul along with her coat. I was wondering what she might remove next.

"I love walking on the boulevard grass barefoot. It's so soft. You should try it sometime."

I tried to be witty, make her smile. "Not me. I'm afraid of stepping on a bee, or worse yet, dog poop."

On our walk, Susan explained what the meeting with Dr. Flannagan was about, and when she did, I felt like the dumbest jackass in all of St. Paul. Minneapolis, too. Susan knew things about Mandy that I ignored or did not want to acknowledge. She told me how sweet my sister was and how much she looked up to me.

"She even loves that crazy Izzy almost as much as she loves you." Susan unwrapped a Tootsie Pop and gave it to me after she had taken the first lick. "You two boys are always looking out for her, and I don't think you see her suffering. She also has a big crush on Izzy. Francis, that's why I want you to meet my father. I think Mandy needs more help than you, Izzy, or I can give her. Someone needs to help her with her fascination with fire before she hurts herself."

I learned that Susan knew things about my family that even I did not know. In my heart, I knew Susan would not hurt me, Mandy, or my family, but why should she get involved? I felt ignorant, vulnerable, and exposed when she told me more.

"So, you know about Mandy's playing with fire?" I asked.

"I only know about her dangerous fascination with fire, and about just one fire. The one at the park that she accidentally started, which Izzy took the blame for."

"Oh my God, Susan! Izzy lied to me about starting the Cherokee Park fire?"

"Yes, Francis, but only to protect your sister and your family. You already lost one sister to fire, and then you lost your grandmother to cancer. Izzy said your family was having a tough time, and he thought he was helping by covering up the Cherokee Park accident."

"You actually talked with Izzy?"

"Yes, I did. Miracles do happen, Francis. When we were through, he called me Susan for the first time. I think he knew that I really don't despise him and realized that we just started annoying each other back in fifth grade and it got out of control. Francis, he even touched me, shook my hand. He made me laugh when he asked if he could still call me Suck-Up Sue occasionally so he would have something to say in confession."

"Wow. Maybe he won't be so jealous of my being your friend anymore."

She was holding my free hand. I did not want her to let go,

but she reached down to the grass and plucked a big yellow dandelion and handed it to me.

"I promised Izzy, and you, too, that no one needs to know about the park fire. Not even my father. No one got hurt, so the only people who would be destroyed now would be your family, and especially Mandy."

"Susan, that is wonderful. My folks are already under a lot of pressure."

Susan stopped walking and said, "Izzy loves you and Mandy like he did his own brother, Jack. I don't like being an only child. It's lonely sometimes. If I ever have children, it will be at least three or more. Maybe someday, I'll even have friends as close to me as you three are to each other."

I regifted her flower. Placing it behind her ear under a bobby pin, I said, "Susan, you already have that friend. You already do."

"Francis, I'm glad you mentioned your other sister. You don't speak about her to anyone. However, Mandy did. Why she chose me I do not know, but she did. Do you know she does not even know her twin sister's name?"

"Her name was Shannon."

"No, Francis! Her name *is* Shannon! She is not dead. Just missing, at least for now."

"But how did Mandy come to you?"

"It all slipped out when Sister told us to have our former classroom buddies draw a picture of the people they loved most— people they wanted everyone to pray for over Lent. Father blessed the drawings and put them in a big wicker basket in front of the altar through Easter Sunday."

Susan then bragged about how Mandy was great at art. She used paints and colored pencils for the assignment. Most of Mandy's classmates just drew their people with crayons.

"Your sister has a gift, a talent for telling a story with her artwork, and she spent two class periods on it. I wish you could have seen all of them. They were beautiful, in a sad way, but very touching. She told a story way beyond what most children her age could express. I think she was asking for help through her artwork. She gave them all to me after they were handed back."

I was glad Susan had seen the drawings but angry that I had not.

"I'm her brother. She should have painted her story for me."

Susan brushed aside my anger and finished her story before we got to her front yard. "Mandy's picture had your family all close together. Your sister said the two older ladies were her grand-mothers. One was lying on a bed with her eyes closed, and a glass of water was on her stomach. Mandy later told me that it was her fault your grandmother died. She said it happened because she had spilled ice on her."

"Yep. She's right. That's what happened. Just Izzy, Mandy, and I were there. Minutes later, she died in front of us. Nuns were running everywhere. Mandy could not stop crying until Izzy took her down to the cafeteria and bought her an Eskimo Pie. I was on the phone with my father while a kind nun watched over me. It was the worst day of my life, but it was not Mandy's or anyone else's fault."

Susan described the other people in my sister's prayer chain. Our other grandma was kneeling at a Communion rail. Mom, Dad, Izzy, and I were standing in front of the Dairy Queen, all holding ice cream cones. Mandy was in the middle with a cone in her left hand and a garden hose in her right. Then there was a second drawing of herself, in which she was standing alone across the street and holding a torch with a red flame in front of her face.

Susan continued. "I asked her why she drew herself twice."

I sat down on the curb, taking in what Susan was sharing. I put my head in my hands, trying to cover my tears and forgive my stupidity. Mandy was not too little to remember. She remembered that day, no different than I did, over and over.

"Susan, the girl across the street with the fire in her face was Shannon. Mandy is still praying for Shannon, trying to save her from the stove burns!"

Susan tossed her books on the boulevard and sat next to me. She took her jacket and shoes and laid them on top of her books. Then she placed my hand in hers.

"Francis, my father told me about the tragedy the day he met you at the hospital. He told me what you did to save Shannon's life."

My eyes stung from tears. They were burning, and my gut ached. I felt like I might throw up.

"Susan, how come you never said anything to me before?"

"No, Francis! How come you never said anything? You should not keep stuff like this inside. It must have been awful for both of you. I wanted to help, but it was your private business. I did not know you well enough, but now I'm taking that risk."

I looked over at Susan for more help. Her face was a blur. "What do I do now?"

"Well, maybe go to your folks. I went to my father because I was not sure of the right thing to do either. I think my dad can help your family. Just hear him out. If you want to pretend this day never happened after that, I will never bring it up again and neither will my father. He promised me as much."

When I left Dr. Flannagan's office den, I felt relieved and hoped Mom would meet with him too to get help for Mandy. Susan was in her bedroom the whole time, so it was just me and the doctor. Dr. Flannagan insisted our conversation would go no further without my permission.

With his work at the hospital's burn unit, he said he knew some fine people who could help Mandy before her situation became more dangerous. There was a name for her problem. It was called pyromania. It was rare in younger children; it was more likely something that teens or mentally disturbed older children and adults struggled with.

He said he was confident my sister's fascination with fire was not a mental illness, but more so a disorder that could be easily treated. He thought she was using fire to reach out for help or to feel in control. With fire, she could manage it, starting and putting it out, which gave her a sense of power.

"Francis, most of the time children cannot process tragedy like adults, so they hide from it and find ways to let off the stress from a traumatic event, especially if they have no one they feel safe with to share their feelings."

He explained that both Mandy and I had had two huge losses, first our sister and then our grandmother, and that Mandy blamed herself for losing both of them. By playing with and controlling fire, Mandy might think she could have prevented Grandma Rose from dying and also saved Shannon from falling into the flames.

"Catching pyromania early is probably the key to ensuring that your young sister lives a long and happy life," he assured me.

Dr. Flannagan then helped me role-play how to approach my mom about getting Mandy the help she needed. I laughed when he took out a wig and put it on.

"Do I now look like your mother?" he joked.

I parted with his strong handshake.

"Thanks, Doctor. I'll do my best to get Mom to call you and set up a meeting with your friend. We are a very proud family. Even though we have problems with the business, my father will want to pay something for Mandy's helpers."

"Francis, you are an amazing young man, very smart, and you have a solid, kind heart. Mandy and your folks love you very much. You leave the money thing up to me. I have a plan. Not your worry."

Susan walked me down the front steps and handed me an envelope.

"Your sister gave me this artwork yesterday. She had kept it hidden in Shannon's pillowcase. I think you should have it. Maybe it will help you to help her."

"Thank you, Susan, and tell your father thank you for his help."

Susan's back was to her front door so Dr. Flannagan could

not see when she blew me a goodbye kiss.

"See you again soon, Francis, right?"

I tipped my straw fedora toward her.

"I'll carry your coat anytime, pretty girl, but now I've got to practice my acting before I go to my mom."

When I got home, my mom was down in the basement doing laundry. Mandy was in bed. I opened the door and gave my sister the biggest good-night hug of my life. I loved that girl so much. Meanwhile, I was falling into a different kind of love with Susan.

"I love you, Mandy. Sleep tight and don't let the bedbugs bite."

My cute little sister peeked at me from under her sheet.

"And, Francis, if they do, I'll hit them with your shoe until they are black and blue."

I went to my room and opened the envelope. Inside, on pink construction paper, Mandy had drawn three separate frames, like the Sunday newspaper's color cartoons, only this one was not funny. The first box was of two little girls standing on a stool together looking into a fry pan on a kitchen stove with a big pancake in the middle. The second was one girl shoving the other with both hands. The third was the girl who had been shoved lying on the stove with her pajamas on fire.

In the few seconds I was gone, they must have been fighting over my chocolate-chip pancake. Mandy had pushed Shannon, and she placed all the blame on herself for our family losing Shannon.

That night, I slept with the crucifix Grandma Rose had given to me with my typewriter. I prayed to the only person in Heaven who was real to me, the one I knew would understand and could help my family. I asked Grandma Rose to talk to God for me.

I awoke before my alarm sounded, dreaming that Mandy, Shannon, and I were hanging out at Grandma Rose's house, watching Bugs Bunny cartoons on her TV and eating chocolate-chip pancakes for breakfast.

37

Saving Mandy

He heals the brokenhearted and binds up their wounds.

—PSALM 147:3

Sometimes it seems that when one thing goes well, others go haywire. One right, two wrong. The right thing was due to Susan and her father. Mandy's pyromania was getting under control after she began having meetings with Dr. Flannagan's friend, a child psychologist named Dr. Sharon Lee.

Dad, like I had predicted, bucked and moaned, wanting nothing to do with the program when Mom broke the news to him. He even yelled at her. The last time he swore at her was when Kevin crapped on his bowling shirt. I was so proud of Mom. This time, she held firm and did not try to pray the problem away. I'm glad she stuck to her guns, or it would have been up to me, a big kid, trying to figure out a little kid's serious troubles.

I heard my father arguing after a few beers one bowling night.

"Son of a bitch, Eleanor! There ain't nothing wrong with that girl that a harsh talking to and decent spanking won't fix. You know goddamn well we don't have hundred-dollar bills lying around like in *The Beverly Hillbillies*. Even if I did, I'd be dumber than a drunken Baptist to give our money to a head shrinker!"

Mom persisted. She took my father's pack of cigarettes and gambling tickets and threw them in the kitchen sink.

"You listen to me for once, Antonio Paulson! We've got plenty of money for your bowling, beer, smokes, and gambling, and I will

197

pay for Mandy's health and well-being!"

Dad retrieved his items from the sink.

"Besides, my mother is giving us the money, just like she would for any of her grandchildren. No one else will know about her charity but us."

Grandma Patricia was thrifty but not cheap. She scrimped and saved. She even had over three thousand dollars of real silver dollars saved in her safety deposit box, as well as my grandfather's silver coin collections. I figured she would rather have us use the money for good while she was alive. Grandma told me that when she was overly thrifty, Grandpa told her that money was like manure: she should spread a little bit around every now and then, let it do some good.

That was it. Mom won, and Dad admitted it in his own way later when he apologized. It was a happy ending when he had flowers sent to her the next week. That same night, they shut off the TV and went to bed early. They locked their door and turned their favorite radio station up loud.

Together, Mom and Mandy went to several appointments with Dr. Lee.

Mandy said, "Francis, she is so nice. She said I can just call her Sharon with no *Doctor* in front."

At other sessions it was just Mandy and Sharon. I was invited to the last one, to listen, learn, and let my sister know I would always be there for her, no matter what. Dad always had the excuse that he had to work, so he never even met Dr. Lee. He did not like or trust headshrinker doctors.

Mom said that Sharon refused payment, and when Mother insisted on fifty dollars out of the one hundred and twenty that Grandma gave us, Sharon said she would donate it to the St. Jude Children's Research Hospital in our family name.

I was trying to be calm about the two bad things that might happen. It was possible that Susan and Izzy might both go to new schools the next year. Susan's father was up for a big promotion to head up a new wing at a hotshot brand-new hospital in Houston, Texas, but he also had another opportunity at the prestigious University of Wisconsin hospital in Madison. If Dr. Flannagan was promoted to Wisconsin, I could deal with that, but Texas meant I would be boyfriend toast.

Then Izzy informed me that his old man was not wasting any more money by sending him to Trinity Catholic High School, where I would be going. Izzy even begged his old man, promising he would work all four years and pay his own way if he could swing it. I encouraged my friend.

"Maybe you can get one of the scholarships from Holy Family Parish? At least apply. I did."

"No way, Francis. They might give me one just to stay away. All that money will go to smart people like you or your pretend girlfriend, if she does not move. You both deserve it."

I then gave my friend a second suggestion.

"I know Travis's cousin got a scholarship from the brewery because his dad works there, and Travis said his cousin was only a C student. Maybe ask your old man to put in an application."

Izzy looked at me like I was from outer space and then said as much.

"Hey numb nuts, what planet are you from? The SOB hardly looks at me, and if the brewery did give him the money for my education, he would drink and gamble it all away."

38

Frank and Izzy

JUNE 1968

*And He said to them, "Follow Me and I will make you
fishers of men."*
—MATTHEW 4:19

I had a great dad. Izzy did not, but he looked up to Frank like he
was an adopted uncle after we made brittles together. Frank built
Izzy up and tried to give him confidence.

He told Izzy, "Just think of me as your chuckle uncle." Izzy
liked that.

Frank loved fishing and tried to get Izzy back into it. In
December, when we worked together, Frank would treat us to
burgers at the White Castle. He said, "My wife hated this place,
but now she is no longer here to tell me no, so your supper is
on me!"

One time Frank even brought his tackle box to the restaurant
and gave Izzy a few of his prized collection lures.

"These Lazy Ikes, Dardevles, hooks, sinkers, and bobbers
will get you started, Izzy. I've got doubles. Don't much need two
of everything. I have a rod and bait-casting reel collecting dust.
It's yours if you want it. Izzy, you are too old for that cane pole

that Francis says you use."

After Frank's wife died, Frank went fishing with his younger brother each summer. His brother never married but was devoted to his old wooden rowboat and five-horsepower Montgomery Ward's Sea King outboard. They both traveled all over Minnesota to fish and camp from Memorial Day through Labor Day.

Frank told us, "Our goal is to catch at least one fish on every one of Minnesota's ten thousand lakes."

Frank and Al, his brother, camped in tents. Frank showed me pictures of huge metal stringers of bluegills, crappie, northern pike, and walleye.

"We slaughtered them! One giant pike busted my line before Al could get the net under the monster," he boasted.

At Christmas, Frank gave a large package of frozen fish to all of us at the store: the clerks, packers, and the chocolate dippers. He added a bottle of Mogen David wine to wash them down with. He even set our family up with extra fillets, including some trout that he smoked himself.

Izzy and I were invited to a day of fishing with Frank and Al after school was out. Izzy almost said yes, but he was still afraid of getting in a boat again.

"Maybe next year, Frank. I have my paper route customers to take care of, you know?"

I knew that Izzy could get a sub. He seemed sad and unsure about his decision not to go with us. I went and had a blast. We caught our limit, and Al was great at cooking shore lunch for the three of us on his camp stove. He even brought along a fresh lemon and his homemade fry breading. I had my fill and thanked them.

"This is better than any fancy restaurant, Mr. Al."

"Thanks for the compliment, young man. When they jump from the water and into the pan, the fish always taste better, especially with good friends," he said.

We cleaned up our picnic area, putting the fish guts on a

rock out from the shore for the gulls or otters. I went for a quick swim, and then we pushed off in the boat to fish again to replace the ones we ate.

We caught our limit again well before sunset. On the way home, we all snacked on Cracker Jacks in Al's truck, and after we got gas, Frank and Al let me ride in the boat the rest of the way home. I waved at people like I was in a parade. It was a good day, but I missed Izzy being with us.

The next day, Izzy showed up on his bike early in the morning after his route, quizzing me on every detail about our fishing expedition. It seemed like he wanted to live it through me. I wanted to lecture him and did.

"Izzy, sometimes you have to take a risk. Frank likes us, and it pissed me off you were not there. Together, we would have cleaned out the lake. Rocked the day!"

"Francis, I really wanted to go, but I could not show up without the gear Frank gave me."

"What happened to the rod, reel, and lures? Did you lose them?"

"No. My old man found them when he was drunk. He ransacked my room and wanted to know where I stole them from. He took them away, but at least he didn't beat me."

"Izzy, I'll talk with Frank. Ask him to call the old man and explain."

"The old man is not your problem or Frank's, and it will just make it worse for me. When I challenge him, he doubles up on his beatdown."

I decided I would double my efforts to get my best friend back in the water, swimming, fishing, and canoeing again, and away from his crazy old man, at least for a couple of days. Maybe by Labor Day he would join Frank, Al, and me.

39

Losing Susan

JUNE 1968

Love bears all things, believes all things, hopes all things,
endures all things.
—1 CORINTHIANS 13:7

It started as one of the best Monday nights in my whole life. Susan and I were at Joe's sharing a malt on a date my mom had finally approved. Mom dropped us off before she drove to church to bake cookies for the Father's Day Mass with her Rosary Society friends. Dad, Frank, and Mandy were still at the candy factory.

Joe featured a few greasy breakfast offerings: runny eggs, limp bacon, and hash browns with Cheez Whiz on top. Each meal came with a side of Wonder Bread toast and grape jam. The only bread Joe sold was Wonder Bread.

Joe was the nicest Lutheran that Izzy and I knew, as well as the only other Lutheran we knew besides Candyman Frank. Joe liked Izzy, and Izzy liked Joe. Izzy was never a smart-ass with Joe. My buddy said that he might even turn Lutheran someday and quit praying to the Virgin Mary because of Joe. Once, he asked Joe why he sold only Wonder Bread.

"Wonder Bread? Because it's full of vitamins! You boys will

never have to swallow peas or carrots again. The missus even makes our turkey stuffing with it. She dries it out in the toaster first." He told us his missus made him turn Lutheran before she would marry him. "I was not much for going to church until I met her."

Joe came from behind the register to take an order for Susan and me.

"Joe, my friend Susan and I will share a chocolate malt, unless you have strawberry. That's her favorite."

Susan smiled at me for trying. She knew only the Dairy Queen had strawberry.

"Well then, Strawberry Sue, let's see what old Joe can do."

Susan blushed. "Chocolate will be fine, sir. Francis was just teasing me."

Joe was starting to have fun at my expense. "Well, Francis, they say teasing means loving, and I don't want to disappoint your friend. I've got frozen strawberries the missus picked in back. I'll blend up my vanilla malt with some strawberry soda syrup and those frozen berries just for Susan."

Joe told us it would take a few extra minutes to whip up our order. He plopped down a bowl of potato chips and two ice waters for us.

"The chips are on the house, while you wait."

Joe had only two choices to go with his chips for lunch or dinner: Oscar Mayer wieners or the grilled cheese made with Cheez Whiz. Both were messy to eat, and both were served on Wonder Bread buns or toast.

There were no fries at Joe's. He didn't have a deep fryer, just Old Dutch potato chips. Joe's brother-in-law worked at the Old Dutch factory and gave him a good deal on the seconds, the ones too thick, thin, or burnt around the edges. I liked them better than the good ones.

Joe also had just two ice cream flavors: chocolate and vanilla. His malts were dynamite, the best in St. Paul, but most summers

I did not have enough allowance to afford them. They butt-kicked the malts at Dairy Queen and were served in tall, pretty glassware, not wax-lined paper cups. I thought it was funny that *Woolworth's* was etched in the glass. Joe bragged to Izzy and me that he had found fifty of them at a swap meet for two dollars.

"Young men, that is just four pennies each. No need for me to get out of sorts if you boys drop one and it shatters."

His malts did not skimp on size either. One would satisfy two adults, maybe four children.

Izzy used to complain about Susan because she never went to Joe's, just the Dairy Queen since they had strawberry malts.

"She can keep herself and all her lame friends over at the DQ. They're all morons. Normal people do not wreck their ice cream with fruits and vegetables," he said.

I told Susan that Joe always treated Izzy extra nicely. "I think he knows things at home are not all whipped cream and fizzes for Izzy."

Joe always threw a couple of extra sour balls in Izzy's penny candy bag. Joe did not even call our parents the afternoon I distracted him with my candy purchase while Izzy came in the store wearing Jack's sunglasses and Chicago Cubs hat, the brim covering his whole forehead and the sunglasses hiding his eyeballs. Izzy slipped a quarter in the vending machine, yanked the knob for his pack of Old Gold Filters, and then ran like the wind.

Joe brought out our tall, frosty pink treat with two straws and then handed me one long silver spoon.

"The spoon is for you to fish out some of the bigger strawberry chunks. You know, the ones that won't fit through your straws."

"Looks great. Thanks, Joe!"

"You are welcome, Francis, but don't go advertising. I'm doing it only for you and Strawberry Sue. She reminds me of my granddaughter—pretty red hair, nice smile, just like Pamela's."

Susan removed her lips from the straw, her hazel eyes on mine.

"Francis, I'm so going to miss times like this."

"Miss? What are you talking about?"

She put her lips back on the straw, did not say anything for what seemed like forever. Then I noticed the tear on her cheek.

"My father is being transferred back to Texas. I just found out yesterday. We are selling our house and will be moving to Houston, where my dad will be the head surgeon in the new hospital's burn center."

Susan's mom barged through Joe's front door in a huge hurry.

"Sorry," she said, thrusting two dollars into Joe's hands. "Kids, we must go to the hospital right away. There has been a terrible fire."

40

Hell!

FATHER'S DAY WEEK, 1968

For everyone will be salted by fire.
—MARK 9:49

Dad had called Frank on Sunday, a full week before Father's Day, to see if he would come in and help out that week.

"I'm in a bind, Frank. I'll even throw in a case of beer and a hundred-dollar-payout All-Star Game gambling ticket."

Dad had placed a small ad in the *Pioneer Press* advertising our gourmet Father's Day mixed nuts assortment with a 30 percent off coupon. We ran out of nuts on Saturday, just a day after the promotion began.

"Francis, maybe we will turn this business around. Someday when you own it, it might be worth something. It pays to advertise, they say, and maybe they are right."

That Monday evening, the night of my date, my father left Frank in charge of the factory and asked him to watch Mandy, then he drove to the bowling alley to buy rounds of drinks. His gambling ticket had just won fifty bucks from Cigar Ron's Twins-versus-White Sox board.

Father's Day was our sixth best sales week after Christmas,

209

Easter, Valentine's Day, Halloween, and Mother's Day. The rest of the summer stunk, so it was one last shot for a good take before laying off the chocolate dippers and packers until we could hire them back after Labor Day. That's when we would start kicking in again for Halloween, Thanksgiving, and Christmas.

Mom counted out the register. We took in over two hundred eighty dollars—a daily record for June. She cashed out, wrapped the money in butcher paper, and hid the dough in the backroom freezer until dad could refigure, pull out his money for petty cash and gambling tickets, and then make the drop at the bank Tuesday morning.

Mom shut off the outside lights, then rushed me out the front door and yelled toward the kitchen. "Frank, thanks for watching Mandy, and when Antonio comes back, remind him not to forget to pick up Francis and Susan from Joe's soda counter before going home."

Mom was already running late to help bake cookies at church, but she did not complain and still picked up Susan and dropped us both at Joe's. Mandy stayed back at the factory napping on a canvas army cot in the middle room by the candy-cane table. Sometimes Mandy pretended to sleep so she could stay back with Frank instead of running errands with Mother. Frank liked having her around too.

Dad lost track of time buying rounds at the bowling alley and was late, so Frank mopped up the kitchen and must have remembered that we had run out of roasted cashews for our mixed nuts. It was a big seller, and 25 percent of the mix was cashews, not the much cheaper Spanish peanuts.

Once, after we finished making a small batch of cashew brittle for Christmas, Frank asked Izzy what the name of the half-moon-shaped nut was, which was also poison if not roasted.

"You mean cashew?" Izzy said.

"God bless you, Mr. Izzy!" Frank said laughing, and he pressed a piece of warm fresh cashew brittle into Izzy's palm.

Frank must have fired up the coconut oil in one of the smaller copper kettles. These were used only for roasting cashews so they did not pick up the peanut flavor from the large kettle we used for roasting the large redskin peanuts, as well as the smaller Spanish peanuts.

What happened after that we will never know for sure. All we know is what my sister, the fire chief, and the police sergeant told us.

Mandy was sleeping on the portable cot when two men, one fat with a ski mask, and one all skinny and dirty, bashed in the front display case window with a baseball bat. She woke up at the noise and started crying. When they heard Mandy, they came after her.

The skinny one yelled, "Shut up, little shit, or we'll kill you and the people in the back too!"

Mandy was screaming. The fat man swung the bat at her and tried to hit her in the head, but she scampered back under the candy-cane table. The fat man was too big to get under the table or reach her with his short, stubby arms and hands. The skinny man began trashing the store, looking for the money.

Frank was in the back kitchen, but he heard the commotion over his radio and the loud candy-furnace exhaust fan. He knew something was wrong, grabbed his large, long peanut brittle butcher knife, and ran to the front, leaving the hot oil unattended. He could not see Mandy and thought she was kidnapped.

The police officers said the crooks had probably been staking out the store for a while, and when they saw my parents counting out the cash at the end of each day, they planned their moves. They hit us that day because they assumed no one was there.

The robbers found the day's receipts and left. Mandy was weeping, terrified, and cowering under the long candy-cane table. She would not move or speak as Frank tried to coax her out.

The fire inspector verified that the hot oil in the back room boiled over, and, as Mandy witnessed, there was a flash, then explosions like lightning and thunder together. The firebomb lit up the whole store. The inspector thought there were more eruptions and toxic smoke when the cleaning chemicals caught fire.

Mandy told a fireman, "Mr. Frank hooked my sweater and pulled me out."

Frank used the store's long awning hook to snag her out from under the table. It was the one we used to lower the canvas on the front window when sun reflected in the glass, so it did not melt the chocolate showcase displays.

Frank pushed Mandy out the front door, telling her to run around the corner and tell Mike at Lund's Hardware to call the fire department and police.

The firefighters found Frank's body with his face wrapped in aprons, which he must have dipped in water. One of the fire extinguishers was found near his collapsed body. They thought he ran back to the kitchen and scalded his hands on the only fire extinguisher he could get close to, but it malfunctioned, and the foam did not come out. The smoke was too intense, and the exhaust fans kept sucking the flames toward the back door, blocking his exit.

Giving up on trying to save the kitchen and our business, Frank made it to the front, where he collapsed on the floor by the caramel-cutting-and-packing tables, not far from the cash register.

Two firefighters also lost consciousness and were taken to the hospital in a second ambulance. A team of physicians, headed by Susan's father, was working on Frank.

41

My Candyman Friend

Greater love has no man than this, that a person will lay down his life for his friends.
—JOHN 15:13

The firefighters were still pouring water on the roof, trying to save what was left of our factory. Mom got Mandy from Mr. and Mrs. Lund's store, took her home, and tried to soothe her.

Susan's mom had a hospital parking pass and knew her way around, so she, Susan, and I skipped past the emergency room. She got us a seat in the burn center's small gathering space while we waited for news of Frank. I thought it was odd that there were no magazines nor a drinking fountain in the waiting room. Just two ashtrays full of cigarette butts.

It seemed as if we waited forever, my nostrils burning from the hospital's ammonia and antiseptic stinks, all mixed with stale smoke just like at the Jazinski Funeral Parlor. I watched nurses come and go. I was in shock.

My date with Susan had gone so well, each of us sharing bits of ourselves with the other. We talked about our families, the war, the Beatles, our school, and our favorite Christmas gifts. Mine was my IBM electric typewriter. Susan's was a doll her grandmother brought back from Ireland. We spent the time just enjoying each other's company and sharing a malt. Then came her bad news followed by worse happenings. How fast our lives had just changed.

Dr. Flannagan came into the waiting room first. He shook my father's hand, hugged his wife and daughter, and put his arm on my shoulder. Then he addressed my father.

"I'm sorry, Mr. Paulson. We just lost Mr. Zelman, and we need to contact his family. Do you know how we can do that?"

I started to cry. Susan gave me a tissue.

"What happened, Dad?" Susan asked. "Did he suffer?"

Dr. Flannagan said, "No, honey, the burns were just to his hands and arms. He escaped the main fire. But he inhaled a lot of smoke before he made it to the front door, and even more when he passed out. His heart quit, and we could not make it start again."

Then the doctor looked at me. "I am so sorry, Francis. We did all we could for him."

Susan scooted close to me on the brown vinyl sofa. She was almost sitting on my lap and kept holding my hand after my dad went with Dr. Flannagan to give him the information for the death certificate.

Frank only had one son and a daughter-in-law. He must have told them that I liked to write poems and stories because Frank's son asked if I would read a poem of my own at his father's funeral. I was terrified, but I worked on it for the two days before the service. I practiced it on Susan beforehand.

She said, "Francis, it is splendid. You have a true gift."

Frank was a Missouri Synod Lutheran. I had never been in a Lutheran church before, but it was not that different from a Catholic one, except there was no Jesus nailed to a cross. No crucifixes were to be found anywhere—just a plain old cross and no suffering Jesus in that church. It even lacked holy water to cross myself with. I thought that was odd.

Mom instructed me that we were to sit through the whole service and not say the prayers or sing the hymns, as they were not Roman Catholic. I forgot, and when they said the Our Father,

I chimed in. It was almost the same as our Catholic Our Father.

The minister approached my seat and escorted me to the lectern for my reading. He adjusted the microphone to my height. I was nervous, but I just thought of Grandma Rose and Frank up there in Heaven watching over me. Then I looked out and saw Susan. She nodded her head and smiled.

Izzy's old man was too hungover to bring Izzy to Frank's funeral, so while I was reading my poem, Izzy was still riding his bike from the other side of St. Paul.

I read my poem calm as a smooth flowing river, with no rapids or rocks in my way.

My Candyman Friend

His strong arms stirred and poured hot bubbling treats from shiny copper kettles,
Sometimes dodging his kettles' eruptions of boiling-hot sugar lava.
"My Taffy Tattoos, not scars," he boasted,
The largest was from a batch of candy canes.
"I call it Peppermint Patti," he told me once while laughing.
His sweet treats
Peeked out of children's Christmas stockings.
Wide smiles spread across tiny faces when sampling their Christmas morning breakfast.
My candyman friend filled Easter baskets for people he never met.
Easter Joy, for He is Risen.
My friend made his tasty hard work into play,
Always humming, whistling, singing.
One Saturday, three of us tried to break The Peanut Brittle Record.
That day, my candyman friend taught me there is more to our journey than
Cooking one more batch, earning one more dollar, and making life go faster.
They say Heaven is full of love and more cotton candy than a person

could ever eat.
My candyman friend never made cotton candy.
"Just a poor excuse for a real confection," he said.
All I know for sure today is that . . .
When I join my candyman friend at the end of my journey
Together, we will break that record.

Izzy got there late but just in time to see the undertakers place Frank in the long black hearse for his final ride.

After Frank's funeral, in the darkness of the early morning, I was jarred from my sleep. I sat up in my bed in a mind fog and tried to remember what was troubling me. It was my dream, a persistent dream, one that kept circling over and over all night and into the morning.

I was holding one of the candy factory's red fire extinguishers with my left hand. It was normal in size, exactly like the ones we hung our soiled aprons on, but the letters on the service log were gigantic, written in thick black marker, taking up the whole front side. They spelled *MFP*, my initials. In my other hand, I held a gigantic eraser, like the ones the nuns used on our blackboard. I was trying to scrub away my initials, but they would not rub off.

42

Trip On!

FOURTH OF JULY WEEK, 1968

Let perseverance finish its work so you may be mature and complete,
not lacking anything.
—JAMES 1:4

I was still nine dollars short for the August canoe trip. The equipment rental price had increased. When I called, the outfitter guy said, "Sorry, sonny. Increased insurance and my land taxes went up. The crooked politicians in St. Paul just hammered you and all of my paddlers with a three percent sales tax, so you got to figure that in now too."

I replied, "Mr. Mudrick, my father says that's how they get ya. A nickel here, a dime there."

I was not sure how I would raise the extra money, but I told him to hold my reservation and I would mail him my five-dollar nonrefundable deposit. I thought he would tell me to go take a hike, thinking that a young kid would never deliver his cash, but I also sensed he liked me and wanted to keep me on the phone.

"Hey, Francis P, no worries on your deposit. Also, I won't charge you and your buddy for life jackets or for the shuttle ride if you cannot arrange your own. I have another group starting higher upstream, so I'll be going by the Nevers Dam drop-off anyways. If you bring your own fishing tackle, poles, and bait, that will knock off another three dollars and twenty cents. As for the tax, I've got to add it in. No choice, unless I want the governor to close my doors."

"I understand, sir. My father owns a candy business, Rose's Fine Chocolates, and he is not happy about the new tax either. Dad says there are only two things sure about life—death and taxes."

"Francis P, your family owns Rose's? I love their dark-chocolate seafoam candy. Could never find it when I moved my canoe outfitting business from Maine to Minnesota. You guys call it sponge. Strange name if you ask me. We named it seafoam on the coast. Every time I go to St. Paul, I stock up."

"That recipe came from my candymaker friend Frank," I said.

"Francis P, do you know what bartering is?"

"Yes, sir. When two people trade and both win."

"Right, Francis P. I propose a barter between you and myself. If you deliver me two pounds of dark-chocolate seafoam, I'll trade out the rest of your bill, except for the three percent you still owe the governor, and we won't tell him about our barter. We can save that tax and buy us a free soda pop."

I laughed. "Our secret, sir."

"Then it's a deal, Francis P! I get my chocolate fix and save on gas driving to the Cities, and you get a price break on your canoe trip."

I felt like I was reborn. I cleared my throat, making it sound deeper so as not to give away my soprano-boy joy.

"Thank you, sir!"

"And Francis P, tell Frank how much I enjoy his seafoam!"

"I can't do that," I said.

But before I could explain, he hung up the phone. My problem was solved! The trip was paid for, except for the governor's cut, and my father would never miss the two pounds of seafoam. I'd try to pay it back someday with the other funds I owed.

Dad got both editions of the St. Paul newspapers every day: the *Pioneer Press* in the morning, and the *Dispatch* in the afternoon. I only read the *Dispatch*, as the morning paper was always a mess and sometimes smelled like the bathroom.

We had one toilet in our home. Dad read the morning paper sitting on it. When my sister and I got up, we brushed our teeth over the laundry room's utility sink in the basement, awaiting our turn once Father completed his morning readings.

This Fourth of July morning, Mandy sat on a metal stool next to our basement basin, holding her crotch with one hand and flicking her broken cigarette lighter with the other. She was waiting to hear the upstairs flush so she could run and pee.

The lighter had no fluid, but she liked watching the sparks flying from its flint. She probably got blisters as she was all jacked up for the Fourth, and her two bowls of Cocoa Puffs for breakfast did not help.

"They are my baby sparklers," she said, flicking the sparks at my face.

Dr. Flannagan's friend, Dr. Sharon Lee, said it was OK for Mandy to flick the lighter as there was no real flame inside, but when it came to real sparklers, Mandy needed to be with an adult to supervise and avoid danger.

Mandy asked, "Francis, will you be my Fourth of July fireworks adult today?"

She looked so uncertain, like I might tell her to go take a hike. I so loved her baby-blue eyes. She played them on me all the time, getting me to say yes.

To Mandy, the Fourth was more fun than Santa Claus, the Easter Bunny, and Disneyland all rolled into one party package. She would count down weeks before. "Happy Fourth of July week, Francis. Happy Fourth of July eve!" Then, before the sun rose on the big day, she would jump on my bed with her metal pistol, several rolls of caps in her free fist.

"Get up, lazybones! Happy Fourth of July!"

I would put her off until most neighbors were awake, and then we'd go outside and shoot up the neighborhood.

My folks put on a big backyard picnic every Fourth with our aunts, uncles, and cousins. The men smoked and drank beer, while Dad burned hot dogs and burgers. The men, Izzy, and my older cousins played horseshoes. The younger boys and girls played croquet. Usually, the adult women just sipped Tom Collins cocktails and gossiped, probably happy they got out of cooking once per year.

After lunch, Mandy led the parade of cousins to Cherokee Park to shoot off illegal firecrackers and bottle rockets. Izzy had used his paper route money to buy them off Travis, and Travis had gotten them on his family's trip to South Dakota.

Izzy and I followed right behind Mandy during her procession. Two of my older cousins, Judy and Jill, were in high school. They were put in charge by our folks to make sure things went well.

Judy was very funny and always cracked me up. One year she dropped my father's huge watermelon on our driveway while pretending it was a basketball. She quickly brought it inside and put several Band-Aids along the crack. The following year, when the adults were not around, she blew up a watermelon with a cherry bomb for us younger cousins.

Judy and her sister, Jill, were the elders among us young punks, so they took up the rear to make sure no one strayed or got lost.

Izzy was walking backward, looking down the line, and he fired a round of caps from his pistol and shouted, "The Worm is our official Fourth of July Betsy Ross Parade Queen!"

At the park, we gathered at our secret location, forming a huge circle while Mandy passed out contraband to all of us. Last year, I scorched my thumb, and it got all black from a backfired bottle rocket. It hurt like hell for a week. I hid the blistered burns from Mom behind a big Band-Aid. This year my sister brought along a small bag of ice cubes. Handing them to Izzy, she said,

"Save these for my brother. Just in case."

I'm not sure about everything that happened between Dr. Flannagan's friend, Mom, and Mandy, but I was happy that this Fourth of July we had a great time, and no one burned their thumb off. Mandy barked orders like she was a marine master drill sergeant.

"Francis, light each sparkler with this candle. Izzy, make sure everybody puts them in the water bucket when they are finished burning."

Izzy ignored her and put his out in the dirt, not the bucket.

"What is your job, Betsy Ross Bossy Worm?" he said.

Picking up Izzy's dirty sparkler, she jabbed it at his belly and then put it in the water. "My job is to make sure you are safe!"

After dark, all the parents drove to the Cherokee Park bluffs with lawn chairs, where we watched the professional fireworks from the two sister cities, each trying to outdo the other. St. Paul's were blasted from Harriet Island, just downstream from the park. They were magnificent showers, but it was so close to us that the sounds were intense, deafening. Upriver, the displays came from Minneapolis's Nicollet Island and could not be heard, but the nonstop array of color and rockets was as good as St. Paul's and usually lasted longer.

Mandy sat between Izzy and me on the grass. She handed us an Orange Crush and a bag of popcorn she had taken from the adults' metal coolers and snack boxes.

"Thanks for watching me today, guys. It was fun!"

Izzy threw a popcorn kernel at her. "And thank you for finally being safe with all your dynamite," he told her.

Mandy got up, snuck behind Izzy, and startled him with a handful of ice cubes that she slipped down his T-shirt. Then she took off running, yelling, "Francis said you were not safe today, Izzy. Said you burned your belly button!"

Izzy socked my shoulder hard.

"Hey, I didn't do it!" I yelled.

"I know, but I can't hit a girl, even though you look like one with your Orange Crush lipstick."

My sister had lost her dangerous habit with fire. It was shaping up to be my best Fourth of July ever, and I also knew I had enough money to get Izzy back to the river. Life was good. But I wished Susan had been there with me to share the day and the evening fireworks. I was fantasizing about kissing her behind the pavilion under the exploding skies when Mom, hysterical, jerked me out of my fantasies.

"Francis, where is Mandy? We can't find Mandy!"

Everyone scattered, combing the park for my sister. Dad ran across the baseball field and to the nearest home and had them call the police. The cops were there within minutes.

They formed a search plan and handed flashlights to a dozen men. They suggested that Mandy had probably gotten lost in the dark with all the excitement, and they reiterated that the park was safe and it was unlikely she was abducted.

I interrupted the officer.

"Sir, she is not lost. Mandy knows this park as well as anyone in our city. We spend most summer Saturdays here and down the banks of the river fishing or hanging out in the caves."

The word caves alarmed the older bald-headed cop, and he pointed down the bluff to where smoke and a fire glow were now visible. He summoned a fire-and-rescue truck on his radio, and the three police officers and their German shepherd descended the bluffs to the river's edge. The older officer told the other searchers to stick with the plan at the top of the cliffs.

I had downed three Orange Crushes and had to urinate badly, so Izzy and I went to the park outhouse, which had been rebuilt after the fire. The door was locked or jammed. It would not open, and that was when we heard Mandy yelling inside.

"She's over here!" Izzy screamed.

Three football players from Henry Sibley High School ripped the door from its hinges.

Mandy emerged, looking shy and embarrassed but smiling. "Thank you, guys. Did I miss the grand finale, the big booms and sprays at the end?"

43

Testing the Waters

JULY 1968

When you pass through waters, I will be with you; through rivers,
you will not be swept away.

—ISAIAH 43:2

I did it! I had graduated from eighth grade with honors in June. My canoe funds were secured, and our outfitter reservation was ready to rock and roll.

I was still consumed with regrets and worries about having been blind to my little sister's dangerous dances with fire, and I still wasn't sure if Izzy would actually get out there and enjoy the lakes and rivers with me again.

But Izzy finally gave in.

"OK! I'll do it! Since I lost Jack, there is no one I'd rather go canoeing with than you. Maybe we'll have one last good time together before high school starts and you run off to Texas chasing a lost dream while I wither and die at public high school."

"Izzy, you're not going to prison or Vietnam, just to public school. And yes, I'm the one losing someone special, not you. I love Susan in a whole different way than I love you. Trust me, that is good for all three of us."

Izzy confided that he was not afraid of water for himself, but ever since Jack had died, he had been having night terrors that all involved others drowning, even me.

"I never died myself in those, but once my foot got tangled in weeds in the mucky bottom of a deep pond. I could not free it, and my lungs were shot from smoking. I felt them expanding out of my chest, and I thought they would burst, all full of water and blood. Before they exploded, I kicked free and swam toward the surface. When I got there, a sheet of ice had formed, and my fist could not break it. I woke up holding my throat, and I was coughing, gasping for air, and drenched in sweat."

I decided Izzy should start out by spending time on calmer waters first, so each remaining Wednesday in July, we hung out at Phalen Lake's beach. That is St. Paul's largest lake. It stretches into Maplewood, the suburb next door.

"Izzy, they have lifeguards there. The sand is soft, and the bay is calm," I reassured him.

He found a Wednesday substitute for his paper route, so we biked to the beach and played volleyball. After a game with other kids our age, we checked out the cute older girls sunning on the big dive dock at the edge of the safety buoys.

Izzy rated the girls' bodies like he was a judge at the Miss America pageant, insisting that the winners the past three years all wore similar suits.

"Red swimsuits with red high heels win every year, no matter what color hair they have or how big their knockers are," he claimed.

We clung to the dock's sides, inhaling the scent of the wet cedar planks and sneaking peeks at the ladies' bodies. Then we dove under the dock, straining our eyes between the slits to see if we could catch a glimpse of more skin from that angle. Izzy would whisper his number scores to me. "Francis, it doesn't get any better than this. Just think for a moment. Here we are underneath, with all those hot babes lying on top of us!"

The bad boy in me encouraged him.

"Right, but which one is your favorite? I think the girl in yellow with the big sunglasses looks real pretty," I said.

Izzy corrected me. "Canary Carrie? Are you nuts? She's only a five. Loses points for a one piece and no toenail polish. Now, Sock It to Me Sherry, the chick with the red-and-white polka-dot bikini, she has a body to die for, and her short hairdo shows she has confidence, probably wrestles well too, if you know what I mean."

"OK, Romeo. So how many points does Sock It to Me earn?"

Izzy used his palm to push water up into my face.

"If you'd wash out your blind eyeballs, you'd see she is a strong seven. I'd have to have a conversation to give her a higher rating. She looks hot, but I can't get the total picture until she speaks. Could be dumber than a doorknob."

I laughed. "And Sherry told me your tiny dock doesn't quite reach the water either. I'm curious, what does it take to earn a ten, Izzy?"

"Very simple. Any babe on that platform wearing a cellophane bikini would rate a ten."

Izzy started climbing the ladder to strike up a conversation with Sherry to get her to speak. I followed, and when he approached her, I shoved him off the dock and swam like a shark, beating him back to shore.

We always ate lunch at the same picnic table in the shade under a large elm. Izzy had made peanut butter sandwiches at his house, with no jelly as it would make the bread soggy. Our bottles of Orange Crush were from my fridge and warm as piss by lunchtime. I never bothered with ice.

We brought a dime or two for when the ice cream truck rolled through the parking lot dinging its bell. I got a Fudgsicle, and Izzy got a Malt Cup. One time it was a new driver, a pretty college woman. Her dark hair was done up in a bun and tucked in under her ice cream hat, which was in the shape of a cone. She usually worked in the office, but on this day, she was driving the route because the regular guy was on vacation.

Izzy tested out his ice cream joke on her.

"Hi, ma'am. My name's Izzy, and I want to own a truck of my own someday. Did you have to go to sundae school to learn how to serve ice cream, wear the hat, and ring that bell?"

She took the bait, without missing a beat.

"No, little boy! But I learned how to crush nuts."

Izzy was thrown for a loop and almost left his treat on her counter, but he recovered like he always did.

"You mean for sundaes, right?"

"Not always. That's fifteen cents. Ten for the Malt Cup, and five more for me putting up with your lame joke."

44

Minneapolis Parade

END OF JULY 1968

Everyone who hates a brother or sister is a murderer,
and you know no murderer has eternal life residing in him.
—1 JOHN 3:15

Izzy was almost begging.

"Francis, help me, please? My old man is making me go to the parade, and my mom said I could bring a friend. He and the guys at the brewery are driving the Hamm's Beer float."

The float was a favorite every year at Minneapolis's annual Aquatennial celebration. The company spent big bucks having it professionally decorated. It was over thirty feet long and eight feet wide, and it featured a massive statue of the black-and-white Hamm's Bear mascot sitting on a giant beer can. This year they added a beaver chewing on a pine tree. If it fell, it would crush the bear's head. They figured out how to get water pumped and flowing through a pretend river around a beaver dam. We watched as the men poured in the blue dye, getting the water to the sky-blue tone they needed. The Hamm's Beer jingle, the same one that was in all the radio and TV commercials, blasted from the float's large megaphone speakers:

From the land of sky-blue waters,
From the land of pines, lofty balsams,
Comes the beer refreshing,
Hamm's, the beer refreshing,
Brewed where nature works her wonders,
Aged for many moons, gently mellowed,
Hamm's, the beer refreshing.
Hamm's, the beer refreshing.

Izzy begged me to go help pass out candy and to ask my mom if he could stay at our house for the weekend. He said his old man would be mean after drinking on the float all night.

"My mom is visiting her sister in Rochester. She promised to help after my aunt's surgery at the Mayo Clinic. My aunt has lung cancer. She switched to Lucky Strike filters from Lucky straights a year ago, but it was too late."

I knew Mom was OK with Izzy hanging around. She knew things with his old man were rotten. She liked Izzy. Izzy would easily strike up adult conversations with Mom about just about anything. Mom even knew Izzy snuck smokes. I knew she saw him out back once, but she never challenged Izzy or lectured me about it.

In a way, Mom took over for Grandma Rose with Izzy. She was like a stepmom to him. Izzy hated his old man, but he loved my mom almost as much as he loved his own. I just could not figure out why his mother stayed married to the old man, failing to protect Izzy. Izzy said it was because she was Catholic, and Catholic women can't get divorced.

"Even if their lives are shit. No can do," he told me over and over. "Pope says so."

The parade started out smooth, and the crowds were having fun despite the hot, humid July evening. The floats were lit with multicolored bulbs, and thousands of kids and adults lined the route. Izzy's old man and his beer buddies were in a brand-new

Ford pickup truck, sipping suds and taking turns driving.

I yelled at Izzy through my oppressive bear mask, inhaling the stench of my own breath.

"You did not tell me we had to wear hotter-than-Hell bear suits to do this. I can hardly see, and it smells like a steamy, moldy bathhouse in here. My glasses are fogged."

My bear head muffled Izzy's reply, but I'm sure some little kids heard him swear.

"Shut your cakehole, Baby Bear Fran, and I'll buy you two Orange Cs when we are through. If you see Goldilocks, give her a Tootsie Roll, a grind in her butt, and a French kiss."

We were marching alongside the float with a dozen other brewery brats, listening to the same drumbeat and jingle over and over and placing candy in eager young hands. A couple of twin girls who looked to be about three years old started bawling when we approached them.

Their mom was way cool. She laughed. "Don't worry, bears, you're OK. They'd have the heaves if you were clowns. You're doing a good job. Must be hot under those masks."

It was hot across America that week. There were race riots in Detroit and Chicago, and then they happened here.

It started when two policemen roughed up a couple of ladies. The police arrested them, taking them to the station. The *Pioneer Press* later said the women got into a fight along the parade route, maybe over a guy or maybe because they were just drunk as skunks.

The ruckus took place two blocks behind our float, near the Brady High School marching band. The gals started screaming and tussling in the middle of the street, pushing the marchers and their instruments to the sidewalk.

The parade continued, but word got out about the cops roughing up the women, and an angry group gathered on their behalf and started marching across the bridge to Plymouth Avenue. Minneapolis was no different than Detroit, Chicago, or LA.

After the parade, on the drive back to my house, Izzy's old man kept ranting about the incident.

"Those SOBs ruined everyone's clean fun. Should not have come to our parade!" He pulled into our drive, still grumbling, getting in his last words. "You boys get some sleep. I'll be up all night with my gun. If they come to St. Paul, they will regret it. Hope your friend Clinton is not one of them."

When we got out of the car, Izzy sighed. "What an asshole."

We watched the riots on TV for two days. Some of the rioters committed assaults, vandalism, and arson. Many looted all night. It was happening only sixteen miles away from my house. Ten Jewish-owned businesses were burned. A Molotov cocktail was thrown at the home of a Jewish city councilman in Minneapolis. The mayor dispatched his police force with riot helmets and shotguns to take back control of the neighborhood. Then he had the governor call up six hundred members of the National Guard who worked around-the-clock shifts to gain control of the streets.

Firefighters were pelted with rocks while trying to save buildings. No one died, but many were hospitalized. Only thirteen were arrested, including two boys our age.

The excitement kept Izzy and me up late talking both nights that weekend. I was troubled by the violence and could not fall asleep, even after Izzy started snoring.

On the second morning, my father woke me before Izzy got up. He took me into our kitchen, handing me a glass of fresh-squeezed orange juice along with a glazed donut.

"Francis, when Izzy wakes up, have him talk to your mother. She is good with things like this."

"Things like what, Dad?"

"Izzy's father is in jail. They let him make a second phone call because Izzy's mom or aunt did not answer at three in the morning in Rochester. He needed bail money. I offered to help, but he said it was his problem, not mine."

I took in my dad's eyes. They looked more hopeless than sad

or worried.

"Dad, we were with him, and he was angry when he dropped us off, but he is always that way. What did he do that they put him in jail?"

"Well, I wondered the same thing, Francis, so I called the police station and talked to my friend there."

Dad poured me another glass of orange juice, motioning for me to sit down and drink it.

"The cop bowls in the same league as I do," he continued. "He said Izzy's father was crazy drunk and threatened some teens near his house shortly after midnight. He had his gun, and he even shot it into the sky to scare them off as he approached their van. I guess he thought they were coming from Minneapolis to riot, but they were just local kids necking and playing loud music."

45

Kiss

AUGUST 1968

How can a young man keep his way pure?
By keeping it according to Your word.
—PSALM 119:9

After eighth-grade graduation, Susan moved to Texas with her mom to live with her aunt and uncle while her father stayed back to sell their home and prepare for his promotion at the new hospital in Houston. Her mother was still the top fundraising organizer in Texas for St. Jude Children's Research Hospital.

Susan once met Danny Thomas and Lucille Ball at a Houston charity event. I thought that was way cool. Mr. Thomas was a devout Catholic and a long-time friend with Lucy and her husband Desi Arnaz. They all worked at the same TV network.

At the charity event, Mr. Thomas gave Susan an autographed prop from one of Lucille's funniest episodes, in which Lucy and Ethel took a job in a chocolate factory to show their husbands they could earn money too. It was an empty black-and-white chocolate box that said *Kramer's Kandy Kitchen* on the front with an embossed picture of a candy kettle and a wooden paddle. Both Lucille Ball and Vivian Vance had autographed it. When Susan opened the box, there was also a small sequined purse with a note from Mr. Thomas saying what a wonderful person Susan's mom was and how she had helped so many kids at St. Jude with her volunteer work.

That sad day in June, I biked over to Susan's house to say goodbye. I pretended I was happy for her family, but I was all torn up inside. I was going to miss her. She saw through me and tried to make me laugh.

"Thanks for coming over and helping my mom and dad, Francis. I'll be back in August to annoy you at least one more time."

I forced a weak smile.

"Susan, I don't know if I can hold my breath that long."

We had become close, and I wanted to be much more than her friend. I wanted to kiss her, see what it was like. We shared just about anything when others were not listening or chaperoning us. We talked about losing our grandmothers. I spoke freely about missing Shannon, trying to help Izzy, and my shame in not realizing the seriousness of Mandy's fire play.

One night on her back steps, she held my hand and said, "That's what I love about you, Francis. You try to protect and take care of everyone. Like an adult. You don't look for flaws or expect perfection. That is your gift. You are a giver."

That was the first time a girl used the word *love* on me. That night I wrote her exact words down in my journal.

Susan had taken Mandy under her wing too, like the little sister she never had. My mom even let Susan paint Mandy's fingernails and toenails. My sister did not wash her hands for a whole day, afraid the polish might come off. Mom did make her remove the polish before Sunday Mass.

Susan was patient and kind to Izzy after she knew about his old man beating on him and his fear of water. She encouraged me with my plan to get him on the river canoe trip and helped me with some good ideas.

Izzy was still unpredictable. Even though I thought he had

gotten over my liking Susan, he was still jealous of my friendship with her, like I had to pick between the two of them. I started the only fistfight of my life while hanging out with him one day in the cave. After drinking one of his old man's beers, he said, "Anyone that hangs with a skunk weasel witch like Suck-Up is worth less than a wet turd."

I was already depressed and blue about losing Susan, so I shoved him. He shoved back. Then we went at it with fists and arms flailing. I won only because I was not drinking. I pinned him to the cave floor and made him eat sand.

After the fight, I felt awful and could not sleep. We avoided each other for two weeks. Then he just showed up at my house on his bike on a Sunday afternoon, chucked me on the shoulder, and handed me a small brown paper bag.

"I'm so sorry, Francis. Susan has been nice to me. I guess I'm just jealous that she is your best friend now, not me. Friends again?"

I laughed when I opened his gift and saw an Orange Crush and a gigantic rubber dog turd he had bought at Woolworth's. That was my Izzy. How could I ever go on without him?

When Susan came back to St. Paul the first week in August, we talked on the phone when we could, but there were always people around. My favorite meeting was the one we had at Joe's sharing a malt the day Frank died. Before Mrs. Flannagan arrived, Susan insisted on paying because she knew I was saving up for the canoe trip. A few days later, I received an anonymous envelope in the mail. When I opened it, President Jefferson was starting at me from his two-dollar bill.

I wanted to go on a real, longer date, a nice date, alone, just the two of us with no Joe nor anyone else around to chaperone, but my mom said movies were out. And besides, I was flat busted. The last time we had been completely alone was the night Frank died.

Mom said, "You are way too young for a movie date with a

girl. Stuff happens in the dark that should not. Sixteen or seventeen might be a proper age to be left alone in private for that long."

Susan was always curious about the big Hamm's Beer bottle on top of the brewery that Izzy and I climbed into once. I showed her a short story I had written in my journal about that climb. She said she wanted to taste the spring water that flowed all year inside the brewmaster's fenced-in garden patio.

Two weeks before the canoe trip, while Susan was still here with her folks to close on the sale of their former home, the two of us rode our bikes to the spring on a hot Saturday morning.

Susan was wearing white shorts, white sneakers, and a powder-blue button-up blouse. Her top button was undone, and when she was not looking, I tried to sneak peeks and see if her mom had bought her a bra yet. I wondered what it might be like to touch her blouse and accidentally-on-purpose maybe just brush by her breasts with my fingers.

Susan was gleeful, and that made me happy too. She tied her red hair in a ponytail with a rubber band.

"Francis, let's put our heads under the spring and get all wet. I'm all sticky. It's so humid today."

Grabbing my hand, she pulled me to the spigot, dunked my head under the cool flow, laughed, and then ran like the wind.

She giggled. "Tag, you're it!"

Susan could outrun me if she wanted. She was wearing decent sneakers. Besides, she was athletic and had long legs with cute freckles. But on that day, she let me catch her on purpose. Dragging her back to the fountain, I drenched her head until her long hair dripped enough spring water down her blouse that I could see the outline of her bra.

We found a patch of grass and lay on our backs, holding hands and drying ourselves in the hot sun.

"Francis, I need an adventure. Show me how you and Izzy climbed up that billboard and inside of that big beer bottle. I might even let you kiss me in there, as long as no one from the street can see us. I don't want to get caught. My dad would never let me see you again if he knew we climbed up that high."

"Deal! Let's climb!" I said.

I was one step behind her. We scaled the metal braces high above our city toward the bottle's opening at the very top. Susan placed one foot before the other, making slow, steady progress. I loved steadying her and touching her bare ankles, and I could not take my eyes off her bare legs. I wondered what color panties she was wearing underneath her white shorts.

The last ledge was the trickiest.

"Francis, I'm so afraid right now. Are you?"

"Not really. Just don't look down."

"Francis, what are you thinking? Right now? I'd give a penny for your thoughts."

"Susan, I really can't say."

"Why not?"

"I have my reasons."

"Just tell me one. Please? If you do, I might let you kiss me inside the bottle."

"Well, OK."

I could feel her bare skin when I steadied before the last three metal braces, and I let my hand linger for a few moments while I replied.

"Susan, I was thinking that I have never kissed a girl before. I might not be good. You might not like it."

"Well, try me. I like you, so I know I will like it. If it makes you feel better, you would be my first too. What else are you thinking?"

"Well, my main thought is not a proper one, and if I tell you, you may never kiss me."

"Francis, I wanted you to kiss me in the chocolate room at your candy factory, and you did not let me. I trust you, and I will kiss you if we get into the bottle safely. You do want to kiss me, right? Tell me. What are you thinking? It can't be that bad."

"Well, I was wondering as I was climbing behind you and touching your legs . . ."

"Oh, yes. I liked your hands on my ankles."

"I wanted to touch them and your legs much longer. Is that a sin?"

"Oh, Francis, you are so naughty. But touching my legs is hardly a sin. I will still kiss you."

"Well, is wondering what color panties you have on a sin?"

She turned her head so her eyes met mine.

"Of course, it is not a mortal or a grave sin. Maybe just a venial, smaller one."

I winked at her. "Good! Then I'm just a little sinner."

"Oh, and, if you really need to know, I'm not wearing underwear today."

"What?"

"I just don't like how they creep up on me when I ride my bike."

Susan leaned into the opening, her buttocks brushing my face.

"Oh my, I see it. I can almost touch it," she said.

"See and touch what?" I replied.

"Someone put a wooden ladder here so they could climb up and out from the bottom."

Susan sounded excited, pleased, knowing we would not die stuck in the bottom of a beer bottle. I had forgotten about the ladder. Izzy's brother and his friends had hauled it up and left it there for others to use the summer before he died.

"Be careful, Susan. I'll wait until you are at the bottom, and then I'll follow."

In the bottom of the bottle were candles and a box of matches. Susan lit the largest one before I landed.

Her eyes were happy and bright in the flickering light. The freckles on her nose glowed too.

I teased her. "I'm glad you lit that candle because we are such a perfect match."

She put her finger to my lips to shush me and whispered, "Now come closer, Francis."

I did.

She put both arms around my neck and said, "Pull me in tight and kiss me like you may never see me again."

So, I did. There was something about my first kiss with Susan that I will never forget and always treasure.

46

Mom Trouble

END OF AUGUST 1968

Remember the Sabbath day, to keep it holy.
—EXODUS 20:8

Dr. Flannagan moved his family to Houston so that he could run the fancy new hospital's burn center. I received only one postcard from Susan. It was a picture of the Astrodome. On the back, she drew a picture of a beer bottle with a candy-cane straw sticking out of it, and she signed it, *Your Friend, Susan. PS. Every time I see a candy store or a beer billboard, I smile.*

Mom threatened to take me to our priest because I sassed her and slept in until noon most days. Even Izzy couldn't cheer me up. He tried hooking me up with a cousin of his at a bonfire. She was funny and pretty too, with long dark hair and deep, dark-brown mysterious eyes. She pinned me behind the giant oak and gave me a long, wet kiss. It was different from Susan's; I did not get aroused.

What kept me going was Izzy and our canoe trip. When I was engrossed in thinking through final details, it kept my mind off Susan and my despair.

Like a jigsaw puzzle, the last piece of my plan fell into place.

Travis and his dad were driving by the outfitter on the way to their hunting shack. They were headed there to spruce it up and build a new deer stand. I trusted Travis with my desire to get Izzy back in a canoe and on the river again.

Travis said, "I know Izzy's old man is a jackass. I'm happy to help."

Izzy and I lied to our parents. We said we were going with Travis and his father for some river fishing, but I forgot about the one thing that would make my mom cancel our journey.

She almost nailed me to the cross after I cut our grass and started airing out my sleeping bag on the backyard clothesline.

Handing me a glass of lemonade, Mom said, "Francis, where will you and Isadore be going to Mass on Sunday morning? You know, on your fishing trip? You certainly cannot give up the Lord's Day for a few hours of fun and a stringer of fish."

I responded quickly, pleased with my fib.

"Mom, no worries. I have it covered. If there's not a town nearby with a Catholic church, I will get back in time for the late evening Mass at the St. Paul Cathedral. That is, if you will drive me."

"And what if you are not back in time?"

"Well, one time, Travis said their truck broke down, and when he told our priest why he had missed Mass, Father said to go to one of the daily Masses the following week. You know, make it up, like a missed test."

Mom fell silent. I think I aced her quiz with my quick thinking. Finally, she flashed me her "I trust you" smile, but not a full 100 percent smile, before speaking again.

"Well, OK then. I like Travis. He's responsible, but you two keep Izzy in line. I'll give him a ride to Mass too."

Izzy and I met their truck at sunrise under the High Bridge. Travis and his yellow lab jumped out of the cab, the dog eagerly licking and greeting us.

Travis said, "Are you two numb nuts ready to roll? I washed

out the truck bed really good! I'll pay a nickel for every fish scale you find!"

The rusty bed still smelled like fish. We tossed our fishing poles, packs, and then ourselves over the side and staked out our positions. Izzy pushed his back against the cab's window, wanting to ride backwards.

Travis put his dog in the cab's jump seat next to his father and then jumped in back with us and sat across from me.

"I'm back here with you clowns. My dog, Peter-Less, will ride up front with my dad."

I laughed. "Peter-Less?"

"Yeah, we adopted him last summer when our other hunting dog, Scooter, died. If you looked, you'd see he has only half a dick and one testicle, just like Izzy."

Izzy turned to Travis. "No shit, Sherlock?"

"I shit you not. He caught it in some barbed wire as a puppy. Can't screw, but still pisses like a racehorse."

We hunkered down in the truck bed, and Travis's father took off. Izzy took out one of his Cuban cigars, unwrapped it, put it in his mouth, and then aimed his spritzer, spraying Travis and laughing.

"That's for disrespecting my balls. I have two of them!"

I had planned every detail like General Patton. I bought our food, got some ice at Joe's, and snuck one of Dad's issues of *Playboy*, the one with Marilyn Monroe on the cover, out of his hiding spot in our garage. Izzy swiped two bottles of beer from his old man and slipped them in my cooler.

Flashing the Cubans a second time, Izzy said, "Beer, brats, babes, and two long Castro turds—thanks to the Worm and Cigar Ron!"

I winked at Travis, then asked Izzy, "They're a year old, Izzy. Will they flare like dead leaves when we light them?"

Izzy snapped back, "You ass-cracks don't know squat about fine tobacco. It's like fancy French wine or cheese. The longer the wait, the sweeter the taste."

I felt on top of the world: true freedom was ours, cruising the dirt river roads with no cars behind to eat our dust. Every now and then, Izzy looked at me, then Travis, and flashed his wide smile along with his middle finger. Travis whipped out his squirt gun and nailed Izzy right on his bare right nipple.

"Bull's-eye. Travis one. Izzy zero," I said.

Izzy retaliated with his perfume baptismal sprayer.

"I baptize you both—the breast-ever a-holes I ever met at Holy Family."

We were only a few miles from our drop-off. Izzy had not said a word for a long time. He just stared at road dust. Suddenly, he turned and pounded on the cab window, motioning for Travis's father to stop.

The vehicle slowed to pull over. Izzy jumped out and fell, and his face hit the gravel. He held his head with both hands as if it might explode, then he pulled himself to his knees and vomited.

When it subsided, he mumbled into the dirt.

"I'm sorry. I can't do this canoe trip. My head and guts are going against me."

Something had gone haywire really fast, and Travis and I did not know what to do, but Travis's dad took charge and put a cold rag on Izzy's face. He gave him a canteen of cool water.

Then he started asking Izzy a bunch of questions.

"Isadore, what did you eat for breakfast?"

"Leftover sour cream raisin pie."

"What have you had to drink so far today?"

"One cup of instant coffee, sir."

Travis's father laughed when Izzy answered the last one, which made me think things were getting better.

"Izzy, can you tell me the names of your two friends who are here with us now, and the name of the president of the United States?"

Izzy was speaking softly, but he wasn't throwing up anymore. "The president will be Eugene McCarthy, but it is still Lyndon Johnson."

Izzy pointed first toward Travis, then me. "These guys' names are Gilligan and Gomer's Pyle."

Travis's dad gave me a wink and went on to say that people who eat leftover cream pie and coffee for breakfast, do not drink enough water on a humid day, and are not used to riding backwards in trucks on bumpy roads can get dehydrated and sick.

He thought Izzy had gotten dizzy, sick, and disoriented but would be OK if we sat tight for a bit in the shade and he cooled down and drank a lot of water. Travis's dad went back to his truck and brought back some cheese sandwiches for us all to share in the shade.

Travis handed Izzy half a sandwich, refilled Izzy's canteen with water from his own, and, splashing some at him, said, "All three of us now baptize you Dizzy Izzy."

Izzy rode the rest of the way up front in the cab, and Peter-Less took his place in the truck bed with us. Travis's father dropped us off at the canoe shack, and we arranged to meet their truck downstream at Franconia Landing on the Minnesota side of the river on Sunday. The outfitter told us where to secure the canoe and said as long as there was no damage, he would not charge to pick it up.

Travis's father shoved a five-dollar bill in my palm. "Francis, I want you to take this," he said. "Consider it a tip for all the hard work you did this summer for the stockyards. Go buy yourself a new pair of jeans that smell like denim, not carp!"

He gave Izzy a dollar. "And this is for not throwing up in my front seat. Fish smell is much more aromatic than puke."

I planned for the two of us to paddle most of the day and then make camp near the Taylors Falls bluffs where the Jack tragedy occurred. Izzy looked hesitant, but not fearful, as he pulled the straps tight on his orange life jacket.

I steadied the canoe, holding it by the gunwales. The sand and water welcomed my bare feet. Izzy grabbed his wooden paddle, waded out into the water, and carefully positioned himself into the bow of the freshly repainted green wooden canoe.

Izzy yelled, "Let's put the ash to her, moron! You take the rear. You loved Susan's rear when you climbed that billboard. See if mine looks as good."

Izzy knew how much I missed Susan but was happy that he now had me all to himself. I was feeling sunny inside as the sun warmed my outside. I was on the river with my buddy. Izzy was giving canoeing a chance again. We were almost adults, on our own. No nuns were around, and our folks had no idea where we were or what we were doing.

Izzy stopped paddling near Fisher Creek, playfully back-splashing me with his paddle.

"I baptize you Old Man River, the patron saint of Paddling Pecker-Woods."

I dipped my paddle deep, then lifted upward, dousing Izzy until his life vest was sopped and a small pond was forming in our bilge.

"And I baptize you Dizzy Izzy, the Barfing Big Bad Bastard!"

Izzy turned his head and, looking over his shoulder, said, "Hell, Francis, I'm having a good effect on you. You're finally starting to cuss."

Setting my paddle across my lap, I grabbed the coffee can under my seat and bailed the water around my bare feet.

"Izzy, *bastard* is not swearing. We looked it up in the dictionary, remember?"

He shot back, "Yeah, but *fuck* was not in that Fuck and Wagnalls dictionary. Just say it once, Francis. *F-U-C-K. Fuck!* I know you can do it. It's a freeing experience, just like skinny-dipping. You can go to confession when we get home. Whisper it. Your mommy is not around to make you gargle with soap and vinegar like my old man makes me do."

Pulling back my paddle, I nailed Izzy with another soaking. "Have it your way, moron!" I was laughing. "You are one big bad ugly rekcuf!"

Izzy stopped paddling, twisting his neck. He was clueless. "What the hell is that supposed to mean?"

"Figure it out spelling-bee loser. Unscramble backwards, you big bad ugly rekcuf!"

When Izzy figured it out, he almost choked. Then he was coughing out his bubble gum. Splashing me back, he yelled, "That's cheating, dipshit!"

Then Izzy paused and stopped paddling, like he was in a trance or deep, serious thought.

"Francis, you know, Jack told me that the letters *F-U-C-K* stand for *foul unlawful carnal knowledge*. So, I asked him, 'What the fuck is that?' He said it's when a guy slides his salami in his girl's hot zone when they're not married. It was unlawful, back in Greek times. Then Jack lectured me about how President Johnson and Vice President Humphrey were Vietnam War fuckups."

He switched his paddle to the other side and drew out long, deep strokes. After a few minutes, he talked about his brother again.

"You know, if Jack were alive this weekend, he'd be rioting in Chicago and supporting Senator McCarthy for President, not canoeing with us."

Izzy was now freely sharing things about Jack, something he rarely did. We paddled around another river bend. I noticed a fresh spring trickling into the river. A family of mergansers was frolicking upstream. I motioned for Izzy to silence his paddle and watch.

"Jack would love this," Izzy whispered. "He would jump out to that moss-covered rock and fill his canteen up with that pure, ice-cold spring water."

"Let's do it!" I said.

I nosed our canoe to the shore, steadying the ship with my

paddle. Izzy hopped out and filled his canteen. Then he filled his Twins cap and put the cap back on his head. The cool water cascaded down his neck and shoulders. He jumped back in and got situated. I pushed off and we headed down the swift-moving river.

"Izzy, in some ways, you are a little bit like Jack. I mean in a good way. Maybe his standing up for his beliefs helped you to be firm on yours, even though it got your ass in a sling at school now and then."

"How so?" he asked.

"Well, the first year I met you, you refused to dive under your desk if we got nuked. Sister was pissed and tried to humiliate you and make you conform."

"Oh yeah, I got a good whack with her pointer and then had to deal with the G-Man's wrath too. My old man topped it off by beating the snot out of me."

I rested my paddle on my knees again and watched as an osprey circled overhead hunting for fish. I pointed to the sky. Izzy's eyes followed. He knew how to be silent sometimes. The sighting was a bonus, and we both marveled at the osprey's effortless glide. Then it dipped for its lunch, a large fish that struggled to free itself from the bird's talons.

After the osprey disappeared over the opposite riverbank, I finished my thoughts.

"Izzy, what I'm thinking is that maybe you taking a stand made some of us think about the reality of war, especially nuclear war. I know it did for me, even though I will never have the balls to challenge a nun like you. That was real leadership you showed, just like Muhammad Ali and Dr. King."

"Really?"

"Yes, really."

After talking about Jack, we paddled silently until we ended up sideways in the current, stuck on a midriver sandbar. We both got out to stretch and pee. Izzy peeled an orange for himself.

"Wash your hands before you give me a piece," I said.

"Hell, Francis, my piss tastes better than orange juice. It is the nectar of the gods. You should try it sometime."

I patted myself on my back for a small victory. Izzy was talking about his brother, and my insides said that was good, like when Mandy started talking about Shannon and Grandma Rose, which led her back to feeling normal and finding harmony after her dangerous fire play.

Izzy stood up in the water and walked out from the sandbar. The water was up to his nipples.

"Hey, Francis, let's go nakey in the lakey. We can walk upriver and float back down to this sandbar."

He dropped his trunks, tossing them in the canoe, and walked up the shallows on the Minnesota shoreline. I followed. He was going swimming again, showing no fear. We continued hiking upriver, then edged our bodies out into the higher water midstream. The water was now above our waists. We were careful not to step on clamshells; it hurt like hell when we did. Izzy had always been a good swimmer. He could float on his back like a log. It made me happy to see him doing it again.

The weather was perfect, as was the view, like the ones they put on nickel postcards at every Minnesota and Wisconsin lakecountry tourist stop—a deep blue sky with a few puffy, cottony lily-white clouds forming sky art.

Sparkling ripples surrounded us. The river's sandy bottom massaged our bare feet. Both banks were lined with tall white pines, cedars, a few willows, and aspens. The wetlands and backwater bays were adorned with end-of-summer wildflowers. I inhaled their scent; they were nectar sweet. The blue-and-purple water irises were my favorite. They reminded me of Grandma Patricia's garden.

The current changed again. It was meandering, slow, and safe. The outfitter had said it was dangerous only with severe rain or when they opened the dams upriver.

He had lectured us on safety. "You two voyageurs make sure

to pull my canoe out at least fifty feet up from the river's edge when you camp. Flip it over and tie it down with these ropes, and you will not owe me ninety-nine bucks for a new one."

Izzy was floating on his back a tad upriver from me. His feet were pointed toward my face. He shouted, "Hey, Francis! Do you know how to play submarine with a girl?"

I shouted back, "No, how?"

Arching his back, he forced his penis above the water line and said, "Up periscope!"

When he caught up to me, he told me that Jack had taught him the joke while they were swimming, the same day he had died.

All I said was, "I'm so sorry, Izzy."

We repeated the float two more times, then put on our trunks while the sun dried our bodies. We snacked on the peanut butter sandwiches I had made.

Our life vests were uncomfortably soaked, so we left them in the bottom of the canoe to dry, and we continued paddling bareback. I started to feel burned from the sun, so I put my wet vest back on. Izzy's was still under his seat. We had fishing poles but never used them. We just kept chatting, enjoying each other and the afternoon, as we continued easing our way downstream toward camp.

The river suddenly narrowed, dropping rapidly and introducing us to dangerous flows not marked on my map. The peaks of canoe-eating boulders stared me down, foam frothing over their tops and hiding jagged edges below from view.

Dropping to my knees, I tightened my fists on my paddle and screamed, "Izzy, put that vest back on! Now!"

He reached for it, but lost it, his paddle, and himself into the river's furious flow.

47

Overboard!

John was baptizing in Aenon, near Salim, because there was so much water there, and people kept coming to be baptized.

—JOHN 3:23

Crack! My stern ricocheted off a boulder, almost tossing me, too. A chunk of green wood went flying. The small breach was high, so the boat did not take on water, but chaos followed.

Izzy was out of sight, somewhere downriver. Without him paddling up front in my bow, I didn't have the power to maneuver. I was alone. No one was nearby to save either of us. The rapids seemed never-ending. My heart pounded. My arms flew and grazed my face, knocking my glasses into the bilge.

I was running out of options, terrified that we'd both drown. Not being able to see is a death warrant for a captain. In desperation, I screamed, "Jesus, Mary, Joseph, Saint Francis! Save us!"

I removed my right hand from the paddle's neck and plunged my hand into the water behind my knees while I continued paddling with my left arm. I felt for my eyeglasses. I grabbed them and put them on. I was back to two arms and two eyes, but I could not see Izzy. I saw only glimpses of his life jacket bobbing without him in it.

I slipped through the last V in the river's rapids, just a narrow slot between two boulders. I beat that flow. It was now behind me. I was sweating like a pig despite being drenched with cool water.

253

I took a deep breath and rested my weary arms. I had barely survived the river's angry shitstorm. But had Izzy? Where was my
best friend? And was he dead or alive?

48

Panic

Out of my distress I called to the Lord, and He answered me;
I cried for help and you heard my voice.
—JONAH 2:2

Before I could search for Izzy, the river bit me again. It had the last say. When I paused, my boat turned broadside and got tangled in branches that had fallen in a storm. The willow's angry limbs grabbed my bow, tossing me and the rest of our gear into the water, just like the river did to Izzy.

The St. Croix River was in control again. Its current was again deeper and stronger. I could not stand. I caught another glimpse of Izzy's orange vest stuck downstream on a log, but there was no sign of Izzy.

"Izzy! Izzy! Izzy!" I screamed, choking and spitting out water. I flipped on my back, positioning my feet downstream to avoid bashing my skull on a rock and drowning. My clumsy, cumbersome life vest was soaked but still doing its job of keeping my face above the drink. I could not hear anything above the roar of the upcoming Devil's Hell waterfall.

I desperately angled myself toward the Wisconsin shore, which was where the canoe was trapped upstream, still wedged under branches, but I kept getting sucked toward the Devil's Hell.

I prayed the short prayer, the easy prayer: the Hail Mary. If I survived, I dreaded telling Izzy's folks that their remaining son had died on the same river where Jack had died.

I was exhausted, but my prayer was answered by a minor miracle. With three last desperate, massive kicks, I made it to the shallows and was able to stand in the current. I started slushing my way upstream to the trapped canoe. It was upside down. A bunch of leafy branches obstructed its full view. Just above the shoreline's tall reeds, behind the canoe, Izzy's head popped up. I could see only his face. He was smiling.

"You OK?" he asked, breathless himself too.

Before I could respond, he coughed then wheezed, "After I fell in, I swallowed a crapload of water. Thought I would drown. Was terrified. But made it to shore."

He put his arm around my shoulder, caught his real voice, and continued.

"I tried to see you but could not, so I started hiking upriver barefoot, as fast as I could, cussing every time I stepped on rocks or clamshells. That's when I spotted our canoe trapped under this tree but without you nearby. Francis, I thought you were dead."

I now knew what it might feel like to get a second chance at life. It was like finding out you were not really dying of cancer, that they had just mixed up the test results.

Izzy started breaking off branches to help free our boat so we could flip it over, drain it, and do our best to repair it. I pitched in, but I had trouble snapping even the small branches. An awful, sandy, river-water aftertaste remained in my mouth. I started to shiver from the shock of how close we had come to finding out if there really was a Purgatory, Heaven, or Hell.

I snapped out of my haze when Izzy playfully flogged me with a long leafy willow branch. I put my arms up, defending my sunburned torso. Izzy quit and said, "Francis, don't take this the wrong way, and don't try to kiss me, but I love you like a brother. Just like my real brother, Jack. I cannot imagine my life without having you as a best friend."

I grabbed his willow whip and tossed it into the river's flow.

"Me too," I said. "No kissing you. Only Susan for me, but I love you back like the brother I never had."

Once we had freed our ship, we checked for leaks. It floated with no seepage, so we hugged the shore and looked downstream for our gear. Our food cooler was tied under the center thwart. I thought I had lost it, but it had not popped out in the swamping, so we would eat after all. But we had lost everything else. Izzy was more worried about whether the cigars were still dry than he was about us having food.

"Look! Whatever it is, it's orange!" Izzy shouted, pointing downriver. "I think it's my paddle and life jacket."

We rescued both along with our main gear pack, and we began safely paddling again. If the rest of my map was accurate, we were at the portage around Devil's Hell waterfall and near the Taylors Falls cliffs, where I was planning for us to camp.

Our outfitter had warned us about Devil's Hell. He marked both takeouts on each bank so we could safely portage around them.

"You boys don't be foolish. Pull out at the first portage. It is three hundred and eighty rods. Remember, a rod is a canoe-length. This is a good workout for young bucks like you. Trying to go downstream farther to save a few steps killed two men last year."

He circled the first of two takeouts, as well as the second right near the falls, with a black marker and then underlined his circles and continued his stern fatherly lecture.

"The sheriff said sometimes guys, and even teens, with a few beers in them take chances that can mess them up bad, even kill them."

He then handed me the map with his notes and continued his instructions.

"Make sure to look for the caution signs. They put them on both sides of the river. You'll see those first, before the actual portage path signs. Start easing your canoe to the shore you are closest to. The Forest Service had the second set of signs made after last year's tragedy. But sometimes the law or even God can't fix stupid."

The sun would soon be easing over the river's western bank; it was already showing off a pink sky. Despite our slow pace, we were on schedule. After our portage, it was only a few more minutes of a leisurely paddle before we pulled our freedom machine out of the flow and dragged it up onshore to a secure place for the night. We pitched our tent and set up camp on the Wisconsin side of the river, figuring we would catch the rest of the evening sunset while eating dinner.

I had wrapped our sleeping bags in plastic sheeting, so they were dry. Izzy held up my dad's *Playboy*. It was soaked, and Marilyn's face on the cover was now gone, probably floating toward the Gulf of Mexico.

Izzy held up what was left, just part of a wet boob.

"You are so screwed, Francis. What are you going to tell your dad?"

I gathered more firewood while Izzy erected a rain tarp over our sitting area near the fire pit. He took out a flint, and showing off, he started our campfire with it. He then busied himself by lashing ropes around our two wooden paddle handles, and then he slung them over a tall cedar limb, raising them about twelve feet from the ground.

"What in the hell are you doing?" I asked.

According to Izzy, Jack had told him about two Canadian paddlers who survived class four river rapids on the Churchill River in Canada by using one three-foot-long paddle because raccoons had chewed their paddles in half while they were sleeping. Izzy looked proud of his invention as the paddles swung above our heads in the breeze.

"Jack said critters like raccoons like the salty taste from sweaty hands or maybe even the resins they cure the paddles with."

I noticed how close our paddles were to getting scorched by

his now larger blazing fire. The flames were licking at the paddle blades.

"Good idea, Einstein, but if they drop another foot, we will be paddling with a three-foot pile of ashes."

Not wanting to admit he had miscalculated, Izzy said, "No problem. I zipped the spare the outfitter guy gave us inside the tent."

The firewood simmered into glowing red coals. Izzy set a can of baked beans from Joe's down into the outer edge of the embers, and he jammed a couple of wieners on long sticks. He opened our beers. Mine was cool and welcome after a hot day on the river, especially since I had forgotten my Orange Crush in Travis's truck.

After dinner, Izzy whipped out the cigars. Peeling the foil away, he revealed the dry Cubans from Rich Grandma's funeral.

"You know, these have become illegal since the Cuban missile crisis," he said, and then he pulled out Cigar Ron's lighter. "I sleep with this puppy. My *Playboy* lighter girl. She will be worth money someday."

"Right," I said. "But I thought you might toss the cigars. I figured they got wet."

"No way, numb nuts. Fortunately, we kept them high and dry in our cooler. You are planning to smoke one with me, right, Francis?"

I ignored him.

"Seriously, friend, it's a Cuban! Fidel probably rolled it himself. I'll show you how to smoke. Just puff. No inhaling like I do with my other smokes. You are breathing in more smoke right now from this campfire than you will when you're smoking Cigar Ron's Cuban turd."

Izzy thought he had to convince me, but I'd already made up my mind weeks ago that I would smoke, and we would talk long into the evening.

"I don't know, Izzy. Susan said she would never kiss a boy

who had smoke breath."

"Well, she is not here. She is in Texas with her mom and her rich dad doctor, and all you got was a postcard, unless she sends you her white underthings for old times' sake."

"How do you know they were white, genius?"

"Because I dropped my pencil once when the nun made me sit next to her, and I looked up her uniform skirt."

"I should kill you!"

"White and tight, buddy. Your old girlfriend was a good girl, wearing virgin panties."

Izzy took our metal dinner plates down to the river to scrub them clean with water and sand. When he came back, I fed the fire more wood.

"You know, I really think I loved her," I said.

"Yeah, I know. I'm sorry, Romeo. Maybe there will be a worthier Little Mermaid that will slither up the riverbank and into your sleeping bag tonight."

49

Lost and Found

Be kind to one another, compassionate, forgiving each other,
just as God in Christ also has forgiven you.
—EPHESIANS 4:32

We saved the cigars for stargazing after dark. Izzy dragged our sleeping gear out of the tent, and when the sun faded behind the western horizon, we started climbing up the jagged hillside to the top of Jack's Cliff and laid our sleeping bags on a large flat piece of granite so we could watch the night sky come to life to entertain us.

The rock was smooth, wide, long, and flat enough that we could stand and move around or even lie down, look up at the sky, and sleep if we got tired. If the mosquitoes got nasty, we would take our flashlight and make our way down to our tent.

"This rock, this cliff, was Jack's favorite place," Izzy said, smoothing out his sleeping bag. "He came here often after he was old enough to drive. When he took me here, it was my first time." Izzy paused and then continued, "And his last time."

Izzy sat on his bag, crossed his legs, and gazed across the river.

"Jack loved this spot, Francis. He said it was romantic at night when he took his girlfriend here, impressing her with his knowledge of the planets and constellations."

"Back home, Jack taught you about them too, right?"

"Sure did. And now I'll teach you, Francis. If you tilt your

261

head down between your knees and look down, you might even see Uranus."

I chucked him on his shoulder. "Ha, ha! My anus is none of your business."

Izzy's willingness to razz me and talk about his brother encouraged me to try to get him to open up more. I put my hand on his shoulder. "I'm sorry about Jack, Izzy. He was nice to me, too. Gave up his top bunk whenever I slept in the bedroom you two shared. Always took the floor in his musty sleeping bag with all those antiwar stickers glued to it. My favorite was the one that said *Make Love Not War*."

Izzy took in my comments, then he removed his cap and put it on his head backwards to keep the gnats off his neck.

"My old man is a mean drunk, Francis. Jack was like my real dad. I could talk to him about anything. Girls, sex, music, books, drugs, and religion. But near the end, he never stopped bitching about the war. When they called him to go to 'Nam, I thought he had his ticket out. I figured he'd move to Canada and work for a canoe or fishing outfitter near Thunder Bay, not that far from Duluth. He would be done with the old man and the war, and I could still visit him in Canada by taking the bus, or with a car once I got my license."

Izzy took my hand off his shoulder and gave it a squeeze. He looked at me with weary eyes. The starlit sky did not help brighten them. Letting my hand drop, he raised an angry voice that echoed.

"That drunken cocksucker donated all of Jack's stuff—his baseball card collection, albums—every last goddamn thing went to the Goodwill after his funeral!"

The echo of *funeral . . . funeral . . .* bounced back at us from the opposite cliffs. Izzy stopped yelling, and then he spoke in a soft, sadder tone.

"But I hid Jack's camp gear. He loved camping. He was an Eagle Scout. Imagine that. A war-protesting, LSD-using Eagle Scout."

I was shocked.

"Jack dropped acid?"

"Yes, but mostly he just smoked pot. He even left behind some LSD cubes and tabs in his camp cook kit. I brought some with me. Might try them myself, or else feed some to that annoying red squirrel. The little shitass that raided all our salted peanuts."

I was sure he was bluffing, just trying to get a rise out of me. Glancing upward, I noticed the northern lights were coming out to play while Izzy explained his brother's drug use.

"I don't think Jack used acid more than a couple of times. He said he was curious, not an addict. You know, just wanted to see for himself what all the buzz was about. He told me not to bother when I was older, and if I did, he would kick my ass. Claimed I could have dreams in my sleep that are as good, if I trained my mind right."

Izzy then stood on our rock and pointed to the sky, flapping his arms like he wanted to fly up to the Milky Way and visit our night's light show.

"The first time he used, Jack said he was alone and had a good trip. He said he grew long clear light wings, as fragile as a dragonfly's, but longer, and stronger than an eagle's."

While flapping like he was a giant bird, Izzy's hat flew off. I caught it before it went over the cliff. Stopping abruptly, he sat down and kept on explaining his brother's dream.

"So, Jack started flying toward Canada, looking down at a landscape of magnificent Minnesota hills, rivers, lakes, and rich, lush valleys with waterspouts shooting out everywhere. Massive fountains, a kaleidoscope of colors. He said the water sprays would put Old Faithful and Niagara Falls both to shame."

I interrupted. "Jack's visions seem much better than the bad LSD trips I've read about."

"Maybe, Francis, but when he flew to the Minnesota and Canadian border just north of Grand Portage, he crossed the Pigeon River that separated Ontario from Minnesota, and right below him, floating down the river, was Noah with his ark full of animals. He said all the birds were on the top deck and staring up at my brother flying high above them. In unison, they flew off Noah's ark and right up to Jack to lead him into Canada. The head bird was a common loon. It called out the whole time, a musical symphony that was so beautiful, it made Jack weep."

Izzy stopped speaking when I inhaled a mosquito and started coughing.

"Sorry, Izzy, I just inhaled a bug. I'm not making light of Jack's dream. Actually, the loon is my favorite bird."

"Really? Then you and Jack have something in common—the common loon. He made it his spirit animal for life. He read that the Ojibwa people chose a spirit animal that they adopted and looked to for guidance."

Izzy stopped talking and took out his *Playboy* lighter. He lit both cigars, handing me mine. I took a small puff and tried to make smoke rings, but the breeze messed them up. I enjoyed the aroma from the tobacco smoke mixing with the night air much more than the harsh taste on my tongue.

"Thanks, Izzy. Don't stop, please tell me more. I'd like to know more about Jack."

"OK. So that night was only about two weeks before he died. We even talked about dying, and Jack had it all figured out. Maybe he did, but I don't think he meant to die so young. It had to be an accident, a mistake. Right, Francis?"

I nodded, then Izzy brought up his LSD again. "I would like dreams like that. Figure maybe I'll try half an acid stamp or piece of a cube. You know, experiment. It can't hurt me any more than this cigar."

"Izzy, that stuff can be wicked. Tell me you are joking."

"OK, I'm joking."

"Izzy, do you even know what a bad trip is?"

"Yeah, it's when I go to the G-Man's office, get suspended, and then my old man shit-kicks my ass and breaks my finger."

"Well, that too. But I saw it on Cronkite. People freaking out in Haight-Ashbury in San Francisco. One guy clawed his eyeballs out. Another girl jumped off the Golden Gate Bridge."

Izzy did not say a word. He just took our flashlight and walked away. I thought he left to take a leak back in the woods behind our rock, but he was gone for much longer than a one-minute piss.

Then it hit me. Maybe Jack's death was not a suicide when he jumped off this rock into the Devil's Hell waterfall. Maybe he had been experimenting with acid and had lost his balance during a bad trip.

Izzy finally came back and sat down. I snatched his flashlight and turned it on him. His eyes were bloodshot.

"You didn't!" I yelled.

His chest was heaving, and he was having trouble breathing, and it was then that I realized he had excused himself not to urinate or take drugs, but so he could cry. He was too proud to do it in front of me. I removed my red bandanna from my pocket and handed it to him to dry his eyes.

"It's OK, Izzy. There's no harm in having a few tears."

Izzy wiped his eyes, calmed himself, and then tied the bandanna around his neck like a cowboy. "Do you know the last thing Jack said before he leaped?"

"I'm so sorry, Izzy. What were your brother's last words?"

"Well, Jack strips off his T-shirt and steps out of his trunks. He is buck naked. Then, he takes a running start to that other rock, right over there, and looking over his shoulder at me, he shouts, 'My one last skinny-dip!'"

Izzy took a long drag off his cigar, blew a few smoke rings, looked at me, and then continued. "Francis, at first, I thought it was funny. I did not know how deadly the churning foam and rocks below us were. I still hear his echo bouncing off these cliffs every night before I can sleep. 'See you next year,' he joked, before his body slammed into the river."

Izzy seemed eager to share more, so I just listened. He said that one night after his old man passed out upstairs, Jack brought a six-pack to their basement bedroom and gave a beer to Izzy.

"Jack lectured me. 'Just this one, Izzy,' he said after opening it and passing it to me. 'OK, Jack, just this one,' I said. 'That's right, little brother, pace yourself, unless you want to turn out to be a drunk like our father.'"

Izzy said Jack went to the garage, and when he came back, he smelled like weed. Jack drank a couple more beers, and the two of them talked until sunrise.

Izzy turned away from me and said, "I so respected my brother, and I loved him more than ever that evening. Jack told me one story after another. I kind of figured it was the beer and marijuana talking, but I did not care."

Jack then gave Izzy a sex talk about girls and love. He told Izzy about the first time he was inside a girl, and he said a guy should not try to rush it and that it should be with someone special, maybe even a girl you want to marry.

Izzy said, "The first time Jack had intercourse with his girlfriend, it was in her folks' station wagon. It was parked in her parents' garage. He thought it was really nice for both of them, until she pulled away and ran inside crying. Jack said he felt awful that something so beautiful had gone sideways so fast."

After Jack drowned, Izzy's old man blamed him. Izzy said that the old man had always drank before, but he did not get as drunk and was never as mean as he became after Jack's death.

"Hell, when I was little, he never even drank that much at the brewery, and there you can have all the free beer you want during lunch and on break. Some guys drank all day on the job, and it was no big deal."

Izzy said his old man had started out slow at first with a case of beer per week, then a case every two days. Then there was the whiskey bottle under his front car seat at work. His boss went to move his car and found the pint. He tried to fire him. The union saved his job, saying it was Izzy and some bad friends who had been partying in the garage the prior evening.

Izzy said, "To me, it made no sense that bosses let their workers drink free beer on the assembly lines all day, but then they would fire my old man for some whiskey in the parking lot. I guess they figured beer was Kool-Aid and hard liquor was bad."

Izzy's old man got cautious after that. He drank more than any man should, but he just did not get caught. But he was all over Izzy like buzzards on roadkill.

I kept listening. That's all I knew how to offer. I wanted to fix my friend's pain, to make him laugh again. That was what Izzy was always doing for everyone else. Humor kept him focused and sane.

Izzy described the days after Jack's funeral. "After we buried Jack, I could not cry like everyone else. I was numb, thinking of Jack, all pasty faced with flies and army ants walking across his rotting forehead. He was all locked up inside that steel box, then lowered into a concrete box with a huge pile of shit-colored dirt next to his new home. His prison, a dark, black, cold hole, with no escape should he wake up. If there ever was a Rapture, he would not get sucked up into Heaven. All I could think was that a few days ago, we had been paddling our leaky canoe, bailing, laughing, swimming, enjoying the summer and each other—and now I had no Jack."

I was silent. A faint voice in my head gently called out to me saying, Be still, Francis. Just listen.

When Izzy and Jack shared a room, Izzy said they talked about serious stuff. Izzy's favorite discussion was about death and dying. His brother thought it was dumb that people buried their dead. He claimed that soon there would not be room on the planet for all the dead bodies.

Izzy said, "Jack loved science fiction, NASA, and outer space. He always said that when he died he wanted to have a jet pack put on his corpse and get rocketed into space. You know, like the one

George Jetson wears. He insisted it was a way to bypass Limbo and Purgatory and go directly to Heaven."

Izzy waved his cigar above his head toward the sky. The cigar's tip started sparking red.

"Jack said if he did not live in Minnesota, his next choice was to be buried at sea. He figured the sharks would get a free meal, and he would not be stuffed in a casket, covered with dirt."

Izzy paused and then said, "I told Jack that Lake Superior is big like an ocean, so just have them dump your ashes at the French River Lake Superior rest area. Jack laughed and said, 'No sharks, no deal, little brother.'"

I took a short pull on my cigar while Izzy kept sucking on his. He continued sharing more Jack memories.

"Anyways, we both decided that when we croaked, we wanted to be burned and have our ashes sprinkled somewhere special. I wanted mine scattered on the banks of the Mississippi or on this river, as that is where my best days were spent with Jack, and with you too, Francis. Jack wanted his sprinkled on I-94, the freeway, figuring all those car tires traveling through St. Paul would take him out west to places he had never visited, like Montana, Idaho, New Mexico, and Arizona."

Izzy said they talked about donating their eyes to science before they were both cremated, as neither of them needed glasses. "Jack would give only his eyes though. He wanted to keep his heart and brain."

Izzy said that Jack went spastic and had tears from laughing when Izzy told him that he would donate all his organs except for his sex organs, as having someone experimenting with them would be gross. After Jack had caught his breath and stopped laughing, he said, "Little brother, if you are donating everything to science, what would they burn? Just your sperm worm and nut sack?"

Izzy wanted to talk more. I told myself not to try to fix it, just listen.

"During the wake and funeral, my old man peppered me with questions I could not answer. 'What's wrong with you? Don't you love your brother? How come you did not write a note or put a photo into Jack's casket like your mother and I did? Your shirt and tie are wrinkled. Does your mommy still have to dress you, comb your hair?' After the funeral, the questions stopped, but my old man was still speaking to me without words. He just ignored me most of the time. Francis, those were great times talking with Jack, just like you and I are doing now. Why did my old man not cook me his chili on my birthday?"

"What chili?"

"Well, my mom does most of our cooking, but on birthdays, the old man would go to the store and make a big deal out of doing whatever we wanted for dinner, and the whole family, including my two closest cousins, all had to eat the same thing, no complaints."

Izzy said his mom always ordered lobster, the only time all year they all tasted lobster. She wanted a fudge sundae instead of cake for her dessert, and his old man even made the fudge sauce himself.

Izzie's cousin, Monica, requested banana pancakes with Spam and angel food cake with butter frosting and candy sprinkles on top. Jack's meal was the most work. He would order a full turkey dinner with all the trimmings and apple pie à la mode.

Izzy said, "When my birthday came, about nine months after Jack had passed, the old man did not ask what I wanted for my meal. I just wanted him to start loving me again, maybe show it by making his homemade chili. That is what I always asked for. He used to grate real Parmesan cheese on top, and he bought the expensive, good, crusty Italian bread from Giovanni's bakery downtown. Before his really bad drunken days, he used to let me take a sip of his beer, making me feel special, and would allow me to sit in his chair at the head of the table. He bought balloons and tied them to the back of his chair, which was now my birthday chair."

Izzy set down his cigar, drew his knees into his chest, and wrapped his arms around them like he was getting cold.

"My mom was not a chili chef, but she tried hard. She bought a few cans of Hormel chili from Joe's and threw in some lean ground beef. You know, she tried to doctor it up a bit. It was OK, but it was not my birthday chili. Francis, the point is that he continued the tradition for everyone else, but not for me. What is that supposed to mean?"

I offered the only thing I could think of. "I'm not sure, Izzy. Maybe he is blinded by all the alcohol? The liquor is a cover for his bad judgment? He bought you and Jack that old canoe. He put it on top of his car and dropped you off at the river. He forgot the life jackets. He should have gone with his sons, but he chose to swill booze at the VFW instead. You were a kid, and in a moment's time, you were forced to be an adult telling the sheriff where to look for your brother's body and where to find your old man."

Izzy was getting weary, and so was I. We snuffed out our cigars, still saving the stubs for later by wrapping them in tinfoil. We crawled into our sleeping bags and lay entranced by the stars and northern lights above. After a long silence, Izzy spoke one more time.

"My father messed up big the day Jack died, but he did not kill Jack, and neither did I."

It was the first time Izzy had called his old man *father*.

"Izzy, this is the first time I heard you say *father*. You mean your old man?"

"No, my father. He's not a dad like yours, but he is still my father. That awful night after I left the beer-can art on your porch, I went to our cave alone, feeling all empty inside. I could not stop crying. In that cave, I was desperate, but my father had given me a gift despite all his hate, rage, and anger. After I safely walked out of our cave, I decided that if I'm ever a father, I'll be a great dad."

I needed to know what happened in the cave.

"Safely? Why were you in our cave at night alone?"

"Well, my old man was drinking hard all day. He kept dogging me about everything, even my haircut. Told me if Jack had been there, Jack would've taught me how to clean up myself, comb my hair, be a man. Both my mom and your mom were at Holy Family baking for the school fundraiser."

"Oh, Izzy, I remember now! I went to watch Dad's team bowl and ended up in the bar working on a poem for class. Ginny kept running out booze to the bowlers and giving me nickels to play pinball."

"Francis, on that day, the old man should have beat me until I died. At least then it would've been over. The put-downs kept coming. I kept refusing to cry, and I wouldn't show any weakness. He broke me. I came up with a plan to fix it forever. Make sure another day like that one would never happen again.

"When he went to the bathroom, he passed out, so I went into his bedroom closet and grabbed his pistol. He kept it loaded in a shoebox on the top shelf. Mom did not know it was there. He used to hide his backup booze in that box, but I discovered that he had started hiding his gun there too, the one that got him arrested.

"I put it in my pants pocket, and then I went to the garage and grabbed a blanket to muffle the sound. That's when I saw my wind-chime art in the garbage can. He had left the metal lid off so that I could see the Christmas gift I had made for him on top. He had left the fucking lid off on purpose!"

Izzy was defeated, hopeless, and I wasn't sure in that moment that I had any hope for him.

"Izzy, why didn't you come to my house? You could have stayed with me. After getting home from bowling, I found your note and cleaned up your prize-winning art. I hung it from my ceiling. Mandy still comes in every night to see it glow when I light it up. My whole family loves your creation, Mandy most of all."

"Thanks, Francis. I thought you might like it, so I pedaled over, but no one was home, so I left it on your porch."

"Izzy, I'm glad you did not follow through, but I understand how you were driven that far. I might have shot your old man myself if I had been in your shoes."

Izzy sat up in his bag, looking surprised and shocked.

"Oh no, Francis! I would never kill or even hurt my father. Jack was a pacifist, against violence for any reason, just like Dr. King. But I felt so low, I planned to start a fire in the cave, take all of Jack's leftover LSD, and blow my own brains out. If I was a bad shot, the carbon monoxide from the fire and the drugs would finish me off."

Izzy's story frightened me to my core, but there was a calm inner voice coming from the depths of my being that steadied me. The voice spoke ever so softly: *Be still . . . listen . . . breathe, Francis.* It was Grandma Rose's voice.

"Izzy, I care about you. Funerals suck, and going to yours would have destroyed me. I'd spend the rest of my life wondering why I could not help."

"You actually did help. The Worm too. Even your grandma."

"How so?"

Izzy started speaking clearly, with focus. "Francis, I was so alone. It was dark. I was exhausted from the all-day beatdowns, too drained to even start a fire, but I was still strong enough to pull the trigger. I decided not to take Jack's drugs. I just put the barrel in my mouth, pointing it upwards toward my brain."

The soft voice came to me again: *Francis, breathe . . . just listen. He will be OK . . . trust me.*

Izzy rolled from his back onto his side, facing away from me, and let out a deep sigh.

"Then, I made my desperate plea, Francis. My final pathetic prayer. Call it what you like. You know, like them born-again Bible-bangers do when they go on the stage, and the preacher and Jesus save them, and then they all fall over like dominoes?"

"You mean like that Billy Graham crusade in Minneapolis?"

"Yep, kind of like that. I talked to God one last time and asked him why my father hated me so. Then, a bat flew out of a crevice and startled me, and I dropped the fucking pistol. It went off when it hit the cave floor. Echoed like a son of a bitch. I started crying like a baby. Thought I was going nuts."

Izzy said he had been on the blanket he'd brought along, flat on his back, and could feel the cold from the cave floor penetrating his bones. He rolled over onto his side, like how he was positioned now, and crushed whatever he had last jammed into his pocket. It was a small baggie of leftover peanut brittle he had saved from our day making candy with Frank.

Izzy said, "So I opened the bag and started jamming the crumbled brittle and peanuts into my gullet. I had not eaten all day. It was like manna from Heaven. I stopped weeping, and I thought of the good times I had shared with you, like that day with you and Frank trying to break the record, and that hot summer day with the Worm and you, when she was naming those damn carp as we buried them right outside the same cave I was trying to kill myself in. I started crying, then laughing, remembering the way you had chased those cute girls off the bridge when they saw your puny muscles."

The voice came to me again. It was even softer and more assuring. *Be present. Use your gifts,* the voice said.

"Francis, I think Jesus, God, and your grandma sent that bat to save me. After my plea, I felt a comforting wave like a surge of heat, light, and energy coursing through my whole body. I knew if I could have more days like that with you and the Worm, life might be worth living again. My art project was just a pile of beer cans after my father crapped on it, sucking all the hope for his love out of it when I'd made it special for him."

My words started coming freely now. It was almost like someone else was speaking for me.

"Izzy, remember the Little Sisters of the Poor before my

grandmother died? What did Grandma Rose say?"

"I do remember that day well, Francis. I also heard your grandmother in that cave telling me I was an ace. Like she was lying next to me on that cold floor. She said you, me, and the Worm, we were all aces, right?"

"It's true, Izzy. You are a pain in the ass at times but a true ace once someone takes the time to know and love you. Did you at least offer Grandma Rose some of your brittle? Or did you just eat it all yourself?"

"Sorry, Grandma Rose and Grandson Francis. I pigged it all, but she is in a place where she can make and eat all the peanut brittle in the universe if she chooses. She might even break that damn record!"

I sat up. Izzy rolled over and sat up, too, scooting closer to me. We were eye to eye.

"Please don't tell anyone about the cave, Francis. I get in enough trouble without others worrying I'm going to pull a Judas."

I was trying hard not to sob myself, knowing how close I had been to losing him.

"Francis, I even started going to Mass again. I decided tonight that I'm going to confession at a different church when we get back."

"Why a different church, Izzy?"

"Think about it. Trying to murder yourself is a whopper of a sin, and a new priest won't recognize my voice. I want to be sure I'm clean and get rid of my sin, but when that surge of light and heat went through me, I knew I was forgiven by a higher power, a force more loving and forgiving than any beer-guzzling priest sitting in a small, dark guilt-go-away confessional box."

The night was ending, and dawn was breaking. A new day. A new beginning. Izzy stood and pulled my red bandanna from his neck and rubbed it across his face as if trying to erase his final salty tears.

To distract me from his emotions, he pointed to the eagle still perched at the top of the largest pine on our cliff. The majestic bird finally took off toward the heavens. When it was just a speck, no longer visible, I thought I heard Izzy sob, "I love you, Jack."

I wrapped my arms around Izzy and held him for several seconds.

My best friend handed me our backpack before we descended to our campsite at the base of Jack's Cliff.

"I guess, like that eagle, I had to fly through some shit to grow," Izzy said.

"Me, too," I replied. "But I still want to beat the snot out of you for what you almost did in our cave. I'm no replacement for Jack, but I think of you as my brother. Maybe you will adopt me someday."

He did not even pause. "Deal, Brother Francis. But can we add the Worm to our deal? She's a hoot!"

"Yes, if she approves, but under one condition."

"What is that, Brother Francis?"

"That you never, ever try to make Mandy say the word *rekcuf.*"

We started hiking down the bluff toward our canoe.

Despite all of the hardships, snags, and obstacles we had endured, I would never trade my journeys with Izzy, Susan, and my beautiful little sister Mandy, even for all the peanut brittle in Heaven. Only Izzy could save Izzy. And during that night on our canoe trip, I prayed he did—or at least got a great head start.

We greeted the river's bank. Izzy began lowering the canoe paddles from the tree. I started pulling up the metal stakes from the tent we had never slept in. I tossed the last one with a huge wad of mud on it at Izzy.

THE END

For He satisfies the longing soul
and fills the longing soul with goodness.

—Psalm 107:9

EPILOGUE

They are not lost who find healing and peace by searching for truth,
sometimes questioning their faith, and also occasionally indulging
in the food of the gods: fine confections.
—FRANCIS PAULSON

IZZY'S MANNA-FROM-HEAVEN PEANUT BRITTLE

2 CUPS WHITE CANE SUGAR
1 CUP CORN SYRUP
½ CUP WATER (DO NOT USE HOLY WATER)
2 CUPS RAW SPANISH PEANUTS
1 TSP SALT
3 TBSP BUTTER
1 TSP VANILLA
1 TSP BAKING SODA

In a deep saucepan over medium heat, stir first three ingredients with a wooden spoon and cook to 236°F.

At 236°F, add peanuts and salt. Stir continuously until temperature reads 270°F.

At 270°F, add butter. Stir until temperature reaches 305°F. Remove from burner.

Add vanilla and baking soda. Stir quickly as mixture foams, then pour onto a greased or buttered baking sheet or greased or buttered marble surface. Spread with a pallet knife, forcing peanuts to the edge of the mixture. Flip the brittle over while still pliable and spread as thin as you like with your hands or utensils.

Helpful Hints

1. Work fast before brittle hardens.

2. Brittle is seasonal. It won't keep well in hot, humid weather.

3. Brittle doesn't like refrigeration. Keep in an airtight container.

4. Never put snow or ice on your marble (unless you are a pro).

5. Make sure pennies, jewelry, and false teeth do not fall into your candy.

FRANK'S HOT-LAVA BUTTER ALMOND TOFFEE

3 CUPS WHITE CANE SUGAR
4 OZ CORN SYRUP
¼ CUP WATER
1 LB BUTTER, CHOPPED
¾ TSP SALT
12 OZ RAW ALMONDS, CHOPPED
1 TSP VANILLA
1 TSP BAKING SODA
TEMPERED MELTED CHOCOLATE (OPTIONAL)
ADDITIONAL ALMONDS OR PECANS, GROUND OR SLIVERED (OPTIONAL)

Stir first three ingredients in deep saucepan over medium heat until mixture reaches 250°F. While mixture cooks, wash interior sides of pan using a brush dipped in water. Keep stirring to prevent mixture from scorching.

At 250°F, add butter. Bring mixture back up to 240°F. Add salt and raw almonds.

Stir briskly, dodging any hot-lava butter toffee balls. Cook to 308°F.

Remove from heat and stir in vanilla and baking soda. Pour onto greased or buttered baking sheet or greased or buttered marble slab. Spread to desired thickness with pallet knife. Cut into squares while pliable or break into pieces once hardened.

Covering in Chocolate

Once toffee cools, dip in tempered chocolate (milk or dark). For tips on tempering, consult YouTube or call Martha Stewart. While chocolate is still wet, dip toffee in ground or slivered almonds or pecans. Bring a box to your dentist.

ACKNOWLEDGEMENTS

No writer successfully publishes their debut novel alone. My gratitude and appreciation to all who encouraged me to get this story across the finish line, like my Minneapolis Loft authors, teaching artists, and mentors, especially Kate St. Vincent Vogel, Mary Carroll Moore, and David Housewright.

Thank you to my collaborators at Beaver's Pond Press, Kerry Stapley, Taylor Blumer, Jay Monroe, and Alicia Ester, as well as my volunteer BETA readers that were with me through many drafts: Charlie Purfeerst, Tom Diedrich, Lori Dorfman, Thomas Barton, Sheryl Peterson, Greg and Vicki Baker.

A special kudos to www.kaxe.org and Michael Goldberg's *Stay Human Radio Hour*, and there is no forgetting my favorite high school creative writing teacher, Mary Alice "Ma" Stifter, who made me memorize Strunk and Whites' *Elements of Style*, then smuggled me our school's banned copy of JD Salinger's *The Catcher in the Rye*.

I thank my life-long paddling partner and bowman Jim George for decades of on-the-water adventures. You probably looked for yourself in parts of this story—but it is fiction, Jim, just fiction.

There is also one special person who always had faith in my journey even when I doubted it myself. Thank you, Sharon Gahan, you are loved by many, including this author!